WHITE CRANE BOY

KU JIN

Translated by
WU JIAMEI

Sinoist Books

Published by
Sinoist Books (an imprint of ACA Publishing Ltd).
University House
11-13 Lower Grosvenor Place,
London SW1W 0EX, UK
Tel: +44 20 3289 3885
E-mail: info@alaincharlesasia.com
Web: www.alaincharlesasia.com

Beijing Office
Tel: +86(0)10 8472 1250

Author: Ku Jin
Translator: Wu Jiamei

Published by ACA Publishing Ltd in association with the Liaoning Children's Publishing House

Original Chinese Text © 白鹤少年 (Bái Hè Shào Nián) 2017, Liaoning Children's Publishing House, Shenyang, China

English Translation © 2020, ACA Publishing Ltd, London, UK

ALL RIGHTS RESERVED. NO PART OF THIS PUBLICATION MAY BE REPRODUCED IN MATERIAL FORM, BY ANY MEANS, WHETHER GRAPHIC, ELECTRONIC, MECHANICAL OR OTHER, INCLUDING PHOTOCOPYING OR INFORMATION STORAGE, IN WHOLE OR IN PART, AND MAY NOT BE USED TO PREPARE OTHER PUBLICATIONS WITHOUT WRITTEN PERMISSION FROM THE PUBLISHER.

The greatest care has been taken to ensure accuracy but the publisher can accept no responsibility for errors or omissions, or for any liability occasioned by relying on its content.

Paperback ISBN: 978-1-910760-79-6
eBook ISBN: 978-1-910760-80-2

A catalogue record for *White Crane Boy* is available from the National Bibliographic Service of the British Library.

1
CAN A GOOSE ALSO WALK INTO A TEXTBOOK?

"Look at that stone! There is an obvious crack where the stone lies tight against the fine sand in the stream. The water is not deep, about the depth of one and a half hands. The fine yellow sand below the crack looks smooth, which apparently is a sign that a crab often goes in and out through it. Besides, the crack has a wide opening, spacious enough to put an open palm into it. There must be a big crab in the burrow under the stone!"

When he was wondering about this, he was already standing in front of the stone, his long legs looking so slim. He kept his footing, composed himself, and stooped down to reach out his small hands and lift up the stone suddenly. Indeed, a big crab was nesting inside the burrow under the crack, a really big one about the same size as the palm of one's hand. When he was trying to catch it, the burrow immediately filled full of water and at once formed a small whirlpool. Clear water became muddy and the crab disappeared from sight within a second.

The colour of the crab's shell was almost the same as the flowing water. If it should walk sideways on its eight feet, it would disappear into the stream. Quick as a wink, he pushed the stone aside. With a plopping sound, the stone fell into the water and splashed a lot of water on his face, some getting into his eyes. He was forced to close his eyes but the two small hands were still busy working. Groping inside the muddy water, he felt he had caught something in his hands. It must have been the crab he was looking for. He scooped it out of the water together with the fine sand.

At that moment, a young girl was singing *shan'ge* (mountain folk songs) nearby:

> Long legs short, long legs tall,
> Fall down on the field ridge when the rain falls.

He tossed his head and shook off the water from his eyelids. Blinking his eyes for a while, he then opened his eyes to look in the direction the singing came from.

A girl about ten years old with a blue backpack on her shoulder was standing on the riverbank ten metres away from him. She winked at him as she sang the song. He was a little annoyed. "You…"

"You, you, you what? Silly Tian!" The girl smirked. "Say a bit more, can't you? I bet you can't string two characters together!"

The boy who was greeted as Silly Tian looked somewhat angry and tried desperately to say something, his head stiffly tilted to one side and his face choked purple. After quite a while, a word rushed out of his throat, "Huang!"

"Huang, Huang what? My name is Huang Xiaoqiu. If you are good, say it clearly and completely! Stop calling me Huang!" The girl interrupted the boy rudely and pointed at her nose, saying, "I went to school at seven and now I am in the second semester of the third year. Look at you, Tian Shi Bowa, you are ten and a half years old, half a year older than me, but you still can't go to school! Ha! Ha! You are just a silly boy with long legs like a clothes prop! Look at yourself, face choked red with effort. You can only utter one character! Given two days, you couldn't even finish half a sentence. Ten and half years old! Can you wear a backpack and go to school happily like me? I guess you couldn't even if you were twenty years old!"

It seemed that Huang Xiaoqiu was telling the truth. Tian Shi Bowa, the boy called Silly Tian, stood there dumbly, eyes wide and mouth opening into a big "O".

"Hey, you are not happy with my making up a *shan'ge* about you? Silly Tian, I am about to compose a song." With a triumphant smile on her face, she began to sing about Tian Shi Bowa again:

Long legs short, long legs tall,
Catch a crab to be roasted over the fire.

As the youngest daughter of Carpenter Huang in the village, Huang Xiaoqiu was totally different from her elder sister Huang Xiaochun who was gentle and quiet and enjoyed being alone. Huang Xiaoqiu instead often spoke in a coarse voice, like a boy. Born into a rich family, she was well-fed and grew up to be very strong like a naughty calf - talkative, restless and mischievous. Now, she stood beside Tian Shi Bowa as she talked all along.

"Tian Shi Bowa, what is in your hands?" With a strong southeast Chongqing accent, Huang Xiaoqiu was thinking about playing a trick on Bowa. She wanted him to open his clasped hands. She said bluntly, "Nothing unusual, right? Open your hands and show me what it is!"

Slow to react, Tian Shi Bowa looked at her and hesitated whether to do as she had told him or not. In his mind, he admired Huang Xiaoqiu very much because she could go to school. He at last opened his hands slowly. Although he didn't mean to please her, he regarded her quite favourably. The big crab trapped inside was freed. The fellow's eyes bulged and, looking around, it moved its eight feet a bit to check the surrounding environment, and then began to walk sideways.

Bowa worried it might run away so he wanted to close his hands.

"Wow, what a big crab! You are so good. Let me have a good look."

Before Tianshi Bowa was aware what she was doing, she quickly reached out her hand and stirred inside his hands. The crab dropped into the stream with the sand with a splash and disappeared immediately.

"Ah!" Bowa shouted.

"Ah! Ah! Ah! Silly Tian!"

Huang Xiaoqiu turned around and ran away, giggling and making a grimace. She shook her hair back and skipped on her way as she proudly recited a poem in the Mandarin textbook:

Goose, goose, goose,
Neck bent, it sings towards the sky.
White feathers float on green water,
Red webbed feet make clear ripples.

Huang Xiaoqiu went to school in high spirits, leaving Tian Shi Bowa standing in the stream awkwardly with his hands open.

He should have been very angry but, strangely, he wasn't at all. He felt it was nothing unusual when Huang Xiaoqiu sang a *shan'ge*, nor did he feel sorry about the loss of his big crab. He was attracted by the poem recited by Huang Xiaoqiu in Mandarin, which he felt was so pleasing to his ears. He heard it clearly like 'goose, goose, goose' and 'red webbed feet make clear ripples' and he still remembered it clearly too.

What was it all about? Goose? How could a goose walk into a textbook?

Tian Shi Bowa stared straight at the blue backpack on Huang Xiaoqiu's back until she turned a corner and disappeared.

For no particular reason, Tian Shi Bowa did happen to have a pair of long legs, about one or two inches taller than other kids of his age. Unlike other kids in the village, his legs grew faster than the rest of his body. When he stood among the other children, he was half a head taller than them. Nobody could explain why. It might have been innate but it could not have been genetic because his parents both had very normal legs. His mother was very worried about it and often said to others, "What should my Bowa do about it? With such a long pair of legs and a slightly built body, he can't even walk steadily!" This was indeed how Tian Shi Bowa walked, unsteadily, and he easily lost his balance. On rainy days, small paths along the White Crane Stream, especially paths through fields, became very muddy after the rain. When Tian Shi Bowa walked on the path, he often slipped and fell over, and was black and blue all over. That's why Huang Xiaoqiu made fun of him just now.

Besides, Tian Shi Bowa was a *jianzi*, a local term for a stammerer. Strictly speaking, Bowa was not a stammerer because for a *jianzi*, either he could not complete a sentence or he had to stop a few times while he was speaking and then stammered again until he finished. As for Bowa, he was different. He would be blocked after he uttered one single character and after quite a while he was able to enunciate a second one. Sometimes, even if it had been quite a while after he had spoken the first character, he still could not continue. He was just blocked there, wanting to express himself but unable to. Except for his family or people who knew him quite well, it was very difficult for other people to understand him. That's why he himself never thought about going to school and even his family and the other villagers all believed it was impossible for him to do that, although his family could afford to send him to school.

But today, and particularly at this moment, as Tian Shi Bowa stood in the White Crane Stream and watched Huang Xiaoqiu skip all the way to school after she had deliberately let go of the crab in his hands, for the first time he very much wanted to go to school.

2
PAINFUL DESIRE

The Xiaonanhai area in Bamian Mountain in Qianjiang, southeastern Chongqing was about 1,000 metres above sea level. Even in April during spring, the temperature difference between day and night was still very large. During the day, dazzling sunshine, like a bright gauze, blanketed green mountains and trees, and touched lakes and rivers, bringing warmth to all living creatures. A lot of women took the opportunity to wash clothes and quilts and many young men went swimming naked in the river. But at night, the temperature would drop so low that one had to put on a sweater or even a cotton jacket. Many households therefore, would often keep firewood inside the stove burning all night in their heated room.

The heated room in Tian Fashui's home needed a bit more firewood. Tian Shi Bowa's grandma was old and she had arthritis too. If there was no fire in the room, she could not even dare to sit on the bench. Behind the living room was the heated room inside which the fire pit was always burning with beech tree stumps in April. Beech wood is hard. When its stumps are dug out of clefts in the rocks, they burn for a long time because it is harder and stronger than the average wood. One beech tree stump can keep a fire going for a day and a night, and is easy, convenient and efficient. In the evening, a kettle of water was heated on the fire pit for tea and for the heat as well. When it was time to go to bed, wood ashes would be spread over the open fire for safety on the one hand and to keep it burning longer inside the ashes on the other hand. This method could keep the fire in the pit for three days and three nights. The next morning when one scraped away the ashes, the charcoal was glowing red from the fire; very convenient for picking one up to light the stove for cooking breakfast.

Thick bluestone slates were laid out and stacked neatly around the fire pit and on the upper side of the slate was a smooth surface chiseled by the stonemason, as wide as a palm, on which small things like a packet of matches, tobacco leaves and a small tea bowl could be placed. At this time of year, adults either went to pick mushrooms in the mountains, picked corn on the mountain slopes or harvested rice in the field; no one sat by the fire pit. As for children, well, Tian Shi Bowa was the only child in his family, they were not afraid of cold. Thinking about all the living creatures in the White Crane Stream on the previous night, they would get up early and go to catch fish and crabs in the stream the next day.

Tian Fashui, Bowa's father, would usually help Bowa's mother Li Runlan with the supper after he had picked corn in the field and returned home.

After supper, Li Runlan began to prepare food for the pigs. She added some corn flour into the pot with some dishwater left inside or some wheat bran to cook first, then she put a basket of plant leaves into the pot, stirred it a few times and cooked it together. When it was ready, she used a water ladle to scoop the mixture into a pigs' food bucket with a handle on one side. A full bucket of pig food! It would have been very challenging even for an adult man to carry and walk a few steps at one time. But Li Runlan, slender but sturdy, could hold a full bucket of pig food and walk more than ten metres to the pigsty, which other people found quite amazing. Bowa, however, knew his mother was using her strength skillfully. Yes, Li Runlan was good at using her strength smartly. Tian Shi Bowa once watched his mother when she did that. She usually moved her apron to her right thigh first, then held the handle of the bucket tight with her right hand and pressed the bucket close to her right thigh. As she moved her right thigh, the bucket moved as well and at the same time she leaned her body to the right lightly and stretched out her left hand to keep her balance. It was almost her whole body that pushed the bucket forward. In this way, how could she not carry the full bucket comparatively easily to the pigsty?

That's why the pigs his mother raised each year were all very big and fat and she had two pig pens with four pigs! Two pigs were kept for the New Year banquets during the spring festival season, the year-round cooking oil for the whole family and gifts for relatives and friends, while the other two were to be sold to cover day-to-day expenses.

When his mother went to feed the pigs, his father switched on the dimly-lit electric bulb. He and Grandma sat in the wooden chair beside the fire pit. He scraped away the ashes on the stump bonfire, grabbed a handful of homemade tea, put it into a Buddha-belly tea kettle with a handle, added a ladle of water and put it on the open fire to brew.

Making tea in this way was named stewing by people in the White Crane Stream community. When the tea kettle boiled, people moved it away from the open fire, lifted it and poured the tea into a small china bowl, drinking it hot, one bowl after another. When there was only one third of the tea left in the kettle, they added one more ladle of water and brewed it again on the fire. This could be repeated several times. When they needed to leave the house, they put the lid on the tea kettle, and moved it away to keep it a certain distance from the open fire. After a busy day outside, one was sure to be thirsty. When they went back home and sat by the fire pit, they poured out a bowl of tea, tried it on their lips, and if it was neither hot nor cold, but warm, it was perfect to gulp it down. Then one stroked one's belly and breathed a sigh. What a comfortable life it was!

Tea brewed in this way was called stewed tea in the White Crane Stream area. No matter who passed a household, they would be greeted like this: Hey, feeling tired? Come on in and take a break with a bowl of stewed tea.

The tea kettle was boiling noisily on the fire. Tian Fashui held the handle, lifted it up and poured out two bowls of tea. After putting the tea kettle back, he held out one bowl of tea for his mother. He said, "Grandma, please have a bowl of hot tea."

Like his son Bowa, Tian Fashui addressed his mother as Grandma. Bowa had been thinking about going to school for a whole day. He knew it was useless to tell anyone in the family about this except his father who had the final say on everything. He didn't do it during supper because when his father was hungry, he would not listen to him but just ate his food whole-heartedly; neither did he do it when his father was busy brewing tea on the fire pit after supper. Bowa waited patiently and quietly beside the door of the heated room, waiting for the right moment.

Grandma took the bowl and said, "Let's drink." She blew on the hot tea and tried it with her lips. Too hot for her! She pursed her lips and placed the bowl carefully on the edge of the fire pit.

Father had one bowl for himself. Probably because he had been working in the fields all day, he was indeed tired and thirsty. Beyond regarding whether the hot tea might burn his mouth or not, he slurped the tea while at the same time blowing on it. Within a minute the bowl was empty. "Well, perfect!" He exhaled, reached out his hand to scratch the back of his head, and moved his bottom a few times on the chair to find the best and most comfortable position. Feeling relaxed, he picked up some tobacco leaves and put them on the stone surface, preparing to wrap a cigarette for himself as a treat and to refresh himself as well.

Bowa felt it was the right moment. He called out.

"Father!" Bowa walked over to stand on the other side of the fire pit, looking straight at his father opposite.

"Goodness!" Tian Fashui's hand was shaking a bit, as if he had been shocked by the sound. He opened his eyes wide and looked in the direction of his son. Under the dim light, he had been busy drinking his tea and rolling his cigarette, and he hadn't noticed when Bowa had come to stand beside the fire pit. "You spoke all of a sudden. It really startled me!"

Although Tian Fashui didn't treat his son in a very careless manner, he thought he knew his son very well. He was busy rolling his cigarette, not asking Bowa why he had called him. Bowa at that time was somewhat reckless. He held back for a while, looked at Tian Fashui and at last called out, "Father."

"Beating you with a stick three times would not make you speak out. What are you calling for? I am right here!" Tian Fashui sounded a bit impatient, as his voice thundered throughout the room.

Bowa was feeling timid and didn't know what to say next.

Grandma took pity on her grandson. She waved to Bowa and called out, "Sweetheart, come over here."

Although Bowa was not the apple of his father's eye, he was always the best grandson as far as his grandma was concerned. With his eyes still on his father, Bowa staggered over to his grandma, who took him in her arms, put her arms around his waist, let him sit facing the fire pit and asked him gently,

"Don't be afraid! Grandma is here. What do you want to say to your old man?"

Honestly speaking, Bowa's father could not have been very old since Bowa was just a little over ten, but why did Grandma ask him to call his father "old man"? Tian Fashui had a daughter who had long since been married and moved out. In the White Crane Stream area, family planning was practiced but one family could have two children on condition that there must be four years between the birth of the first and second ones. Unfortunately, in Tian Fashui's case, four years turned out to be twenty-four because his wife could not get pregnant again after the birth of her daughter. When Bowa was born into the family, Tian Fashui was already in his forties. Now, he was in his fifties. An old man indeed. Bowa was different from the other kids. He could not speak more than two characters at a time and very often it would take a long time for him to spit out one more after he had spoken a character. But tonight it was probably because he wanted to go to school so much that he managed to say more within a short period of time.

In his grandma's arms, Bowa felt a bit braver. He said to his grandma, "*Shu* (book)".

Grandma looked at Bowa in confusion, having no idea what he meant for the time being.

"*Shu* (lose)?" His father seemed to get something. He stared at Bowa and asked, "Are you gambling with those urchins in the village?"

"Nope."

"What did you lose then?"

"*Xue* (learn)!" Bowa was somewhat anxious. He looked at his father, and with great effort, he suddenly said loudly, "learn!"

"Learn? You dare to learn to gamble instead of learning something good at such a young age? I'll break your fingers off!" Tian Fashui glared at Bowa, his eyes as wide as tung tree seed shells.

"No!" Bowa shook his head.

"You dare to deny it? You just said it!" Tian Fashui looked very angry.

He said in a gruff voice, "You dare to learn something bad! Well, go and get that bamboo strip behind the door. You won't remember it clearly if I don't give your bottom a good spanking!"

Tian Shi Bowa started to cry with fright but he could not cry out, his little face twitching. He turned to his grandma and lowered himself into her arms, "Grandma!"

"Tian Fashui, what's wrong with you?" Grandma scolded him loudly as she comforted Bowa in her arms, "Grandson, don't be afraid. Grandma is here. Your dad wouldn't dare!"

Grandma was a little angry. She said to Tian Fashui very seriously, "I am not an old fool yet. Tian Fashui, you can't say you are either, can you? You didn't even bother to make it clear before you scolded him like this. I will get you for this if you frighten him out of his wits!"

"He has always been a bit clumsy. No need to worry about frightening him out of his wits." In front of his mother, Tian Fashui lowered his voice, "I just don't want him to learn something bad."

"You said he has been clumsy. How bad could he learn to be?" Grandma blamed him, "Bowa's reactions are indeed slow but he is still young and you should make it clear first before you jump to conclusions."

Tian Fashui stuffed some wrapped tobacco leaves into the bowl of his bamboo pipe and said slowly, "Make it clear? He is a fool. It's easier to fall than to rise."

"Fool? You said Bowa is a fool?" Grandma was annoyed at that. She said to her son dismissively, "Bowa is a clever boy. You know, when he grows up, he is sure to have a very promising future. You are no match for him, not likely at all."

"No match for him?" Tian Fashui laughed, his furrowed face lit by smiles. "Grandma, you are too fond of him. How could I not know my own clumsy son? Can he climb to the top of Zhongshan's Bamian Mountain like me? Can he climb up Bandengyan to pick black hoof mushrooms?"

"Strength is the only thing you can show off. Bowa is cleverer than you. Let me ask him." Grandma looked at Bowa affectionately and said, "Don't be afraid, my grandson. Tell me, when you said 'learn' just now, you didn't mean to learn to gamble from those urchins in the village, did you?"

"Learn," Looking at his grandma, Bowa was blocked for a while before he tried to say another character, but what he spat out was still the character "learn".

"Yes, learn, learn what?"

"Go to…"

"Go to?" Grandma was very confused, "Go to learn? You mean 'go to school'?"

Bowa smiled, eager to say something, but he was blocked again, and his face turned red. Grandma's heart ached with pity for her grandson. She hurriedly said, "Take your time! Take your time!"

"*Shu* (book)!" Bowa finally spoke the character he had said first. Besides, he made the shape of a book in the air with his hands and repeatedly stressed, "*Shu* (book)".

"*Shu*?" Grandma followed her grandson by making the same gesture and suddenly she knew what he meant. "Go, learn, book, and go to school!" Grandma held Bowa's shoulders happily and asked, "Sweetheart, do you mean you want to go to school?"

"Yes!" Bowa nodded his head immediately.

"What?" Tian Fashui was lighting his pipe over the fire pit. He stopped, smiled and said, "Stop making a fool of yourself in the village! Go to school? Rather the school goes through him!"

Bowa's face froze at once.

Grandma said, "Why can't he? Why can't Bowa go to school?"

"Grandma, you should know the reason." Tian Fashui lit his pipe, drew on it, puffed and opened his mouth, "It is not me who doesn't allow him to go to school; it is Bowa himself who should not go to school. Now you don't need to pay to go to school, it's totally compulsory, you know. But Bowa is clumsy and would only make people laugh at school and bring shame on our family. He can't even speak two or three characters at a time, let alone a sentence. If he was able to learn and read, I would already have sent him to school when he was seven years old."

"Even if he could not say a sentence, he can learn to write. How do you know Bowa can't do it before you give him a chance to try?" Grandma didn't agree with her son and she wanted to back up her grandson. "Since Bowa himself wants to go to school, you will let him try, won't you?"

"It's no use sending him to school. Grandma! Stop worrying about this." Tian Fashui didn't want to argue with his mother over this. He stood up and said, "Why am I trying my best to save money? Bowa is a fool. Everything is OK as long as he has a strong and healthy body. I have to make preparations for his future life."

"But…" Grandma still wanted to say something to her son, but Tian Fashui took his pipe, stood up and left the room.

Grandma sighed somewhat helplessly.

Disappointment written all over his face, Bowa looked at his grandma, tears streaming down quietly.

Grandma wiped his tears away and said, "You want to go to school, do you? Grandson, Grandma knows you do, but…"

Bowa still wanted to say something but he just could not spit the character out at that moment. He was so anxious, with a tense face and bulging eyes.

"Go on, Grandson, don't give up! I know you want to go to school. Go on saying 'go to school'," said Grandma, in the hope that her grandson could speak two characters in one breath and that he would probably learn to say a complete sentence in one breath in the future. If he could do that, his father would allow him to go to school then. She held Bowa's little face, blinked her poor old eyes and tried to cheer up her grandson, "Go on, Grandson."

Tian Shi Bowa puffed out his cheeks, perhaps wanting to speak the two characters *"shang xue"* (go to school), but he failed to say a single character the whole evening although his cheeks turned red with the great effort he made.

3
CELEBRATING SHEBA DAY

Tian Shi Bowa excitedly followed his parents on their journey to a wedding ceremony, and behind his back, the sun began setting in the west.

It was a wedding ceremony held by a fellow villager Huang Mingfu, a banquet to marry his sister Huang Cuicui. According to the custom in their village, after the banquet, all the villagers gathered together to celebrate their traditional bonfire on Sheba Day, a festival of the Tujia people, on which they held large-scale sacrificial and celebratory activities. It was said TV reporters would come to do live recording, which made a lot of people, including Li Chaosong, the village chief, a bit excited.

Tian Fashui walked in front carrying a pole of gifts on his shoulders. They had prepared a few dozen kilos of new rice packed in a newly crafted small crate. He shouldered the load and walked happily with a swing in his step. As he walked along, Tian Fashui felt it was so quiet in the mountains that he couldn't help raising his voice and singing aloud:

> The setting sun shines on the Baiya,
> No happy mood without a shan'ge's company.
> Flowers won't blossom until the arrival of spring,

Fine pulp never comes out if you don't push the grinding
  stone.

"Stop singing like this! It is the wedding ceremony of Huang Mingfu's sister and what's the point of your coming along for the ride? Stop singing in case people should hear and come to rip out your tongue!" Tian Fashui's wife smiled and said in a playful tone with a slight tone of complaint.

"What's the big deal of my singing? In White Crane village, anyone is free to sing *shan'ge* as they want." Tian Fashui shifted the carrying pole to another shoulder and said, "Anyway, it's still a long way to go before we arrive at their home. What's more, they probably want to listen to my *shan'ge* and want to sing one themselves more than I do."

"Bowa is here. It's pollution for kids!" His wife said.

"Bowa isn't old enough to understand. Besides, he can't sing out loud either," said Tian Fashui with some sadness. "Too many people mean more gossip. Some blabber-mouths at the banquet will say my son is a stammerer. It is indeed shameful! I told you not to bring him along but you just wouldn't listen."

"What a father you are! When he wanted to go to school, you said no and is there any problem when I bring him along to have some fun? Bowa likes our Tujia people's hand-waving dance. Tonight is Sheba Day (a day to worship ancestors) in our village. Isn't it good for him to watch and have some fun?" Li Runlan replied. "His grandma has taught him so many dances and he will be happy to try and compete with the others tonight."

When they climbed over the Pine Forest Ridge, they heard the loud noise of firecrackers coming from where the musical band the Huang family had invited was located. Filled with happy feelings, Tian Fashui quickened his step.

The lively atmosphere of the Huang family climbed over the courtyard and reached eight miles away. Near neighbours and distant fellows, friends and relatives, all came and went carrying gifts. What a flurry of activity! Square tables and benches were placed in a neat and orderly fashion with cups, plates and bowls stacked on each of them. The music band they had invited were playing loudly, one song after another, gongs clanging and drums pounding, which produced a more heated and jubilant atmosphere. Three to five women in red and green were standing around a large sedan chair busy decorating it with bright flowers, green leaves and tassels. Men in charge of carrying dowries meticulously placed fine porcelain bowls, plates and vases, an electric kettle, electric iron, electric hair-dryer and electric blankets on the desk, wardrobe, TV closet, dressing table and the washer, one by one and stack by stack to build it into the shape of a pagoda and tied it tightly. Tomorrow morning, they would carry it away. Neighbours in the village who offered to entertain the guests held wooden tea trays, with one cigarette stuck behind their ear and two between their fingers, and greeted guests with good blessings, "Good things come in pairs, have a smoke and have some tea…" Children below the age of ten gathered in small groups, shouting and chasing, climbing and jumping, showing off their unbridled happiness:

Bride and bridegroom, distribute candies and cigarettes; the bride in newly embroidered shoes, gets ready for red envelopes; the bride rides a white horse with red envelopes in her hands.

In the courtyard, Huang Mingfu was exchanging pleasantries with some guests. When he raised his head and saw Tian Fashui and his family with loads of wedding gifts entering the courtyard, he hurried over to greet them.

"Brother Huang, what a blessing on your family! Congratulations!" Tian Fashui's wife Li Runlan spoke straight.

"Oh, haha! Thanks, Mrs Tian, welcome!" Huang Mingfu called his busboy, "Zhao Heiwa, quick, serve cigarettes and tea!"

Tian Fashui and his wife wrote down their names on the signing table and presented the new rice he was carrying and a hundred yuan as well. When they sat down on the bench beside a square table, Xiao Chuanzhang and his wife Sufang came over to say hello, "Fashui, your whole family have come to the wedding banquet!"

"Yes! Yes! You guys arrived earlier," Tian Fashui answered.

Sufang saw Tian Shi Bowa who was leaning on Li Runlan. She pulled him over and said in a very exaggerated tone, "Well, isn't this Bowa?" and as she said it she grabbed a handful of peanuts and candies from a tea tray on the square table and stuffed them into Bowa's trouser pocket, "Bowa, say a few words to Aunty Liao."

Tian Shi Bowa stared at his mother, and then at Sufang, who continued, "He is still that silly, isn't he? Can't he speak?"

Li Runlan pulled her son back and let him stand in front of her. She said, "Who said my Bowa can't speak? My Bowa could speak when he was nine years old. Bowa, say something to Aunty."

Tian Shi Bowa took a look at Sufang, compressed his lips, puffed out his cheeks and opened his mouth. Immediately a character came out: "Aunt!"

"Wow, what a lovely greeting!" Sufang appeared very happy but at the same time she seemed to know the secret that Tian Shi Bowa could only speak one character at a time. She began to tease him deliberately. "Never did I think Bowa could speak so clearly. Very good! Bowa, speak to me again and I will give you two handfuls of candies."

Tian Shi Bowa looked at Sufang blankly, not knowing what to do. Li Runlan hurriedly said, "Sufang, have some tea first. My Bowa doesn't speak a lot. Let's have some melon seeds and tea."

Li Runlan spoke incoherently as if she was hiding something, which could be seen through by Sufang. She sighed and said, "Well, my boy Xiao Jianbo went to school at the age of seven. Bowa is nine and a half years old, isn't he? Everything is good about him except one thing that he cannot speak and cannot go to school. It's quite pitiful when I think about it."

"There's nothing to be pitiful about! He is not a big boy yet and it is us who don't want him to go to school for the time being." Li Runlan lowered her head and protected Bowa's head with her arm. She couldn't help shedding a tear when she thought about it.

It was true that Tian Shi Bowa didn't open his mouth to speak before he was nine years old and he didn't even utter a babbling sound. All the villagers called him little dumbo. On his ninth birthday, Li Runlan asked Bowa to go with her, bringing a big bowl, a spoon and a knife. She wanted to get some fresh honey to celebrate his birthday. When his mother lifted the honeycomb out of the bee hive and was going to cut off a piece, a bee flew out of the hive and settled on Bowa's lips. Bees usually didn't have long poisonous stings and it was generally not very painful when a bee stung you elsewhere except on your lip, which could be extremely painful. At that time, Tian Shi Bowa was frightened by the bee and he opened his mouth involuntarily, which startled the bee. The bee lowered its tail and stung him on his lip.

"Mum!"

This instinctive shout was really a big shock! Is there any child who wouldn't cry for his mum when he was in a panic? Tian Shi Bowa immediately squatted down and covered his mouth with his hand after uttering a cry. Hearing the shout and seeing her son squatting on the ground, Li Runlan stopped her work and lowered her body to check Bowa's injured mouth, "Bowa, relax. Mum will squeeze the sting for you!"

After the bee flew away, the poisonous sting remained on Bowa's lip. With a sack of poison attached to the sting, it was very improper to pinch it and pull it out with one's fingers because if one did so, the bee venom would be injected into the flesh which would make the injury more painful and swollen. Li Runlan meticulously scraped with her little finger nail, she had quite long nails, the place close to where the sting was on the lip. Fortunately, the sting fell off smoothly.

"Well, it won't hurt any more!" Li Runlan comforted her son, then she suddenly realised she had heard a cry just now. Was it from Bowa? She wrapped her son in her arms and looked at him in great surprise, "Bowa, my son, was it you who shouted just now?"

The boy was confused by her question. He looked up at his mother, thought about it and nodded his head vigorously.

"Son, did you call Mum just now?"

Tian Shi Bowa nodded in confirmation.

"Good heavens! My son can speak now!" Li Runlan was very excited. She held Bowa to her heart, rubbed his lips and said, "Son, say it again, say Mum."

Tian Shi Bowa moved his lips a bit, and his throat too, but this time he didn't make it. Li Runlan put him on the ground and said, "My son can make it. Come on, one more time. Say Mum."

Her son wanted to do so as well. He puffed out his cheeks and made the utmost effort, face choked red, but finally failed.

It didn't happen again until the next day. Tian Shi Bowa went back home from the White Crane Stream after he had played to his heart's content. The moment he ran into the courtyard and saw his mum who was doing housework under the roof, he suddenly called out again: Mum.

By late afternoon, the banquet was over but no guests had left. Men and women, young and old in the village, and friends and relatives from the other villages too gathered together, some sitting on benches, some standing, or squatting on the edge of the courtyard, smoking, drinking tea or chewing candies, all waiting to take part in the hand-waving dance to be held in the Hand-Waving Hall in Baiheba.

It was on September 19th in the lunar calendar. Night had just fallen; a round moon brushed away a few clouds and slowly climbed high amid the cool evening breeze. It then lingered there for a long time above the Hand-Waving Hall in Baiheba, scattering golden and auspicious light on the courtyard and on the villagers who rushed into Baiheba for the celebration.

The ancient Hand-Waving Hall was still as grand and vigorous as always. Three steps led up to the main hall, a temple-like building with three spacious rooms open to everyone. The lines of its ridges were bold and smooth and on each of the eaves of the four tiled roofs on both sides stood a white crane, stretching its neck and spreading its wings ready to fly.

By convention, worshipping the land gods and the eight kings of Tujia ancestors was the first activity.

Three sacrificial offerings - the heads of a pig, a goat and a cow on a big tray, had already been placed on the ritual altar, in front of which was an incense holder inside which the burning candles and sacrificial money gave off smoke continuously. Guided by the village chief Li Chaosong, the bride and the bridegroom, today's focus, walked into the Hand-Waving Hall, each holding a lighted sandalwood incense stick. They devoutly bowed three times in front of statues of the Earth God and the Great Kings of the Eight Tribes. After the sacrifice, Li Chaosong, on behalf of the Earth God and the Eight Kings, delivered blessings in a very solemn manner as solemn as the announcement of a decree by an immortal. Hoarse as his voice was, his loud and clear blessings filled the air:

Earth God and Eight Kings, please bless the bride and the bridegroom, bless White Crane Stream and its villagers. Bless us with favourable weather and auspiciousness!

With a roar, the bonfire flamed up. All the villagers gathered round.

In front of the Hand-Waving Hall was a huge courtyard paved with bluestones which could admit thousands of people playing inside. Along the edge of the courtyard were placed smooth stone plates carried from the White Crane Stream and wooden benches with a coat of tung oil where people could take a seat for a break after they had danced for a while or when they were not busy after the harvest season.

Under the silvery moonlight, the bonfire piled with the dry wood of beech, hawthorn, sandalwood and pine trees was glowing red. Men and women in the courtyard, as if having long been assigned their tasks, had all reported for duty already, some holding bronze drums and gongs, and some carrying side-drums and drum-set cymbals.

Accompanying the sound of cymbals, the double metres of gongs rang. Within a second, amid the happy double metres, people began to dance. Young lads and maidens were the first to enter the dancing field. Hand in hand, they danced happily, leaning forward and backward rhythmically. They waved their arms and legs to the music, arms swinging freely and feet moving back and forth or right and left, like chickens looking for food or ducks paddling in the river.

With the beginning of Sheba Day, Liu Yixiang, a TV reporter, carried his video camera and started his work.

Li Runlan, like an expert, said to Tian Fashui, "This is the Danbai dance."

Curling his lips, Tian Fashui said, "How could I not know that!"

"Really? Well, tell me what this style means?"

"Are you testing me? You think I don't know? Let me think for a while." Tian Fashui scratched his head but could not work it out after quite a while.

Li Runlan laughed and said, "What's the use of scratching your head? It represents the movement of transplanting rice seedlings in the spring! Even my Bowa knows it."

Tian Shi Bowa, holding his mum's hand, smiled and said to himself, "Of course I know. Grandma often teaches me a lot of gestures and movements of the Hand-Waving Dance."

"Oh, yes, transplanting seedlings, right," added Tian Fashui as if he had long since thought of it.

"One, two, three and four." The rhythm turned into a four-beat quadruple metre, which added some poetic flavour to the joyous atmosphere. The circle formed by the performers became larger and larger. At that moment, a handsome, strong young man jumped out from the boys' group. He wore a brown-red double-breasted jacket with brass buttons and a yellow ribbon around his waist. The most striking thing was the blue silk headgear on his head, piled into a large circle like a rafter on which a garland made from pine branches was placed, a floral crown symbolising a lifespan of a hundred years.

He was the bridegroom.

"Whew! Whew!" The bridegroom made two loud whistles and immediately a prolonged reciprocal sound burst out among the young ladies.

Amid the loud cheers, Huang Cuicui, the smiling bride, flew out of the girls' group. She wore a *jingou* (gold hook) top and a *bafu* skirt (a skirt of eight widths made of red and black checked silk embroidered with flowers or other designs), the colour of the latter was brighter and redder than the gold velvet. The decoration and ornaments on her clothes had very distinctive flavours: hems and cuffs were trimmed with blue banding inside edged with two lines of colourful braid; two watery lotus flowers were embroidered vividly with gold thread on the front of her top. Around her snowy neck hung a silver necklace decorated with many lovely silver ornaments, colliding with each other and jingling pleasantly as she danced. The gold ring on her left ring finger glistened as she danced gracefully and skillfully.

The bridegroom came forward to meet his bride. Holding her right hand in his left hand, they began to dance the *Shuangbai* Dance (an ethnic minority dance of Shuangbai County). They looked at each other affectionately as they danced together, a glance, a smile, or perhaps a twist all full of tacit understanding, so sweet and harmonious.

Ornaments dangling from the brims of their hats flashing and the bottom of the bride's skirt flying up, the bride and her groom danced skillfully, hands and legs moving in harmony, sometimes like transplanting seedlings, sometimes like weeding or harvesting rice, and sometimes like carrying a shoulder-pole. They danced back and forth, whirling about toward each other or sidling away reluctantly. The bridegroom was charming and unrestrained and the bride was elegant and graceful, without the slightest trace of embarrassment or artificiality, and presenting the natural beauty of spring and summer and the artistic beauty of autumn and winter.

After a while, the beat gradually weakened while people's whistles became more and more enthusiastic. Whew! Whew! Whew!

At this time, the bride picked up a particularly large red rose mallow from a round tea tray held by a girl and smiled shyly, ready to stick the flower in the garland on the groom's head. Hooray! The laughing young men and women suddenly rushed forward toward the bride whose hands shook a little and failed to stick the red rose mallow on the garland in time. Just at that moment, the bride and groom were separated by the crowd.

The loud sound of drums and gongs stopped all of a sudden and a silvery and sharp ringing sound burst out, with a lively and funny jingling solo rhythm. The crowd separated in two directions, leaving an open field in the middle. Suddenly, a red light flashed in the open field and it turned out to be a red silk ball that flew into the dancing field like a meteor. Under the dancing silk ball, a pair of small bare feet moved quickly.

It was a 12-year-old boy who had run into the dancing court holding a huge red embroidered ball in his hands. His performance was called 'delivering the silk ball'.

What did delivering a red silk ball mean during the hand-waving celebration in the wedding banquet? A silk ball? Balls also meant testicles, namely boys. This association sounds vulgar but rural people love this. They believe an eight or twelve-year-old boy dancing with an embroidered ball in a wedding ceremony predicts that the bride will give birth to a boy, which indeed sounds a bit sexist but people in villages don't care and this part is still the highlight of such celebrations. The boy was skillfully waving the ball in front of the dragon's head or its tail, left and right, back and forth, and up and down, and the show didn't end until the bride and groom met and held the ball together.

"Mum!" Tian Shi Bowa pulled his mother's hand and pouted in the direction of the dancing field.

Li Runlan smiled and said to Tian Fashui, "Look, your son is telling us he can dance 'delivering the silk ball'."

Tian Fashui laughed, "He may be silly, but he's got some ideas. Good!"

Li Runlan said, "It is good, he only knows some simple movements his grandma has taught him. We haven't ever seen him dance before anyway!"

"Is there any problem with that? Don't you remember Bowa's grandma is the government-designated successor of the hand-waving dance?" said Tian Fashui proudly.

The drum beat faster. The bride was pushed to the front of the dragon's head, holding the rose mallow high while the groom was blocked by the dragon's tail and the boy waving the red silk ball ran back and forth in the middle of the field.

The dancing team formed an arch like a colourful swimming dragon.

The bride, leading the dragon parade, held the flower, smiling, and approached the boy as she danced; the groom who was at the end of the dragon parade, waved his arms and moved his feet quickly, eager to find his way into the middle of the field to stop the boy with the ball. But each of his movements was defeated by the other dancers' *Shuangbai* movements.

When both sides were locked in the tussle, the boy with the red silk ball suddenly uttered a cry and fell to the ground. He sprained his ankle and could not stand up on his feet, the red-embroidered ball discarded. The boy's parents, together with the people nearby, hurried to lift him up and carried him out of the dancing field immediately.

What an ominous incident! The boy delivering the red silk ball had had an accident before the bride and groom could fetch it! That was indeed unlucky!

All cymbals, gongs, drums and bells stopped and the dragon parade stopped their dance as well, dumbfounded and not knowing what to do.

At this critical moment, a boy dressed in red ran into the dancing field. He picked up the ball quickly and started dancing, one hand holding the silk ball and pressing it against his chest, and the other mimicking a duck flapping its wings. His feet moved back and forth smoothly, dancing so elegantly and skillfully.

"Hooray! Brilliant!" The band cheered and loud music burst out again. The surrounding people cheered enthusiastically along with the drumming sound and the dragon parade started their dancing again. The lively atmosphere of the celebration was restored.

Outside the dancing court came a voice, "The boy dancing in the middle right now seems to be Tian Shi Bowa."

Shocked by what they heard, Tian Fashui and his wife looked around hurriedly but their son was nowhere to be seen. They looked closely toward the dancing field and saw that Bowa was indeed there.

"Goodness! What are we going to do?" Li Runlan became anxious, moving her feet toward the dancing court, ready to pull Bowa back.

Tian Fashui was quick enough to grab her arm and scolded her, "What are you doing? Going and getting Bowa back? Won't everyone be embarrassed?"

"Thank heavens! The boy in red has come to the rescue! That's great!" Huang Mingfu recognised Bowa and ran over to express his gratitude to Tian

Fashui and his wife, "Brother Tian and sister Runlan, thank you very much. My family are greatly indebted to you."

"What a good boy he is, it's a pity he is dumb," someone nearby gossiped.

"Who said that?" Li Runlan rose to claim at once, "My Bowa can speak."

Staring at the dancing court, Huang Mingfu heard and came to explain, "Definitely! Bowa will speak quite a lot in the future. Look, with his long legs and moderately-sized body, he is a very handsome-looking boy! How wonderful his dancing is!"

Indeed, it was show time for Bowa in the middle of the dancing court. As young as he was, he was an excellent dancer. He sometimes was a sparrow hawk turning upside down to catch a piece of cloud; sometimes he was a lion crouching on the ground to roll the embroidered ball. He was trying every means to tease the bride and then ran to make fun of the groom with all the skills he had.

Particularly excited, the bride and the groom called into play all the tricks they knew to try to move close to each other. The other dancers, however, were no less inferior in the battle, all stretching their arms or legs to deliberately stop them from meeting each other. The groom was impatient. He held a piece of tree leaf close to his mouth and began to blow it. The melodious call was the groom's anxious heart, which of course made the bride writhe in agony. She looked back, eyes full of boundless affection and swirled standing on tiptoes.

The groom was of course more anxious. He moved his body aside and swirled on his feet as well, running quickly toward the bride.

"What wonderful swirling movements!" Tian Fashui praised loudly.

Exactly! The bride swirled on tiptoes, looking like a blooming red flower, fresh, bright, ardent and graceful; the groom's successive steps and swirls were vigorous, rough and fervent, like wind blowing through pine trees, a flowing river and galloping horses.

"How could they meet each other?" People who watched outside the circle forgot that they would join the dance later and began to worry about the bride and groom involuntarily when they saw they were separated by a wall of men.

"When the best and most joyful part comes, they will meet in the middle," someone said loudly with certainty.

As he said this, the beat of drums quickened. People standing aside were encouraged by the rhythm. They invited Tian Fashui and his wife, ran into the dancing field together and danced happily, feet tapping the ground, arms stretching out and swirling up.

Pump-a-rum, pump-a-rum, Ooh! Ooh! Amid the spirited sounds of drums, cymbals, gongs, bells and even whistles, the dance reached its climax.

When this part was played by the TV station in their prime time, Liu Yixiang, the reporter, narrated:

"Under the bright moonlight and against the glowing bonfire flames, the costumes of the Tujia people are so colourful and dazzling: bright red, peach red, scarlet and rose-pink, grass green, verdant green and emerald green, gosling-goldy yellow, brownish yellow and lemon yellow, all hues, spinning into green mountains, golden rice paddy fields and smiles on people's faces.

"Ah! The entire land and sky is spinning with the beautiful colour and ascending gradually...

"This is far more than a type of dance; it is real life and it is the brilliant flowers nurtured by life itself."

4

SOUR BUT SPECIAL YELLOW PEACHES

Tian Shi Bowa suddenly wanted to go and visit White Crane Village elementary school secretly.

He didn't know where it was but he had heard it was located on a plateau beside Fragrant Stream at the foot of Bamian Mountain. Fragrant Stream belonged to White Crane Village and villagers only needed to climb over two mountain ridges to reach there from where they lived.

The village school had been built for three years, during which time Bowa thought about going there to have a look. When he was seven years old, Li Runlan said to her husband, "Tian Fashui, take Bowa to sign up for the elementary school."

"Sign up for school? Bowa can't even speak! What's the use of signing up? Wait till next year!"

When the next year came, Li Runlan urged her husband to take Bowa to school. However, he looked at his wife and sighed, "To this day Bowa can only speak one character at a time and all the children in our village call him Silly Tian. What's the point of doing that? Students at school will bully him too!"

"But our Bowa is not a fool! Let him try, will you?" the mother pleaded.

"You don't have the final say whether he is a fool or not. All the villagers say that and I am sure the teachers will too," said Tian Fashui. "He is not up to it. Accept it!"

At ten-and-a-half years old, children were in their fourth year of school. But in Bowa's case, it was quite different. Whenever he opened his mouth to say something, his face would always turn purple like a pig's liver and he could only spit out one character still. Would it be right to sign him up for the first year, in that case? The couple looked at each other for a while and wiped away their tears without saying anything.

Although Bowa didn't make any oral protest, he was not convinced at all. He thought, "Yes, I can only speak one character at a time but in fact I have a lot to say, a lot of sentences. They are just blocked in my throat and no matter how hard they try, they just cannot break through as if a small piece of wood is blocking the way. I am very anxious and that small piece of wood is almost bent to breaking point, but those characters still cannot get out…"

Perhaps Bowa was too young to know whether he should go to school or not. He didn't feel wronged about not going to school for the past three years; he just felt a bit embarrassed to meet those primary school students who went to school every day while he himself had to stay at home helping his mum cutting grass for pigs, driving pigs or ducks, or catching crabs in the stream. Sometimes when he saw some students walk over in high spirits on the road, he would immediately make a detour to a small path or lower his head and hide in the grass or in the woods. He felt a bit inferior to them and embarrassed to meet them.

Sometimes when he failed to avoid them, those kids would begin to make fun of him. They chanted:

> Silly Tian, drives ducks on the way; the ducks are in the river,
>   trying to catch fish…
> Sheep are running around; what are you going to do, Silly
>   Tian…

For years he would even hide from those students, so how could he ever think about going to visit the school then?

But because of the poem Huang Xiaoqiu had recited to him, he suddenly felt those simple characters were so beautiful, so elegant and so wonderful that he was fascinated by them and could not get them out of his mind at all. He thought about it when he was catching fish and shrimps, when he was cutting grass for pigs and when he was eating his sweet potatoes. As young as he was, he would even think about it when he was sleeping in bed. He at last decided to go and visit the school without telling anyone in his family.

He never thought his secret visit would give birth to a lot of stories, open up the virgin land of his potential and be the prelude to a wonderful life.

Bowa went there at noon. He didn't directly walk to the school on the main road in front of it, perhaps out of awe of the school or the shame of being unable to go to school. He sneaked out of the woods via the hillside and sat on a large stone, looking down at it.

Some of the students in White Crane Stream elementary school came from a much more distant village named Shangmatou, so they didn't have a noon recess. School began at 9:00 in the morning and ended at 2:30 in the afternoon. The bell announcing the end of class rang when Tian Shi Bowa was looking down at the school. It happened to be a fairly long recess. The moment the classroom doors opened, students tall or short rushed out noisily followed by a slender female teacher dressed in a red blouse and a pleated skirt. She waved towards the students and said a few things to them. Some taller students immediately went back into the classroom and when they went back to join the three-row team on the playground, they all wore a type of grass clothes and hats made of grass braids. A boy student stood in front of the team to lead the dance. Drums sounded on the tape recorder and all the other students in the group began to dance following the boy leading the way in front of them.

Their movements looked more like a fight with some beast, fiercer and more intense as the music went on, the grass costumes on their bodies rustling from time to time.

"Maogusi (hunters covered with hair) Dance! Maogusi Dance!" Bowa knew this and wanted to spit out what had come into his mind but he couldn't even utter a single character. On the full moon night of January 15th, according to the lunar calendar, there was a celebration in their village and Bowa saw his father and the other villagers dancing the Maogusi Dance together which was particular to the Tujia people. What surprised him was students would dance it at school. Curious, he walked down and stopped at a place closer to them to take a look. He was even more amazed when he saw the young female teacher was dancing with the students and to be exact she was learning to dance from her students.

Tian Shi Bowa of course didn't know the female teacher had volunteered to teach in their village from downtown Chongqing in response to a project named the 'Poverty Alleviation Programme'. Her name was Liu Wanyi, of Han nationality, and she had a pair of graceful eyes above a beautiful straight nose. Her face was fair and pink, and she was as beautiful as the cherry blossoms in full bloom. It was less than two months since she had come to teach in this village school and it was natural that she didn't know how to dance Tujia dances. The County Board of Education however demanded that students and teachers in the ethnic areas learn to dance a few ethnic dances and sing some popular folk songs as well. That's why she was learning to dance folk dances with her students.

They were dancing the hunting part of the Maogusi Dance. From setting traps, checking traps and fighting with beasts until winning final victory, they sometimes waved their small hands, holding their breath, sometimes chased after their prey, hurrying back and forth, or sometimes, inspired by the stirring drums, fought with the beasts, each of them putting their heart and soul into the dance. Bowa was fascinated by their dancing. As he was getting more cheerful and excited, he wanted to see it clearly and wanted to be there dancing with them. He moved his feet slowly, and unknowingly he entered the peach forest and then went out of it.

The drums suddenly stopped and so did the dancing. The students scattered and shouted noisily as they rushed in and out of the toilets.

"Hey! Look, there's a man over there!"

"Right, it's a boy like us, in the peach forest!"

"It might be a thief stealing peaches!"

"Yes, possibly!"

"Hey, I know him," Huang Xiaoqiu shouted as she pointed at Tian Shi Bowa. "Silly Tian, stealing peaches! Silly Tian, stealing peaches!"

Teacher Wanyi saw the boy too. Pointing in Bowa's direction, she asked her students, "Who is that boy?"

Still lost in the dance at that moment, Bowa didn't extricate himself from his fantasy until he suddenly saw the female teacher pointing at him and asking her students something. Feeling something might be wrong, he scrambled to his feet and ran into the peach forest. Primary school students are fond of creating a disturbance. Some of them began chasing after Bowa, shouting: "Catch the thief! Catch the thief!"

Huang Xiaoqiu seized on the topic and said, "Teacher Liu, the boy running away lives in the same village as me. He is a fool. He must be stealing peaches."

"In your village? Why doesn't he come to school?" As she asked, she went over to the peach forest to take a look while Tian Shi Bowa had long since disappeared.

"Ha! How could he? Teacher Liu, you don't know." Huang Xiaoqiu giggled and said, "He is a fool named Tian Shi Bowa. We all call him Silly Tian because he can't say more than two characters."

"Silly Tian, stealing peaches!" Some students were still chanting.

"Oh? Was he stealing peaches?" Teacher Liu picked one from the tree and handed it to a boy nearby. "Come on and taste it. Is it good?"

The boy took a deep bite, chewed for a while and spat it to the ground immediately. He looked up at Teacher Liu, wanting to say something but it seemed he was choking and could not make any sound for quite a while, with tears welling up too.

"How is it? Very delicious?"

"Sour…so sour that it sets my teeth on edge!" The boy finally squeezed out the words as he continued spitting something from his mouth.

"Right, it is sour, very sour; exactly. Look at this peach, round and yellow but someone just had his teeth put on edge! This kind of peach is called a yellow peach which is hardly eaten raw and is a particular variety often used to make canned fruits," said Teacher Liu, smiling as she talked. She looked around and continued, "Students, remember not to speak ill of others without thinking. Think about it. Who would come and steal peaches when so many of us are here in broad daylight? Some of you have tasted the peaches. Would Tian Shi Bowa come to steal sour peaches? We were dancing just now and he was watching us quietly nearby. Why did he love to watch it then? You all say he is a fool but how could a fool enjoy watching people dance like that?"

Teacher Wanyi looked back thoughtfully beyond the peach forest, along that small path in the direction where Bowa had just run away.

5
DANCING CRANES

Bowa was quite upset these days.

Honestly speaking, how could a boy of his age have so many things on his mind? Strangely enough, Bowa, the boy who was unable to talk and who looked quiet and dull, had so much at the bottom of his heart which had been haunting him all the time.

Based on what the villagers said, Bowa was born into this world with bad luck.

Ten years ago, on the night when Bowa was born, the midwife came to Tian Fashui's family to help. The moment the hot water was prepared, thunder roared; wind blew violently and it poured with rain. The midwife was a little frightened at the time. She said to Tian Fashui, hesitantly, "What weather! I am afraid it is a bad sign. If something should go wrong with the baby, please don't blame me!"

Tian Fashui's mother said, "Rain brings dragons while thunder brings the phoenix. It is a good sign. Relax. Go ahead and do your work!"

"If you can assist with the delivery of a baby boy for our Tian family, I will thank you with two thick slices of pork!" Tian Fashui added.

The midwife didn't let anyone down. She indeed helped Tian Fashui's wife deliver a baby boy, which made Tian Fashui mad with joy, striking his hands upon the wall repeatedly.

Tian Fashui's mother watched her grandson carefully and noticed that this little thing didn't cry. She told the midwife immediately, "Quick! Spank him at once!"

Now other people came to realise that the baby hadn't cried yet. The midwife quickly held the baby tight by his feet and spanked him with a slap on his bottom, but still there was no cry. She did it again but silence was the only response.

"Break the jar! Now!" a voice suggested. With a loud 'bang', a jar broke into pieces and people all looked at the baby who strangely made no sound at all. Then the second bang came but this little thing was still silent.

"Let me have a look," said Tian Fashui, who was in a panic. He held the baby in his arms, touched its belly, felt it was warm and checked its heartbeat, pounding vigorously. What about its eyes? Yes, the eyes, although wide open, were motionless even when its eyelids were pricked. He asked the midwife, "That's weird! He does not move his eyes. You have experience. Please tell me what I should do? What should I do?"

"It seems the baby is physically normal," said the midwife as she rubbed her hands. "Well, let's try the last chance but it is a bit risky."

"Go ahead, please!"

"Your son seems very unusual and I am afraid he will experience rain and wind before he sets sail." The midwife said, "This method used to work well. Hurry up and take him out of your house immediately. Observe his facial expressions and if he moves his eyes or cries out, look around at once to see whether there are some treasures around. Then burn some incense for him and find him a godfather."

"Got it!"

With a lighter, a torch and some incense in a plastic bag, Tian Fashui wrapped the baby in a thick cotton cloth, held him in his arms and went out of the home.

As the wind howled and the rain fell, Tian Fashui bent his body to protect his son from the merciless weather. He walked along a mountain road, and passed through the woods, gullies and small hills but his son didn't cry at all. When he arrived on a flat mountain road, he stopped to switch on the torch to watch the baby who still didn't show any sign of crying, with his eyes wide open but motionless. Tian Fashui sighed and straightened up, "Good heavens! Why did you come to punish us like this?"

A gust of wind and rain blew across the baby's face. Against the flickering light of the torch, he felt the little thing wiggling its body a bit. He hurriedly switched the torch onto a brighter setting to take a look. The baby boy, his son, was apparently shaking his head and blinking his eyes in response to the howling wind and rain. Obsessed with a vague joy, he covered the baby with his body and shone his torch on his son again to take a closer look. Yes! Yes! This little thing blinked its eyes three times, the corner of its mouth moved a little and the lips parted as if uttering a sound. Tian Fashui thought it was obvious that the baby boy wanted to cry and wanted to say something.

"My son can blink his eyes! He can cry!" Tian Fashui shouted and shone his torch in all directions. He found paddy fields on both sides of the mountain road and in the middle of one of the paddy fields stood a huge rock. He said excitedly, "Rice field is 'tian', my given name too. That huge rock will be my son's godfather."

Tian Fashui used some twigs to prop up a plastic bag as an umbrella. He then took out some incense and candles, lit them and stuck them into the field path. Three multiplied by three is nine while nine means longevity, so he bent over and kowtowed nine times in front of the huge rock.

When they named the baby, Tian Fashui said to his mother and wife, "Tian is my family name while the rock (*shi*, in Chinese pinyin) is the godfather of my son. Since this little thing experienced something, let's name him Tian Shi Bowa, shall we?"

Tian Shi Bowa grew up gradually, a healthy boy with sharp eyes and agile hands and feet, but there was one thing that always worried his parents and made neighbours and the other villagers feel pity toward him and that is that he still could not utter a character when he was already nine years old.

"Why did Huang Xiaoqiu deliberately push my large crab out of my palm into the water? Why can she go to school even though she is so naughty? I want to go to school but why doesn't my father allow it? So many students danced the Maogusi Dance and I can dance too, but why couldn't I join them? Why did they call me a peach stealer although I was just quietly watching them dance? What's the female teacher's family name? She looks very kind anyway. But I saw her ask her students something when pointing at me; did she suspect as well that I came to steal peaches? Although I ran far away, her eyes were still on me, following in my direction. What was she looking at? Will she come and report this to my parents…?"

Tian Shi Bowa had been dwelling too much on this. He worried that the female teacher would come to visit his family so he went out to hide from her very early every day and came back home at noon to stuff his stomach with some cold food his grandma had prepared, then he went out again with a willow basket round his waist to catch crabs and small fish in White Crane Stream. In fact, catching fish and crabs didn't matter to Bowa these days; he had other things on his mind. He climbed up and down the hillsides high and low, walked along the winding White Crane Stream, wading in the river and going back ashore from time to time. He was hiding from something but how was he to know that in life there are always things we can never avoid even if we want to? It was not long after he had left the house that someone walked into his home.

Xiaonanhai was a barrier lake retained after an earthquake in the Qing Dynasty. Many streams from Bamian Mountain converged to become its source, among which Banjia Stream in Daughter Valley of Shisan Village and White Crane Stream from Zhongshan Summit were two comparatively large ones. Upstream of White Crane Stream was named Zhongshan Stream and downstream was White Crane Stream, simply because a lot of white cranes came to inhabit this area. Although it was called a stream, White Crane Stream in fact was a small river. When the water rose, there was a risk that even adults could be washed away. Bamian Mountain was located in Qianjiang District southeast of Chongqing, a place full of steep hills and centuries-old forests, stretching over an area of 480 kilometres. Its main ridge branched into many small hills, among which two wound down with White Crane Stream in the middle, the bold one on the left was called Blue Dragon Hill and the elegant one on the right was known as White Crane Hill. The two hills broadened as they stretched down and at last formed a big square mouth in Baiheba. One *fengshui* master who happened to pass by said admiringly, "The Blue Dragon on the left and White Crane on the right shelter this place side by side; backed by the Black Tortoise behind like a strong fortress born for it; the vast Xiaonanhai in front is a perfect gift from nature, a lake like a jade belt in this area. Jigong Mountain on the other side of the lake is flourishing with trees, majestic and magnificent. All these are in accordance with the saying in *fengshui*, Chinese geomancy, that it is an auspicious place with a Vermilion Bird in front and a Black Tortoise behind. A man of nobility is sure to be born here!"

Would the *fengshui* master's prediction come true? But what kind of people could be said to be noble? Conventionally, men of nobility might be those who had made great contributions, who had special talents, or who had excelled themselves with great love and understanding of this world and those whose wisdom was far superior to that of ordinary people. Never did a noble man appear in this place and would one do in the near future? Quite possibly, since nothing is impossible in this world.

Let's put this topic aside and enjoy the scenery of the White Crane Stream area. Looked at from afar, the White Crane Stream was like part of an ink painting drawn by a highly skilled painter who held a drawing brush, dipped it into the white and blue paint, and painted the White Crane Stream with his full affection and passion. Under his brush, the stream flew from the top of the high Bamian Mountain, wound through hills, taking a turn at some place or gushing down to make a deep pool or hanging down like a waterfall. When it reached White Crane Village, it calmed down and slowed its pace. The land of White Crane Village sloped gently but the whole village still exhibited a hilly topography distinguished by three prominent landmarks, namely, the Tian family plateau, the Li family plateau and the Xiao family plateau, masses of fertile land around the three areas and the Baiheba, the centre of White Crane Village.

The White Crane Stream changed its character after flying down the high mountain. It was no longer impatient and bold but mild and gentle as it wound through. It crossed through woods of horsetail pines, poplar and other types of trees, ran around piles of huge animal fossils and zigzagged into the Xiaonanhai area flourishing with reeds. Bestowed with water, food, snails, eels, small fish and shrimps, some birds flew here to build their nests and settle down while some, such as white cranes, migrated from far away and lived here for a few months. In groups, they flew in the blue sky and sailed across the clear water; they took their time wandering in the creek and rice fields; they enjoyed delicious eels and fish to their heart's content and they spent their nights among green mountains and trees.

Bowa went straight to the White Crane Stream after he left home. At this moment, he was bending his body to catch fish and crabs in the water.

He didn't intend to catch those things in the water these days; he had something on his mind and he just wanted to find shelter in nature and kill time. His targets were all in the stream but sometimes he would look up and stare at the sky. What was he looking for? He actually was looking for a sparrow hawk he had seen in the sky when he came here a moment ago. He wanted to know whether it was still there.

He remembered once his grandma took him to play in the field. She pointed at the motionless sparrow hawk in the sky and said, "It is a *chuangzi* (attacker)," and then she added, "Of course it has an official name, sparrow hawk, and it likes preying on small birds best. People in Wensha Town all call it *chuangzi*."

Although it looked like a medium-sized sparrow hawk, it in fact belonged to the *falconiformes*, a special species like *besra accipiter*, which Bowa didn't know until he went to school. The name *chuangzi* sounds a bit interesting and was easy for everyone to remember once they had heard it. Extremely fond of meat, the *chuangzi* seldom fed on plants and tender grass or corn alike because one meal of birds, insects, rats, hares or snakes would provide it with the nutrition it needed for a week. A meat dish? Was there someone who could cook meat for them? No. One reason they liked meat was because they enjoyed catching prey themselves. To put it precisely, they made a living by their own efforts like a man who ventures out to make his fortune.

Making a living? How? The sparrow hawk can fly particularly fast and is said to be one of the fastest birds in the sky. Like many large birds, the sparrow hawk can glide easily after spreading its wings, flying upward and forward, but this is not its special skill; it has a trump card, that is, it can hover in the sky like a humming bird. Of course, it can only hold that posture for about half an hour because it requires a huge amount of power to fix itself in one spot by flapping its wings quickly and skilfully. After half an hour, it relaxes its body and soars, making a few circles in the sky, and then stops still in another place once again. What is its plan by flying like this? One benefit of hovering in the sky is that it is difficult for other ferocious birds to find it while it can spot its prey very clearly. When its target flies close in the opposite direction, especially in the proper position below its body, it flaps its wings more quickly and attacks its prey. When it is very close to its target, it folds its wings suddenly and folds itself into a bomb shape, its sharp beak charging forward. With a crisp swooping sound, its beak pierces the body of its prey. No bird that it targets can easily escape, and those unlucky enough to be attacked by its beak either die or get injured, which is probably the reason why it is nicknamed Mr Attacker by people in White Crane Village or even people living south of the Yangtze River for generations.

"Mr Attacker, you are good! But you are a bit vicious. Who is going to be your victim today? I hope you don't get anything!" Looking at the sparrow hawk motionless in the sky, Tian Shi Bowa muttered a few words in his heart and bowed his head in search of sawbelly (wild carp) beside the water grass.

The small sawbelly is white all over with a very sharp mouth and small eyes. Tiny and dexterous, they swim very fast and are not easy to catch. But as the saying goes, everything has its nemesis. In the White Crane Stream community, there is an animal which can wait patiently for as long as it takes and once it makes a move, it never fails. These animals are wading birds, among which white cranes, gray cranes, egrets and gray egrets are the best hunters. Look at those white cranes! Standing quietly in the stream, their stilt-like legs look slender and graceful, but with a second look, one notices a pair of yellow eyes set on each side of the head rolling watchfully from time to time. Besides, its dark red long beak stretches out toward the surface of the water very professionally, slanted a bit and motionless. As long as the sawbelly forget themselves and swim to their side, they are sure to be caught by the sudden attack of that long beak and devoured in its belly.

So many white cranes! As long as they stand in the stream, fields, lakeside or the reeds, they are sure to have a good harvest. The setting sun was moving towards the west and groups of white cranes had already stuffed their stomachs full, ready to take a walk, stalk out into the water, stretch their bodies and then go back to their nests to rest, full of joyful feelings. As if they had long since made an appointment, these white cranes began their performance. Some stretched their long necks and raised their wings; some were calling and singing; some were dancing or just spinning beautifully. Then one by one they began to run from different spots, accelerated, drew back their willowy legs and took off in a second as they flapped their wings quickly. When they stood quietly, they were snowy white covered with layers of feathers among which the innermost ones were the black elementary layer. When they spread their wings and flew in the sky, the black innermost feathers were visible demonstrating layers of black feathers along the edge of their wings. With black and white in perfect harmony, they looked plain, bright and elegant, very beautiful and eye-catching.

Those which had already taken off were hovering in the sky waiting for their fellows while those who were a bit late began to hastily follow up. Like wild geese, white cranes could also fly in a V-shaped formation, a bit poetic although this is usually seen during migration or long-haul flights. After feeding, they fly back to their nests, the white cranes flying freely without a care, gathering together like clouds or flying in line or adjusting their positions and harmoniously joining a new team. They never wander randomly or behave recklessly; they just stretch their long necks, spread their beautiful wings and call leisurely to their friends, one forming into a small group here and a small group merging into a large group there, with their cries echoing back and forth among each other. Like dancing elves and intricate paper-cuts, they soar gracefully against a blue sky and white clouds. Bathed in the setting sunshine, their dance in harmony with their tranquil surroundings paints a beautiful picture that is pleasing to the eyes, so peaceful and refreshing, so grand and remote, and so harmonious and poetic.

Bowa untied the willow basket from his waist, rubbed the dirt and grass stains from his hands, found a piece of grassland and lay on his back.

Suddenly he saw the beautiful image of those white cranes flying elegantly and freely in the sky. He was stunned by what he saw, eyes bulging round and mouth wide open. Perhaps he didn't know how to appreciate beauty and could not explain what beauty was, but like some gifted kids or a born genius, Bowa had a good aesthetic intuition. "Beautiful! So fantastic!" Bowa felt a bit relieved by the vast and peaceful picturesque sky above his head. He spoke to himself in his heart, clenching a small fist and waving gently, legs with rolled-up trousers occasionally kicking towards the sky. He didn't care whether the call from the bottom of his heart could be delivered through his mouth or not; he was just fascinated by the scene and cheered again and again exaggeratedly, his mouth wide open.

Just as he was almost intoxicated with the dance of these white cranes, an unexpected thrilling scene confounded him. That Mr Attacker, the one who had been watching and waiting in the sky, flapped its wings with an accelerated speed and flew down. No, it was not flying; it was charging violently. It was now a flying bomb that could almost penetrate armour.

Obliquely below the attacker, a small row of white cranes were flying gracefully. Attention, they were obviously lower in altitude and slower in speed than other flocks of cranes because most of them had only just emerged from infancy and learned how to fly independently.

Keeping its eyes on its prey, that attacker, without any hesitation, assumed the properties of a flying bullet and aimed at one of the little cranes in the flock, ready to launch a fatal attack.

Seeing an unknown object coming at him at full speed, with a swift movement, that little fellow dodged aside instantly out of instinct, which saved his life at that moment.

Mr Attacker had planned to stab its prey in the heart while the movement of this little fellow meant it accidentally hit him in the wing.

The little white crane folded his wings in fear from the sudden impact and fell down quickly. Luckily, he came to his senses and managed to spread his wings dozens of metres above the ground.

The little fellow began to fly again. He struggled and tried to keep up with his companions but his left wing was so badly hurt that it became limp after flapping a few times, with his body and wings both tilting.

He kept struggling and tried his best to flap his wings, wanting to climb back into the blue sky. Oh, what a strong-willed little white crane! He was not giving up but trying harder.

Thinking it had killed its prey, Mr Attacker flew back to search for it at low altitude. Then it saw the wounded prey still flying unsteadily above him, so it fluttered its wings and flew up to prepare a second attack. The wounded little fellow suddenly hit upon a way out of this predicament when he noticed the move of the attacker; he made a sudden move and flew down but affected by his wounded wing, he was not flying down but falling down like an object. He struggled to pull himself up again, but he felt the left wing almost didn't work and his whole body became increasingly weaker, unable to fly upwards at all. He tried a level flight and was forced to descend a few metres. After trying repeatedly like this, he was very close to the ground.

Mr Attacker, as if very experienced, went back to the sky above the little crane and hovered there waiting patiently. This fellow perhaps knew its prey would surely fall to the ground and it wanted to save its energy and wait for that moment when it could peck the little prey to death with its hooked beak and feed on it slowly.

Oh, No! Bowa became anxious. He jumped to his feet and ran towards the little white crane. He ran across the grassland, on the field paths and in the sand, the wind blowing past his ears and his eyes fixed on the little fellow. He ran barefoot with great force.

The little white crane was still struggling but his wounded wing wouldn't work any more and was drooping, unbalancing his whole body. Closer and closer the little fellow came to the ground and at last he was exhausted and fell into a tall reed bush.

Without any hesitation, Bowa dashed into the reeds. He opened his eyes wide and searched everywhere but the little fellow was nowhere to be found. He was very worried and kept asking himself, "If I fail to find the little white crane, that attacker will find and kill it. But I saw him fall into these reeds just now. Where did he go? Right, the attacker is looking for it too; it's flying high and looking farther than me and the place it targets is sure to be the place where the little white crane is hiding. With this in mind, Bowa quickly retreated from the reeds and stood on a small mound, looking up into the sky where the attacker was nowhere to be seen. His eyes moved to a lower altitude and it was indeed a lucky coincidence that he saw the attacker hover above another bush of reeds by the lakeside, suddenly fold its wings and land among the reeds.

Yes, the little white crane must be there. Barefoot, Bowa dashed off toward the reed bush like a flying bullet ejected from its chamber.

6

RESCUING THE LITTLE FELLOW

Never did Bowa feel his legs could be so strong and steady as when he ran and stepped onto the edge of the reeds, jumped onto a boulder and landed by the lakeside. In the past, he had been different. When he walked along the riverside, he always stood sideways and on the field paths, he often slipped and fell. But now, the moment when he ran to rescue the little white crane, his footsteps were so vigorous that he felt he could run like a swallow. He even began to have a lot of thoughts. His lips parted involuntarily and he seemed to hear the nursery rhyme Huang Xiaoqiu had chanted to tease him on that day: *Long legs short, long legs tall; fall down on the field path when the rain falls...* "Fall down on the field path? Well, Huang Xiaoqiu, dare you have a match with me? When the time comes, you will realise who would stumble repeatedly and who would fall flat on their face when running on the field path." In his fantasy looking down on his enemy, Bowa was a bit proud. He felt he could prove himself now and from now on he dared to welcome any challenge with his strong body and steady footsteps.

"Watch closely! Watch closely! The attacker has very bright and sharp eyes and it won't land unless it spots its prey. I saw him descend and land in the reeds ahead."

Bowa put a brake on his steps, squatted down, brushed away the reed leaves and stared with wide eyes to take a close look. "Why couldn't I see it?" When he was about to check around, he suddenly heard continuous cries of fear uttered by the little white crane. Following the sound, he saw the little white fellow jump out from the reeds ahead on the left and run forward desperately. Not far behind him, a grayish-brown object with white spots was chasing close behind him; the sparrow hawk looked like a chicken in the distance.

Well, this little white elf! He had hidden motionlessly in the reeds and thought this could cheat his attacker. But how could he know this attacker not only had a pair of sharp eyes but also had an extremely acute sense of its prey, and had actually spotted the hiding place of this little white crane very quickly.

The little white crane couldn't balance his body because of his injured wing and couldn't run faster because of his stilt-like legs. He ran away in panic, staggering and unsteady and the vicious and ferocious attacker was about to catch him. Bowa grabbed a lump of mud and threw it at it, which startled the sparrow hawk a lot. This fellow sprang to its feet and flew up, spreading its wings and hovering above the reeds.

Hurriedly, Bowa picked up a small stick and walked close to the little white crane.

How could the attacker give up its feast in the bag? In its eyes, there was nothing but its prey and it just turned a blind eye to Bowa who was its enemy and was hitting it with mud. Don't you think it is quite the same as the classic story *A Man of Qi State Sees Nothing But Gold on the Market*? He was too obsessed with what he wanted! The attacker had failed to catch anything until now and it was starving; it was seized by the wilful idea of pecking the little fellow to death and then feeding on it. Looking around, the attacker couldn't find any competitor of its family nor did it spot any enemy like hounds, wild cats or panthers. It was probably laughing at itself for the false alarm that had just been raised and now fixed its sharp eyes back on the fleeing little white crane. Aiming at where this young fellow would run to, it hovered and descended slowly, folding its wings, stretching its legs and landing arrogantly.

The poor young fellow thought he was already out of danger. Instinctively, he moved close to Xiaonanhai, which obviously indicated that he planned to jump into the lake. He perhaps thought he could swim away or dive into the water because the vast lake was a natural refuge for him. No matter how vicious and sly the attacker was, it could do nothing when faced with the surging lake!

Just as the little white crane staggered forward and thought about the imminent achievement of his beautiful dream, the attacker landed in front of him without any warning. The little crane uttered a cry and collapsed in a heap on the ground before he had time to think about what to do. That was too unexpected. Have you ever seen a runaway mouse suddenly encountering a cat staring at him with his eyes wide open? Have you ever seen a goat suddenly meeting a hungry tiger in front of him? Facing the attacker that was sure to win the battle, our lovely little crane had no chance of running away, like the mouse and the goat! There was no chance to slip away and any desire to resist naturally disappeared. The little crane was lying there powerless like a lump of soft mud, waiting for death.

What an ambitious fellow this attacker was right now! You have seen a cat-and-mouse game, haven't you? Staring at its prey, the cat would rather play with its hostage first, pawing it here and there than kill and eat it immediately. A turtle in a jar was sure to be caught within reach. Very complacent, the attacker took a sharp glance at the little white crane and knew at once that this poor loser had given up any attempt to fight back as if paralysed except for an occasional movement of his eyes. Pacing around the collapsed little crane in a very handsome manner, the attacker shrugged its shoulders, fluffed its feathers, and puffed out its chest deliberately, showing off rows of beautiful grayish white markings on its belly. Then it brushed its special weapon, the hooked beak, a few times on its feathers right and left in turn. It seemed this fellow was particular about ritual.

It wanted to look clean and neat before enjoying its feast, a high-quality fellow indeed.

When all was ready, the attacker walked gracefully.to the side of the little white crane. It tilted its head to the right side, then to the left to look, as if studying which part was the best for it to start.

It had the answer. It slightly opened its beak, ready to peck the poor fellow on the neck. Just as the attacker stretched its neck a few times and raised up its beak to peck, a wooden stick suddenly hit it over the head.

The wooden stick fell behind the wind it made. What an alert bird the attacker was! Startled by the roaring wind carried by the stick, its powerful short legs intuitively jumped upward and its left wing stroked a bit; it was already three feet away from the little white crane. And the wooden stick hit the ground with a loud noise, leaving a bowl-sized pit.

Bowa saved the little white crane at that critical moment. Seeing the attacker showed no sign of leaving and continued to stare covetously at the little crane nearby, Bowa chased after it, lifting the stick high in his hand.

The attacker had no choice but to take off, hovering over the reeds again.

Seeing his enemy fly away, the little crane kicked his long legs, stretched his neck and got to his feet staring at the sky. He could not help trembling at the sight of the attacker that was still hovering over his head, eyes full of worry.

Bowa approached the little crane who, as if it were one of us, developed a kind of trust when he glanced at Bowa. Perhaps he sensed Bowa meant safety, something he could rely on. The little crane quickened his steps and snuggled up at Bowa's feet.

Warmed by him, Bowa reached out his hand and stroked his feathers. Then he bent down a bit and held him in his arms. He felt the urge to say something, a lot of things, but he could not manage it, nor did he know what on earth to say. Blocked for quite a while, he at last spat out one character: crane.

7
GOOD COMPANY

Since the last time she had seen Silly Tian, Teacher Liu Wanyi had made a point of paying a visit to Tian Shi Bowa's home. After talking with Bowa's grandma, she knew he was not a fool and knew he could weave baskets, perform folk dances and that he helped his father tend bees quite often. She made a decision that once she returned from supporting an education conference downtown, she would ask Bowa to go to school as soon as possible.

While Liu Wanyi was on her trip downtown, Bowa came back exhausted with the injured white crane in his arms.

Bowa's father saw him first.

When Bowa appeared in front of the house holding a little white crane in his arms, Tian Fashui saw him at a glance. He shouted immediately, "Tian Shi Bowa, you are really a fool! How dare you catch white cranes? Go and set it free! Now!"

Hearing the noise outside, his mother went out of the kitchen to see what had happened. She saw the crane held in Boba's arms as well. She hurriedly walked over to him, bent down and said, "Set it free at once. No one catches white cranes. Why did you do it? Let it go, otherwise your father will spank you."

As she spoke, she reached out her hands, trying to hold the crane while Bowa turned away and muttered, "Wounded."

"Tian Shi Bowa, I told you to set it free." Standing at the entrance of the courtyard, Tian Fashui stared angrily at Bowa. "Didn't you hear me? I will break your arms if you don't!"

"Quick, set it free! Or your father will beat you," Li Runlan urged her son. Bowa reluctantly placed the crane on the ground. Pointing at the crane and looking at his father, he wanted to say something but he just could not get the words out. He looked very anxious.

The little white crane stood on the ground for a little while and began to move his long legs to walk forward. But his injured wing hurt him so much that he could not hold it but let it drop limp with the result that it became a burden on his body and made him stagger on with great difficulty. A few steps later, he collapsed on the ground. Tian Fashui felt something was not right and walked toward him to check. The little fellow, however, uttered a cry when he saw Tian Fashui move toward him; he stretched his long neck, spread the other good wing and with the help of his feet struggled to run to Bowa, leaning against Bowa's feet and crying on and on.

"Tian Senior, look! This little white crane recognises people!" Li Runlan kind of understood what was happening and began to speak for Bowa.

Tian Fashui moved closer to look at the crane and asked Bowa, "You want to tell me he is injured? His wing?"

"Yes," said Bowa, looking into his father's eyes.

"Let me have a look," said Tian Fashui, reaching out to grab the little fellow who, however, cried immediately, flapped his good wing and dodged to the other side of Bowa, trying to hide.

"Ha! Ha! Interesting! The little crane does recognise people. Well, he understands our feelings, an intelligent animal that was worth being rescued by Bowa." Tian Fashui smiled and said, "Son, show me his injured wing."

Bowa squatted and held the crane in his arms. The little fellow spread his wings obediently on Bowa's hands. Tian Fashui checked both sides of the wings carefully and said, "Look, how big this hole is! It has been pierced through. I have seen this kind of wound before. It must be the damned attacker that did it."

Hearing that, Bowa felt great admiration for his father and gave him a thumbs-up. The word "great" was in his mouth but he just could not enunciate the word from his open mouth.

"Sure I am! Who do you think your father is? How could I not know that an attacker left it! What a joke," said Tian Fashui very proudly.

Li Runlan asked anxiously, "How should we deal with the injured little white crane? His wound will get inflamed on such a hot day! He won't survive if we set him free but if we keep him at home, we don't have any medicine for him."

"That's no bother at all. Wild Sanqi (a type of ginseng), radish-shaped Sanqi and plantain all help remove internal heat, reduce inflammation and kill bacteria. All these ingredients are available beside White Crane Stream and I will go there to get some at once." With these words, Tian Fashui went into the room, took a torch and went straight to the White Crane Stream.

Bowa's nervous tension was suddenly relieved. He exhaled a long breath like a grown-up, called out "Mum" and squatted on the ground. The little white crane took a glance at him, staggered a bit and snuggled up closer beside his bottom. Hurriedly Li Runlan asked, "Bowa, what happened to you?"

"Hungry."

"Oh, yes. Definitely! I am hungry too." Li Runlan quickly grabbed Bowa's hand and took him to the house. When they had taken just a few steps, Bowa suddenly shook off his mother's hand and turned back to pick up the little white crane. Together they entered the room.

Sitting at the square table in the living room, Grandma was waiting for dinner. She had poor hearing and was completely unaware of the noise outside. When Bowa came into the room holding a big bird, she was very surprised and stepped over to lean down and have a close look. Then she straightened up, smiled, rubbed her hands and said, "Good! Good! Cranes bring longevity. It is a good sign that my grandson has come into the house holding a crane. It seems I am going to live to 90 years old."

Very soon, Tian Fashui came back with a bunch of herbs. Bowa squatted on the ground. In front of him was a bench where he spread his hands, resting his chin on it, watching his father treat the injured crane. Seeing Bowa sitting beside him, the little white crane didn't make any attempt to struggle and yielded to Tian Fashui. Tian Fashui smashed the herbs and put them on one side first, then he cleaned the wound on the white crane's wing with salt water and applied the herbs to the wound on both sides of the wing. Bowa's mother found some clean used cloth to wrap around the wound. After the treatment, Bowa thought this little fellow must be hungry too. He took out two small fish from the basket and put them close to his beak while the little crane just took a look and turned his head aside without even opening his beak, as if he had no appetite at all.

It was time for Bowa to go to bed. He slept in the neighbouring room but how could he go to sleep while still holding the little white crane? His mother thought about it and brought a small rocking bed Bowa had slept in when he was still a little baby to his bedside. She put some hay inside, picked up the little fellow and placed him into the rocking bed.

What is a rocking bed? In fact, it's a cradle in the general sense. Shortly after Bowa was born, his father went to the mountain, trying to find some rattan with which to weave a cradle for his son. Viewed from above, it resembled a deep basket with a plank of wood forming the bottom of the frame. High in the middle and low on both sides, it would rock from side to side when slightly pressured by hand on one side, really a lot of fun. Inside the cradle, the little white crane lay down, curled up and buried his neck in the good wing. Bowa hadn't fallen asleep yet. Lying on the bed, he was imagining that the injured little crane must be feeling a lot of pain and be unable to fall asleep. He thought he might try rocking the cradle so that it would go to sleep quickly. Thinking of that, he reached out his hand and pressed one side of the cradle. With a rattling sound, the cradle rocked. The little crane however was greatly startled by the sound and stood up all of a sudden, poking his head out of the cradle and crying in panic.

"Crane…" Bowa hurried to comfort him. In fact, he had wanted to say to him it was all right but after he made a few futile attempts in his throat, he eventually gave up. He reached out his hand to stroke the little crane's neck and his feathers. The little fellow relaxed and lay down again, putting his neck back into his wing.

"It is good for Bowa to raise a bird," said Tian Fashui, sitting on the bed as he smoked his pipe, not knowing that Li Runlan had already fallen asleep. "A fool and a silly bird! Neither of them could talk. It's fate that they became acquainted with each other. Life will be easier for them anyway!"

Bowa got up quietly before daybreak. He covered the cradle with a sieve in case the little white crane jumped out. He then held a bamboo crate and went out of the door. The late moon was still lingering on the mountain ridge in the west. Under its dim light, Bowa walked steadily on the hazy road and very soon he arrived at the White Crane Stream.

Bowa rolled his trousers up above his knees, placed the crate into the water grass and stirred the grass wildly with his thin legs. When he stopped and picked up the crate, quite a few small fish and shrimps had jumped inside!

Bowa carried his trophy back home. Hurriedly, he placed the crate on the ground, entered the room and came out with the little white crane in his arms. Standing on the ground, the little fellow stretched his neck staring straight at the small fish and shrimps in the crate. Perhaps he was still a bit shy and dared not stretch out his beak to eat anything but took a glance at Bowa instead.

Laughing to himself, Bowa picked up a small fish and put it close to its beak. With a quick movement, this little fellow quickly caught the fish in his beak, raised up his long neck and the fish disappeared. Bowa pushed the crate to the little white crane who immediately enjoyed the feast eagerly and happily.

8

WHITE CRANE VILLAGE ELEMENTARY SCHOOL

Located next to Xiaonanhai, White Crane Village elementary school was more like a bungalow than a school.

With its painted cement wall and black roof tiles, it was a row of bungalows with two large rooms, one used as a classroom and the other divided into two small rooms for two teachers to use. Each small room was partitioned further into two living rooms. The one in the front was quite multifunctional: a teacher's room, dining room, reference room and meeting room while the other one was a bedroom. What about kitchen and bathroom then? Along one side of the bungalow two small rooms were set up there, one for the kitchen and the other a toilet and storage for spare stuff. On the other side of the bungalow were two small cement brick buildings, used respectively for the boys' and girls' toilets. A lot of peach trees were planted behind and on both sides of the bungalow; in front of the bungalow was a cemented rectangular playground, in the middle of which a thick bamboo platform was erected for the flag-raising ceremony.

There were dozens of school-age children in White Crane Village. In the past, they had to go to study at a school at Xiaojie in Xiaonanhai, which usually took them two and a half hours to get to by boat from White Crane Stream to the town. Besides, the long-term boat fare was too much for a poor family to afford, which meant that, as a result, either many children could not go to school or a lot ended up dropping out of school. Therefore many years ago a school was built in Xiangjiaba which was not very far from the lower pier of Xiaonanhai. Children in Nanhai Village near the lake, in Shuangyan Village on the hillsides of Bamian Mountain and in White Crane Village all studied there. But the schooling problem in White Crane Village was by no means solved once and for all. For one thing, White Crane Village was located near the upper pier of Xiaonanhai which meant that a boat fare to the lower pier to go to school, was still inevitable. For another, adults all worried about safety issues; the boat was not big enough while the children were all quite young, after all. What's more, it still took nearly two hours by road. Five years ago, the county education committee and leaders in charge of education in the town conducted some research into the situation at White Crane Village and decided to build an elementary school there.

Honestly speaking, the school should have been built on Baiheba where the students all lived relatively close, but leaders in the village and in the town were both quite reluctant to give up fertile farming land there. What's more, those fields had already been distributed to villagers and it would have been very difficult to persuade them to give them back. The field in Fragrant Valley was also beside Xiaonanhai, which was collective land belonging to the village. It happened that there was just a piece of flat land available, which had not been transformed into a paddy field due to insufficient water, a perfect place for building a school and a playground for sports. Of course, there was another reason. Many students in Shuangyan village and Tanglian village lived nearby, which made it easier for kids to go to school nearby. A lot of yellow peaches were planted around the school too. There was a story about it. A few years ago, some departments in the city had encouraged villagers to plant fruit trees while yellow peaches, though not good to be eaten raw, could be made into canned fruit. Now they were already ripe but no company came to buy the fruit; they were left there growing wild. The good thing was the green and flourishing yellow peach trees around the school made the air cleaner and the environment quieter. Like a specially designed landscape, it made the village school extraordinarily beautiful.

Shortly after the completion of the school, students from White Crane village and the other villages all came back. With the addition of those who didn't go to school in the past, there were more than a hundred students in the newly built one. The school therefore grouped the first and second years into one class and the third and fourth years into another.

Two teachers were assigned to teach at the school, a male teacher and a female one. The former was a young man in his twenties, a new graduate, who planned to work in the village just for a while and a few years later would be transferred back to the city. The female teacher was nearing retirement age and had no worries at all because all her children were already working. She volunteered to teach in this quiet village free of hustle and bustle to enjoy fresh air for two years.

Two years later, the female teacher resigned as planned but no other teacher was willing to come. The young male teacher kept pestering the school for a transfer, claiming it was so inconvenient to live there, and many other things. As for food, he had to cook for himself; rice and vegetables were not always available and neither was firewood. Irregular meals, cooked or raw, had made him suffer from stomach problems. As for the living place, it was too small and in winter it was extremely cold inside and there was no proper bathroom! No matter where he wanted to go, near or far, he had to walk and when it rained, his legs were sure to be covered with mud. Leaders of the education committee comforted this male teacher and told him new teachers would come and conditions would be improved and that what he should do was to do his job well pending his transfer to the city. The male teacher shrugged and pulled a long face helplessly, thinking to himself that, in that case, he would muddle along.

The male teacher muddled along indeed as he had no choice. Since he was the only teacher in the school, all the students were grouped into one class. When he taught the third year, the others had to do their assignments or sleep in the classroom. Talking was not allowed in the classroom because it would be a distraction to the teacher who was giving a lecture. The teacher on the one hand not only needed to apply his professional expertise, but also needed to be a jack of all trades on the other hand, which meant he had to teach Chinese, maths, English, music, PE and fine arts all by himself. Teaching in this way, how could he guarantee the quality of teaching? Families that were better off or with some other advantages had no option but to send their children to distant schools again. Fifty or sixty students were left but for the teacher, there was nothing different concerning teaching responsibility. No one knew how long that male teacher could hold on.

Thankfully for the village school, things finally took a turn for the better. A volunteer from the Chongqing educational field came. She was teacher Liu Wanyi.

Liu Wanyi was an in-service teacher in Runlan Middle School in the main city area of Chongqing. At that time her school was tasked by higher-level organisations to assign one of their teachers to do volunteer work in an elementary school in poor mountainous areas, someone who was under the age of 30, single and had a comprehensive scope of knowledge. But although so many young teachers met the requirements, none of them signed up. Honestly, Liu Wanyi didn't meet the age requirement for she was more than thirty years old, but she felt very sad when seeing no one volunteer to do this. Just two years! How could they not be prepared to do this at such a young age? Eventually, she signed up. The headmaster said to her out of good intentions, "You have a family; you shouldn't make a decision in a fit of pique; that's asking for trouble. Your husband might be concerned about you."

"Oh? Am I, Liu Wanyi, making a decision in a fit of pique? If they think like this, they must despise me." Liu Wanyi graduated with a well-rounded education and training from a normal university. She admired Makarenko who regarded education as a poem and she had dreams and wanted to pursue a poetic educational life. According to her, being designated to work in a middle school was like using a sledgehammer to crack a nut. Although she could get along well with everything, it was difficult for her to achieve something, which often made her feel depressed. Like this, where was the poetic meaning of education?

In Liu Wanyi's mind, the poetic meaning of education was generated in the impulses of responsibility, mission and ideals while the best way to demonstrate this impulse was "asking for trouble".

She answered the headmaster, "Thank you for your kindness, principal. This time I am going to ask for trouble. I want to know what a village school in the poor mountainous area looks like and I want to do something for the children there. Moreover, my husband understands me. Besides, it is not that far from here and there are two vacations every year too."

Liu Wanyi therefore came to White Crane Village elementary school.

As for the situation in the village school, Liu Wanyi knew something about it in advance. The county education commission had promised her that the male teacher wouldn't be transferred until a new teacher came. Then, except for the inconvenient living conditions, the two teachers would deal with the teaching in the village school. But to her surprise, when she came, the male teacher left. Of course, the education commission didn't break their promise; it was the male teacher's girlfriend in the city that gave him an ultimatum: if he didn't go to work in the city within two months, she would break up with him. For that young teacher, love or marriage was a major event in his life which he could not afford to delay. As a last resort, he quit and went to teach in a vocational school as a contract teacher.

Volunteer teaching, as its name implied, meant to support, help or improve teaching conditions in some relatively backward areas. It should simply have been assisting or sharing some work with others. But now the work that should have been undertaken by two or three teachers was suddenly placed on the delicate shoulders of Teacher Wanyi! Put yourself in her place, it was indeed a suffocating burden.

Cool and a bit cloudy, the foot of the mountain in the distance was veiled by mist and it gradually turned from brown to dark. A few birds flew in after a tiring journey, their wings flapping, and within a minute they disappeared. On the surface of the lake, boats sailed away under the clouds. Wanyi stood quietly beside Xiaonanhai. The evening wind swept across the lake and wafted through her long black hair. Along with the evening breeze, the lingering light of the setting sun shone and stroked her pretty but slightly pale face from the forests and mountain ridges above.

As if a bit depressed, she took a deep breath and exhaled slowly. After repeating this a few times, she felt a lot more relaxed.

She could have left this place without any responsibility. Who had the right to stop her? The row of cement bungalows however seemed to be telling her something and she felt attached to it without knowing why. The fate of dozens of families in this poor village was interwoven with dozens of their children while Liu Wanyi's fate was likewise destined to be intertwined with them in a way, and together they would face difficulties, have a good time and grow. The reason why human beings are different from other animals is that they possess some kind of important spirit unique to mankind. Yes, a kind of noble spirit. She hadn't come to teach in this poor village due to vanity or for personal gain.

Wasn't it rather that a seemingly invisible but strong and stubborn spirit had been secretly pushing her forward?

In previous years, whenever she saw the colourful and luxurious lives of so many children in the city, she would imagine how strikingly big the regional difference was, concerning study platforms and the backwardness of the living conditions of those children in poor villages. Yes, she was guided by some kind of spirit having thought it over and silently made her choice to teach in this village. What was the spirit? It seemed Liu Wanyi could not identify it clearly while life could. It was up to life to explain and give it a definition. Now that she was here, she had to immerse herself in nature and into this life.

Heaving a gentle sigh, she smoothed her hair away from her face and calmly made a decision: to assume this heavy and troublesome burden, to do her duty and to try her best.

No matter how ordinary her words sounded, they were extraordinarily significant! It was a decision full of responsibility and humanity; it was brave of her to sacrifice her small being to shoulder such a huge responsibility.

9
THE BEAUTIFUL SILHOUETTE OF WHITE CRANE BOY

Tian Fashui couldn't wait to set out the next day when he got the message.

As a good beekeeper, Tian Fashui had mastered a lot of bee-keeping techniques. The owner of the apiary he used to work for had migrated to Guizhou, where there were good honey sources and where his business would be better. That owner needed labour and therefore sent him a message inviting him to work in his apiary.

As for working part-time to earn some extra money, Tian Fashui would spare no efforts. In the past, considering the actual situation of his son Bowa, he didn't want to work outside for a long time because he wanted to take care of his son full time. This time he accepted the offer readily because he knew the apiary would take a break during the winter season which meant he could go back home to stay with his son. Besides, he liked raising bees and he was technically qualified to do so. He was sure he would get paid handsomely. That's why he didn't show the slightest hesitation before he left and interestingly he remembered to change the herbal medicine carefully for the little white crane before he set out.

The little white crane was getting better and better and his appetite was getting bigger and bigger too. One day, Bowa caught quite a lot of small fish and shrimps to feed him. After the little fellow had enjoyed his feast, he played wildly with Bowa in the courtyard. Sometimes, he turned around in front of or behind Bowa; sometimes he sneaked under Bowa's legs playing hide-and-seek; sometimes he became so excited that he would flap his wings, flying over the bamboo basket and Bowa's head. When the little fellow was carried away with elation, the herbal medicine pocket wrapped around his wound fell off. Bowa hurriedly held him in his arms to check and found the wound had already formed a scab, and new feathers were coming out on the edge of the injured side.

The little white crane was recovering day by day and he was ready to play in the water. Bowa decided to let him try. He tied a thin nylon rope to one of his legs, then walked toward the stream holding a bamboo basket in his hand. The little fellow, as if understanding everything, hurriedly followed Bowa to the White Crane Stream.

Seeing the stream from afar, the little white crane became excited. He flapped his wings a few times and rose high into the air.

In an unguarded moment, the string slipped out of Bowa's hand and went into the sky with the little white crane. Staring at the little fellow flying freely in the air, Bowa was very frustrated. What bad luck! The little fellow was going to fly away. He told himself that he had been wrong. He had thought the little fellow was unable to fly high for the time being because his wound had not fully recovered. But how could he have known it could and that now it was flying away from him!

Hovering in the sky for a while, the little crane descended toward the White Crane Stream. Bowa hurriedly quickened his step and ran towards the stream.

The little crane wandered in the shallow water, its slender legs moving slowly, so relaxed as if no one was nearby. But he kept turning back to keep a look out, appearing very watchful. He didn't relax to stretch out his beak into the reeds probing for food until he saw Bowa running towards him. He spotted a lot of tender reed roots. Quickly he picked them up, caught them tight in his beak, raised his head and moved his beak up and down, and then stretched his long neck and swallowed those tender roots into his food sac.

Finding Bowa was already in the stream, the little white crane appeared very happy. He greeted him with a loud cry and then bent down again to peck his reed roots.

Bowa had planned to approach this little fellow secretly so that he could grab the string before he noticed it. The little crane's innocence and his intimacy with him therefore made him ashamed of his narrow-mindedness. He stood absently for quite a while, then quickly turned back, picked up the crate and went to catch fish and shrimps in Huishui Bay.

The issue of whether Bowa could go to school or not had been haunting Liu Wanyi. Although his village pals all called him Silly Tian and his father thought school didn't suit him, Liu Wanyi stubbornly believed that without giving it a try no one knew whether it was suitable or not. She could not forget the hope in the eyes of Bowa's grandma and she could not forget the appeal in Li Runlan's words. Liu Wanyi trusted her feelings that it was by no means a coincidence when Bowa showed up in the yellow peach forest. How could she simply ignore the situation and let him live like this? On the day she came back from a meeting in the city, she heard students talking about Bowa saying he was idle all day long and he had recently caught a white crane but wouldn't let it go; instead he wanted to kill it and make a soup with it.

Was it really true? The next morning, Liu Wanyi left home full of doubts and headed for Tian Fashui's home.

The village in September was exceptionally beautiful, with bright sunshine, a gentle breeze, green forests, birds chirping, flowers blossoming and the fragrant smell of crops.

Crossing the Fengyu Bridge over the Xiaonanhai, Liu Wanyi walked down a slope and then another. The White Crane Stream was right in front of her eyes. After she went down the slope, she arrived at the stream and rolled up her trousers, ready to wade through the stream, when she felt something light up in front of her eyes and she was stunned by a picture.

The sun jumped out of the Jigong Mountain pass in the east. Through the narrow passage of dense forest, rays of bright sunlight slanted across the grassland along the White Crane Stream, depicting the beautiful silhouette of a white crane and a teenage boy.

The teenager had a slim figure, wore a yellow sweatshirt and his feet were hidden in the green grass. His body was slightly bent, with two fingers tightly pinching the tail of a small fish and stretching it out straight in the air. The fish hung down vertically under his palm; crystal water drops flew out of its mouth from time to time. Below the fish was a little white fellow whose snow-white feathers shone brightly in the sunshine, reflecting clean and pure light. It seemed they were playing a game. The little white crane, standing on tiptoes, wings spreading slightly and raising his head with a slightly curved long neck, stared at the fish in the boy's hand. The bright rays of sunlight slanted from the top of the opposite mountain and the edges of the dark silhouettes of the crane and the boy were embroidered with a fuzzy golden rim, extraordinarily beautiful and eye-catching.

The crane and the boy! What a delightful contrast! How beautiful, harmonious, friendly and poetic this picture was!

Liu Wanyi was quite unwilling to disturb the peaceful scene but she had to pass by there. Her students' gossip about Tian Shi Bowa that he had caught a crane to make a soup came to her mind again. If that was his intention, why would he bother to catch fish and shrimps to feed the crane? How could he and the crane be so intimate and harmonious? If that were the case, there would be no such beautiful and innocent relationship between them! If she paid no attention to him and didn't help him, how could she call herself a teacher?

Pondering, Liu Wanyi slowly walked behind Bowa. The little white crane stared up at Bowa's hand, sprung up and jumped lightly to peck the small fish. When he landed to swallow the fish, he suddenly saw Liu Wanyi. He was so startled that he uttered a cry and quickly ran a few steps to hide beside Tian Shi Bowa.

"Hahaha!" LiuWanyi was so amused by the little fellow's quick reaction and panicky cry that she couldn't help laughing.

Bowa turned around and found it was Teacher Liu. "Ah!" He blurted out and froze.

At this moment, his feelings were quite mixed. He had seen Liu Wanyi before and knew she was a teacher at the village school. On the one hand, he was pleasantly surprised because he wanted to go to school; on the other hand, he was afraid and uneasy; he wondered what she would think of him after the 'yellow peach forest incident'.

But this "Ah" made Liu Wanyi joyful. Like the other children, this boy reacted the same. Her intuition told her Tian Shi Bowa could talk. His problem was probably due to some articulation barrier or articulation issues. As he grew up, or with some intervention treatment, he perhaps could be healed.

"Are you Tian Shi Bowa?" asked Liu Wanyi.

Bowa wanted to say something but he was so anxious that he could not say anything. He looked at her, eyes wide and face red. In a panic, he nodded.

Liu Wanyi understood his reaction in such a situation. She smiled in her heart and looked at this boy who was called a fool. In this remote poor village, Liu Wanyi had never seen such a beautiful boy with a broad forehead, black eyebrows like lying silkworms and a straight nose. His eyes were a bit small but when he blinked occasionally, a keen and bright light flashed inside his eyes revealing a certain cleverness and wisdom.

"I happened to be passing by," said Liu Wanyi, smiling. "Take it easy, Bowa. I am looking for your father."

On hearing this, Bowa first pointed in the direction of his home, then in the direction of the town. He wanted to tell her his father was not at home. But Teacher Liu misunderstood his gesture as a guide to his home so she said as she walked on, "I know, I have been there before. Go and play with your little white crane."

Bowa's grandma, sitting in front of a tub, was chopping grass for the pigs in the courtyard while Li Runlan was just walking back to the courtyard from the pig pen after feeding the pigs. Wanyi knew it was Li Runlan by looking at her back because she had seen her before.

"Hey!" Liu Wanyi greeted them in the yard like saying hello to her old friends.

"Ah!" Li Runlan followed the sound and found Teacher Liu in front of the house. Like Bowa, she was a bit surprised and uttered a faint cry. She wiped her hands quickly on her apron, swept a few strands of hair back past her ears and went to greet Liu Wanyi with a smile on her face. "Teacher Liu, it is a surprising honour to have you here!"

"It's so nice of you! I am not a rare guest, am I? Remember we chatted with each other a few days ago," said Liu Wanyi as she walked into the courtyard, as if she was an old friend of theirs. She greeted Bowa's grandma, "Grandma Tian, you still look strong and healthy! You are so good at chopping grass for the pigs. Look at this pig grass, chopped so fine."

Grandma Tian raised her head and recognised Liu Wanyi. She stopped using the machete, and propped herself up to rise from the bench by placing the machete against the bottom of the tub. She smiled and said, "No wonder we have such a wonderful morning. We have an honoured guest today! Runlan, go and fetch a bench. Teacher Liu, I'll brew a pot of tea for you."

Li Runlan didn't bring out a bench but a chair instead. She placed the chair in a clean place and invited Liu Wanyi to take a seat.

"Is there another one?" Liu Wanyi looked inside and outside the room as she sat in the chair asking, "That fellow who talks loud and rough. Why didn't I hear any sound from him?"

"Who?" Li Runlan asked surprisingly with her eyes wide open. But when she saw Teacher Liu look around, she suddenly knew what she meant. "Oh, you mean Bowa's old man?"

People in White Crane Stream sometimes would use the term 'old man' to introduce their father or someone else's father.

Li Runlan pulled a bench over and sat on it, saying, "He has left. He has gone to do a part-time job."

"Left? Has he gone far away?"

"Yes, he went to help his friend with an apiary in Guizhou," said Li Runlan gently with a deep breath. "It's good that he is not at home."

"Good?" asked Liu Wanyi a bit surprised. "Do you mean you feel more relaxed when Tian Fashui is not at home?"

"You're right," said Li Runlan. "When he is at home, he is very bossy and you have to listen to him all the time. That is really boring and depressing!"

"Oh, I see." Liu Wanyi laughed as she clapped her hands. She said humorously, "We are both women and I understand. No one will bother you when Bowa's father goes out to work. You can make your own decisions freely, right?"

Liu Wanyi hadn't forgotten her mission today and spoke out directly. Li Runlan was clever enough to get what she meant. She laughed too and said, "Teacher Liu, you truly know what I am thinking about as if you have placed a mirror in my heart."

"Hahaha, we do think alike, concerning Bowa's education," said Liu Wanyi.

"I should have taken the initiative to ask for your help. Teacher Liu, it's so nice of you to care about Bowa's education!" Li Runlan patted her forehead and said, "I am stupid. I felt embarrassed to look for you, thinking that it was totally impossible. It would be good for Bowa to go to school and I want him to go there too. Now is his best chance since his father is not at home. But I need to check that with Bowa's grandma. You know, Bowa is the Tian family's grandson, after all."

"As for this, I don't agree with you. The Tian family's grandson? We are in modern times now. The Tian family's grandson is your son as well."

"You are right, but I am Bowa's mother, surnamed Li and his father is not at home, so I'd better go and talk about this with his grandma." Li Runlan stood up as she said this and waved to Liu Wanyi for an excuse, "Teacher Liu, I will be back in a minute. Don't worry too much."

As she said so she went into the room. A mother could not make a decision for her son! What kind of ethics was this in a rural area! Was it pedantic or wonderful? Was it innocent or backward? What kind of influence would it have on future generations? Liu Wanyi didn't know the answer. She sighed, stood up and went to the side of the courtyard to look into the distance.

In the blue sky, the sun had risen very high and the colourful clouds that had surrounded it just now had faded away with the wind. Under its splendour, Jigong Mountain seemed to have shrunk a lot. Enjoying being touched by the sunshine, fields of corn stood erect, dancing beautifully. When the mountain wind passed, terraces of green rice seedlings bowed down and rose up from time to time as if greeting someone, whispering in their ears or preparing for the flowering and booting of the ears of grain. In the narrow passages on the hillside and corners of terraces were some paths, wide or narrow, looming mysteriously. No one knew who arranged them all and where the paths led.

"Teacher Liu."

Li Runlan came out supporting her mother-in-law. Grandma Tian carried three small bowls and held a pot of brewed tea. Liu Wanyi dragged her eyes away from the scenery in front of her, turned and went back to the chair.

"Teacher Liu, we are very grateful for your help," said Grandma Tian, placing the bowls on the bench, then she poured one bowl half full and asked Li Runlan to serve the tea. She said, "Runlan, you have my word. You are free to make any decision for Bowa. I will back you up. Hurry up, serve tea for Teacher Liu."

Li Runlan immediately held the bowl in both hands and served it to Liu Wanyi. Emotionally, she said, "Teacher Liu, please have this bowl of tea. You are from a big city but you haven't rejected our silly son and keep coming to visit us. Bowa owes you a lot and we all thank you."

As Li Runlan spoke the truth from the bottom of her heart, she became so emotional that she suddenly knelt before Liu Wanyi, tears welling up, "Teacher Liu, you are the great benefactor of Tian Shi Bowa and our family too. We all believed Bowa is a fool without any hope and future. Everyone in the village looks down upon him, and says he is unable to go to school. Thank you so much."

Liu Wanyi was greatly shocked by her action, which was completely unexpected. She quickly laid down the bowl and bent down to lift Li Runlan up. She said, "What are you doing here? How could I accept this? Get up, please get up."

Although Li Runlan got up, her emotions from the bottom of her heart were so strong and forceful that they all rushed out uncontrollably, from her eyes and even her nostrils, flowing all over her face.

In the villagers' eyes, Tian Shi Bowa was a fool, disabled and a perpetual burden. Although Li Runlan forced a smile and pretended that she didn't care in front of other people, she was silent, smothered and depressed when she was alone. Bowa was her son, part of her body and precious to her. He was constantly in her mind, whether big or small things, his smiles, worries and acts, and she would never forget. Now her son could go to school. He could go to school for real! What an unexpected joy! She was overwhelmed with happy surprise and couldn't control herself, falling on the bench and crying loudly.

10
WISH FULFILLED

When Tian Shi Bowa walked into the playground of the village school from the main road right in front of the school, he stopped suddenly. He was a little nervous, his heart pounding loudly. He had never imagined he could walk into the school like this.

Li Runlan had planned to send Bowa to Teacher Liu in person but when they arrived at the main road in front of the school, Bowa turned back and said to his mother, "Back!" His mother wanted to be with him for a little bit longer while Bowa opened his mouth as if to tell her something but he was blocked and could not say one character for the time being, his face choked red. Li Runlan walked on while Bowa stretched out his arms to stop her. Li Runlan thought for a while and understood. Bowa was afraid that the other students might laugh at him when they saw he was being escorted to school by his mother since he was already a big boy.

Li Runlan took out a yellow canvas satchel Bowa's father used to carry when he went out, slung it across Bowa's shoulder and said, "Put your textbooks and exercise books into this." Then she stroked Bowa's face and said, "Yes, my Bowa can go to school by himself."

Alone, Bowa walked on and when he was close to the village school, he turned back to look and found his mother was still standing there looking at him. He stopped and looked at her. Li Runlan knew what he meant, so she waved her hand, turned and left at last.

For Bowa's first day at school, his mother found his best clothes the previous night. It was a blue suit, looking very bright although it was made of synthetic fibre. They had bought it in Xiaonanhai town the year before. Bowa had worn this twice when celebrating the Dragon Boat Festival and the Spring Festival. Later, it was put into a closet for special occasions in case it got dirty. Last year and the year before last, Bowa still could not talk like the other kids so his parents felt ashamed in front of guests and seldom took him with them when visiting friends. Therefore, there had been no chance for Bowa to wear this suit any more. Bowa's going to school was a big event which had reminded his mother of this suit. When Bowa got up in the morning, his mother took it out and tried it on him. To her surprise, Bowa had outgrown the suit. The lower edge of the blazer was just above Bowa's belly button so when Bowa lifted his arms or stretched out his hands, his belly button was revealed. As for the trousers, the waistband could barely reach under the belly button while the bottom of the trousers only reached Bowa's calf; as a result it looked like the capri trousers girls usually wear today.

His mother sighed, "Well, it doesn't look good. We'll have to settle for this." What Li Runlan implied in her words was she was afraid people might laugh at her son while Bowa himself felt there was nothing wrong except that the waistband was too small. When he did the button up, it felt uncomfortably tight. He wanted to leave it unbuttoned since he had an old plastic belt to fasten trousers with anyway, but when he thought about the fact it was his first day at school, he finally fastened the button.

When he entered the school, there was no one in the playground. Probably the students had all gone back to their classroom because noises could be heard coming from the classroom.

One of the classrooms was open and a small room beside that classroom was open too. Where should he go? The classroom, that small room or should he just stand in the playground waiting? Bowa was struggling with which door he should enter. When he felt so embarrassed that he could not bear it any more, Liu Wanyi came out of the small room with her teaching materials having finished preparing for her lessons. She saw him the moment she went out of the room.

"Hey! Tian Shi Bowa! Good to see you here." As she spoke, she walked down the steps towards him as he was still standing in the playground. She took his hand and said, "Come on. Let's go to the classroom."

The whole classroom was filled with loud noises. When Liu Wanyi entered the room with Bowa, it suddenly became silent. All the students were greatly surprised by what they saw. Tian Shi Bowa? How could it be? Was it really Tian Shi Bowa? How could he come to the classroom? They all stared straight at Bowa, wide-eyed.

Liu Wanyi asked Bowa to stand beside the platform and signaled to the class to be quiet. Then she said, "Students, let me introduce a new student to you…"

"No need for introductions. We are from the same village," said Huang Xiaoqiu loudly, slapping her desk with her textbook. "We all know him."

"Oh, don't we have students from other villages? You all know him?" asked Liu Wanyi.

A student with a round face shouted, "Who doesn't know him! He is famous."

"Li Zhaoyue, you are from Shuangyan Village. Since you said you know him, tell me what's his name?"

Li Zhaoyue didn't answer the question. Instead, he winked at the other classmates and made faces first, then he chanted as if he were performing an allegretto, "*Silly Tian, a weirdo, wears a suit revealing his belly button!*"

The whole classroom burst into laughter.

"How could you be so unfriendly to others?" Teacher Liu said, "He is a new student and you should call him by his name."

"Teacher Liu, I know his name," said Huang Xiaoqiu, who loved to seek the limelight, standing up and shouting, "His name is Tian Shi Bowa, he is a celebrity in our village. His nicknames are Stammering Tian, Silly Tian and Dumb Tian."

Again, the whole classroom was engulfed by the roaring of laughter. Some students began to slap their desks, their school bags and their textbooks.

11
THE FIRST LESSON

"Remember, listen attentively, never say or read anything you are not sure about in case people laugh at you." That was the most important instruction Tian Shi Bowa, who had just entered school, received from his mother.

> *The elder brother has 14 yuan and the younger brother has 10. How much should the elder brother give to the younger one if they want to have the same amount of money?*

Teacher Liu wrote down a third-year maths calculation on the blackboard. She read it as she pointed at the question, then turned around to ask her students, "Who can work this calculation out? It's OK to tell me the answer directly."

Bowa worried. How should he answer this question? Was Teacher asking him the question? It seemed yes. Oh, maybe not. She cast her eyes on him just now but moved on to other students later. Should he offer to answer this question? He was clear about what Teacher Liu said but he didn't know the answer. Or those words on the blackboard knew him while he didn't know them.

"Third-year students, do any of you know the answer?" Teacher Liu continued asking and immediately a student stood up.

Oh, it was a question for the third year which had nothing to do with him. Tian Shi Bowa felt greatly relieved.

It was like a party when all the students crowded into one classroom but mutual distraction was indeed inevitable. In this class, there were 32 third-year and 16 fifth-year students. What about the first year? The last time the village school had first-year students was two years ago. Now there was only one student, namely, Tian Shi Bowa.

Theoretically, it was feasible to have all the students study in one classroom but having two teachers was the prerequisite. When some students needed to study in the classroom, the others could be guided to have PE or labour skills training outside. Like this, there would be far less conflict in the classroom. Otherwise, class management was quite a heavy load.

Liu Wanyi was still not quite familiar with these students and she could not turn them loose like herding sheep on the grassland. If anything should happen when one group was given a lecture while the other was left free, she had to be responsible for this. Liu Wanyi therefore was quite busy. She first gave fifth-year students assignments, then gave a lecture to the third year, left them some in-class activities and homework to do, and finally it was the first-year student Tian Shi Bowa's turn.

Teacher Liu gave Bowa private tutoring. She brought a small blackboard and asked Bowa to sit in the very last row. Then she told Bowa to take out his first-year maths textbook and open it. Pointing at what she would teach him in the textbook, Liu Wanyi wrote the Arabic number '1' on the blackboard, teaching Bowa by reading it first herself.

Bowa moved his lips but no words came out of his mouth. Teacher Liu thought he might have felt it was difficult the first time and he hadn't got used to it yet. She taught him again. But Bowa still remained silent despite moving his lips a bit. Teacher Liu wrote '2' on the blackboard and began to teach him, "'Two', now it's your turn. Read." Tian Shi Bowa moved his lips again but he couldn't read.

Liu Wanyi was not mad at him. She looked at Bowa and asked him gently, "Tian Shi Bowa, can you hear my voice?"

Bowa didn't answer but nodded his head. Wanyi was reasonably happy about that. The fact that Bowa could hear and understand what people said

THE FIRST LESSON

suggested he was not a fool. She continued, "I am going to teach you a few numbers. Can you read after me?"

Bowa heard her clearly but he didn't give any response for the time being. He looked at this patient and gentle teacher and thought, "Even if I could read, I can only say one character out loud. If the teacher teaches me the second number, I won't be able to read it for sure. If so, the teacher is sure to be very anxious. My mother told me to listen attentively and never say or read anything I am not sure about. Saying one character is no better than reading none." As he thought about this, he shook his head at teacher Liu.

Without oral communication Liu Wanyi couldn't find out the reason for this at present. She thought about it and decided to try a new method. She said, "Tian Shi Bowa, I'll teach you ten numbers first, then we'll write them down together. Like this, we can remember them. Shall we?"

Tian Shi Bowa immediately nodded his head. As long as he didn't need to read aloud, everything would be all right.

Teacher Liu wrote the numbers from 0 to 9 on the small blackboard. She first asked Bowa to watch while she read the numbers carefully. Then she asked Bowa to take out his exercise book and pencil and began to teach him how to write. She supported Bowa's hand to keep the pencil steady, helping him write down the ten numbers on the exercise book. Each time Bowa wrote one, Teacher Liu would read the number in his ear twice. At last, she asked Bowa to write each number three times at once. Liu Wanyi believed Tian Shi Bowa was sure to remember these numbers clearly after practicing a few times. After all, he was ten and a half years old and these numbers were so simple for a child of this age.

The evening in Fragrant Valley was quiet and graceful. Wanyi walked along the road and enjoyed the coolness by the lakeside. A new crescent moon shone brightly in the sky with a few clouds around dancing softly. Bamboo forests beside Xiaonanhai smelt fragrant, green and fresh. When the wind blew gently through the forest, bamboo leaves rustled and revealed some fine and sparkling light little by little.

Liu Wanyi wrote a diary entry after returning home from her walk.

The moonlight read my feelings and urged me to convey my feelings in the diary.

Tian Shi Bowa came to school finally, a wish fulfilled.

Tian Shi Bowa is an ordinary rural child but is not an ordinary dropout.

He is not ordinary because of his physical defects which have brought him shame, fear and humiliation. It is a spiritual humiliation, so deep that it is already rooted in his soul. He does not have a complete rational consciousness because he is still a bit ignorant but he has been blessed with a persistence in his subconscious world, a valuable persistence to pursue a dream.

It was a pity that he was humiliated the first time he walked into the classroom, although this insult was by no means a hostile act.

It is not necessary to criticise the other students because the blame will be as pale and weak as some stale ideological work. The best carving knife for a sculptor is to feel the palpitation, the throb of a life waiting to be created. If a teacher could read students' unsettled minds, the carvings a teacher would make would be accurate, deep and artistic. Education is instinctive from the inside out and vice versa, it is fundamental to advancement.

Tian Shi Bowa was fearful and uneasy but this uneasiness will have its day to spurt out like the burning lava from the heart of the earth.

In fact, there is a lost child inside the heart of everyone or perhaps in a certain period of time. In your heart, in my heart or in his heart. Think about it, dare we say that doesn't apply to us?

Now, there might be a lost child in Tian Shi Bowa's heart, who right now is lonely and scared, hurt and sad, disappointed and irritated, or just letting him drift aimlessly with the tide. Spare some time and help him to find himself, stay with him and enter his world. Heal him and comfort him. Give him strength and light a lamp for him.

He will become as excellent as the other normal good kids.

It is said Tian Shi Bowa can say one character out loud but why didn't he read it when I taught him in the classroom? I saw his lips move which meant he wanted to say something. Under what kind of conditions will he break through the barrier and read out loud? Could it be occasions when he desperately needs something and longs for something or when something urgent happens that he does that?

The good thing is I have taught him ten numbers today. He wrote the numbers a few times too. If he could learn ten numbers or ten characters a day, that would indeed be great progress for him.

Outside the window, the moon hung in the sky, casting its silvery light on everything. Slender leaves of golden bamboos, oblong leaves of polar trees, and also vines hanging down from cliffs were swaying gently and nodding with smiles in the wind. The moon rabbit narrowed its eyes and sneaked into Wanyi's small room through the tracery, admiring this kind and thoughtful rural teacher. What a tranquil and beautiful night! Wanyi was full of confidence in the progress of the child.

But how could she know that the embarrassment she was going to face during the class the next day would cast a shadow on her confidence.

12

THE SECOND LESSON

Tian Shi Bowa arrived at school a bit earlier than the other students. It was not because he was observing discipline or studying diligently or because he had great ambition; he was in fact afraid of being humiliated by other students on the way and didn't know how to face it. He therefore got up very early and fed himself with a large bowl of corn porridge with some pickles left over from the day before. He finished his breakfast quickly and rushed to school.

In fact, Teacher Liu hadn't got up yet at that time.

Bowa decided to hide himself in a place beside the classroom, the flourishing yellow peach forest in front where not only could he see what Teacher Liu was doing but also he would not have any worry about being discovered by Teacher Liu or the other students.

Teacher Liu began to prepare breakfast in her small kitchen after she got up. Then she did some stretches to loosen up in the yard after she had finished her breakfast. She at last went into her office. Tian Shi Bowa watched, without even blinking his eyes. He waited in the peach forest quietly, squatting there like a cheetah on the African grasslands waiting for antelopes, patient and silent.

When he saw Teacher Liu go out of her small office towards the classroom with a box of chalk and a pile of textbooks, he quickly slipped onto the path below the peach trees and walked toward the classroom with his school bag across his shoulder, looking as though he had just arrived at school.

"Hey, Tian Shi Bowa, you are such an early bird," said Teacher Liu when she saw him and stopped beside the classroom. She continued, "Come on, I want a word with you."

Tian Shi Bowa smiled in his heart. He was full of respect for the teacher and he had fears too, although he pretended to keep calm.

Teacher Liu and Tian Shi Bowa entered the classroom. She said, "Now the other students haven't arrived yet. Let's review the numbers you learned yesterday, then we will begin lesson two."

Like yesterday, Tian Shi Bowa sat at the desk in the last row of the classroom. He took out his maths book, pencils and exercise books while Teacher Liu stood by, placing the small blackboard on Bowa's desk. She wrote a '3' on the board and said, "Please read."

Tian Shi Bowa stared at the number very carefully, lips pressed and eyes blank. Obviously he had forgotten the number he had just learned yesterday.

Teacher Liu wrote '2' on the blackboard while Bowa looked at it in the same manner, his lips not moving at all. Teacher Liu wrote '1' and patted him on the shoulder, "This is the first number we learned yesterday; can you try this?"

Tian Shi Bowa looked intensely, eyes round. He dared not move his lips. He had some impressions, the striking '1' on the one yuan bill. He once tried to read it when his father gave him the money to use. But what did Teacher Liu teach him yesterday? He had totally forgotten how to read it. Could he read it the way he tried with the one yuan bill? No, he couldn't. What if this '1' on the blackboard was pronounced differently from the '1' on the one yuan bill? He couldn't cheat his teacher anyway.

"You don't remember? We just learned it yesterday! It is very simple; how could you have forgotten?" Teacher Liu felt very surprised. She wanted to have a last try. She wrote '0', the first and the last number and said, "Think carefully! How did we pronounce it yesterday? Come on and have a try."

Tian Shi Bowa again didn't read it because he didn't know how. He had forgotten what he had learned yesterday.

"Well," Teacher Liu heaved a little sigh and said, "Let's leave this aside for the time being. Can you write down the ten numbers you learned yesterday from memory in your exercise book?"

Liu Wanyi felt there might be some problems with Bowa's pronunciation so she wanted to test whether there was something wrong with his memory or not. Tian Shi Bowa followed it. He turned his exercise book to a new page, picked up his pencil and began to write but he got stuck when he tried to write down the first number.

"The first number is '1' and the second is '2'," Liu Wanyi reminded him, but Tian Shi Bowa at that time was confused. Whether the '3' teacher Liu wrote on the blackboard was '1' or the '0' was '1'? He was not sure about it. Yes, he could have made a guess and written something down, but he did not. Bowa was an honest boy and he didn't want to do this. He was neither confused nor stupid; he couldn't remember the pronunciation and shape of those numbers he had just learned.

"Tian Shi Bowa, does your family live in Shuangyan Village?"

Bowa shook his head immediately. He gave Teacher Liu a look, feeling confused: my family is in White Crane Village. You came to visit us once; don't you remember? "Your father is surnamed Li, isn't he?" Teacher Liu continued her test. Tian Shi Bowa shook his head like a rattle. He wanted to smile but didn't make any sound when he opened his mouth. It was so funny. It was common sense; how could she not know this? "My mother was surnamed Li and how could my father have the same one?"

"Well, it seems there is nothing wrong with the child, but how to explain what happened just now?" Teacher Liu said to herself, "No more writing down from memory. Please copy down the ten numbers you learned yesterday."

Tian Shi Bowa turned to the page he had copied the numbers on yesterday, looked at it and began to copy the numbers. Very soon he had finished. Teacher Liu took a look at his copy and said to herself, "He wrote all the numbers correctly and very fast too. As for the numbers, they all look neat with clear strokes and moderate strength, quite individual! Let me teach him some new stuff then."

She asked Bowa to take out the first-year Chinese book. Skipping over the phonetic part, she began to teach Bowa Chinese characters. She pointed at the characters 'father,' 'mother' and 'me' in the textbook, teaching him one by one. Tian Shi Bowa nodded his head as he listened but still didn't say anything. Liu Wanyi had planned to teach him the lesson *Quietly*. There were five important characters in this lesson: 'big (*da*)', 'rice (*mi*)', 'earth (*tu*)', 'field (*di*)' and 'horse (*ma*)'. But after thinking it over, she decided to make sure that Bowa could grasp the three characters she had taught him before. She asked him to copy 'father', 'mother' and 'me' three times and she thought this time there would not be any problem for Tian Shi Bowa to do diction. After Bowa finished his copy work, Liu Wanyi asked him to turn his exercise book to a new page and said, "Now let's do dictation. I read a character once only and you write it down."

"Father," Liu Wanyi read it three times but Bowa didn't write it down. Teacher Liu asked, "Didn't you hear me?" Bowa nodded his head, "Then write it down quickly!"

"Why shouldn't I want to write?" Tian Shi Bowa thought. Teacher Liu wrote down three characters just now, but which one was the 'father' in 'my father'? According to the order they appeared, it should be the first one. But he really could not remember what the character 'father' looked like exactly.

Teacher Liu read the second character, "Mother." After a while, she came to the third one. Tian Shi Bowa racked his brains but he couldn't remember how to write the three characters at all.

Teacher Liu heaved a sigh for the second time, a sigh of great disappointment. She felt very frustrated. There might be some special reason for it, but she had just taught him the three characters, how could a student not be able to write them down? If Bowa were her child, she might long before…

At that time, many students came into the classroom. Liu Wanyi said rather helplessly, "Well, let's stop here. You stay for a while after school."

Stay for a while! How helplessly sad the line was. Liu Wanyi was unwilling to give up any school-age child but the prerequisite was that they should be healthy physically and mentally and be able to read and write. If they were really unfit for school and one forced them to come and stay anyway, it was not only a waste of teaching resources but also a waste of others' time. Obviously, Tian Shi Bowa didn't belong here. Liu Wanyi had to make a decision, although it was a bit cruel.

After school, she would send Tian Shi Bowa home and explain to his mother and grandma.

Liu Wanyi stood on the platform for a long time as she looked at her students walking out of the classroom one by one after she had finished new lessons for them and assigned homework. She knew Tian Shi Bowa was still sitting on his seat in the last row waiting for her but her eyes had walked out of the classroom, through the peach trees and settled on the small road in front of the peach woods. She could not help thinking of the hope in Grandma's dim eyes and Li Runlan collapsing on her knees. She didn't have the heart to let Bowa go; she could feel that Tian Shi Bowa was a dreamy child, a kind, polite and pure rural child with some ideas. He had been here for just two days but she was going to send him back. Liu Wanyi's heart was filled with regret.

But she had to face reality. She decided to take him home herself.

Silently, they walked on the small road at the foot of Bamian Mountain, the teacher walking ahead and the student following behind, neither talking.

In a relaxed, uneasy and heavy mood, Tian Shi Bowa was walking along. He felt relaxed because he was walking on a familiar road, so familiar that he would not have got lost even if he had closed his eyes. Also he could go back home to take care of his little white crane. He felt uneasy and heavy because he didn't know what his teacher would do when they reached home. Might she praise him, or make a complaint, or…? He didn't know but followed his teacher cautiously step by step.

Villagers say children are unable to stay quiet when they walk as if they are barbed hooks. They never leave things alone on their way; they either grab some grass or pull some leaves. Tian Shi Bowa was no exception. As he walked along, he left that unease and burden behind. He kicked a stone aside near his foot and grabbed and dragged a long bending vine along from the opposite cliff. He pulled it along and walked for quite a distance and then let it go, causing it to bounce back immediately, hit the leaves and linger there, rustling for quite a while. Teacher Liu heard the sound. She turned back to take a look. She could have smiled but just couldn't bring herself to do it.

As they walked on, Bowa picked up an oak stick beside a fallen and broken tree. He was quite happy because it was as long as a person's arm, like his father's big pipe, big at one end and small the other. It was heavy but handy. Well, if a wild dog dared yell and jump out to bite his teacher, he would be sure to beat it.

It was a pity there were no wild dogs on this road, and neither did Tian Shi Bowa see one in or outside the village either.

The road wound into the fir woods where cedar trees grew tall and flourished, and grass on both sides of the road was luxuriant as well.

Inside the fir woods, a swathe of cool air swept by. They breathed out a hot breath of air at the same time and walked on, refreshed.

Birds sang loudly in the woods and fallen leaves rustled under their feet. "Alas!" Teacher Liu suddenly screamed ahead. She went all weak at the knees and fell on the side of the road near the mountain. Following the sound, Tian Shi Bowa found a green bamboo snake the size of a small bowl that was staring at Teacher Liu with its head rising high.

As quick as the blink of an eye, Tian Shi Bowa was so anxious that he didn't think about anything but rushed forward, jumped up and shouted, "Snake!"

The oak stick hit the snake hard the moment he shouted, which happened to smash the bamboo snake on its most vulnerable point. The snake was still wriggling its body, twisting and winding around the stick. Tian Shi Bowa pressed the head of the snake tight with the stick and didn't let go. Gradually the bamboo snake dangled loosely from the stick, soft and powerless, and collapsed on the ground writhing in a large coil.

Bowa extricated his stick, wiped the end that had hit the snake clean on the grass and looked back at his teacher.

Completely in shock, Liu Wanyi looked pale, her eyes blank. When Bowa walked towards her, she asked him in a low voice, "The snake, where is it?"

Tian Shi Bowa smiled involuntarily. He turned back and pointed at the snake with his stick. Liu Wanyi opened her eyes wide and stared at it for quite a while to make sure it would not move anymore. She tried to stand up with her hands but her legs were not cooperative, trembling still. Bowa went over to support his teacher and let her hands rest on his shoulder. After a while, Liu Wanyi calmed down and her legs stopped trembling as well. She tried to walk a few steps and said, "I am OK now. Not afraid any more."

After she said this, she laughed at herself too. Who was afraid of snakes? Who was really not afraid of snakes? Where did Tian Shi Bowa get such strength? He was still a child after all.

When she recalled the whole scene little by little, she vaguely remembered that loud shout "snake".

Who? Was it Tian Shi Bowa who had shouted just now? Quite unlikely!

He had remained silent for the past two days. Was he able to do that when he saw the snake at that tense moment?

"Tian Shi Bowa, was it you who shouted 'snake' just now?" Teacher Liu asked tentatively. She wanted to clarify the situation although she was not quite convinced of it.

Bowa nodded as he looked at Teacher Liu. Liu Wanyi grabbed both his hands and asked eagerly, again, "You did it? You did shout 'snake' just now?"

When she saw Bowa nod his head again, Liu Wanyi stood up, held Bowa's hand and quickly went out of the fir woods.

"Come on, come with me."

Liu Wanyi found a small piece of flat sandy land, picked up a twig and asked, "Do you know how to write the character 'snake'?"

Bowa shook his head.

"Well, Bowa, let me teach you how to write this character." Liu Wanyi wrote the character on the ground and placed the twig in Bowa's right hand. Holding Bowa's hand, she began to teach him how to do this. Bowa however pushed Liu Wanyi's hand aside with his left hand and held the twig by himself. He quickly wrote down the character 'snake' without any hesitation. A character with complete strokes!

"Wow, great job! Can you write it down from memory?" Liu Wanyi wiped out the character and said, "I dictate and you write. 'Snake'."

Tian Shi Bowa looked at the sandy earth, paused for a while and very soon he wrote it on the ground.

"Very good! Is it the case that as long as you have read it, you can write it down?" asked Liu Wanyi anxiously. She then pointed at a tree near her and said, "'Tree', now it's your turn."

Tian Shi Bowa leaned his head back, something bobbing a few times in his throat. He wanted to say something but he just could not spit it out. He had to shake his head.

After thinking it over, Liu Wanyi pointed at the relatively flat road and said, "I want you to run to that small hill then run back here. Can you do it?" Tian Shi Bowa nodded his head.

"Good! Listen to my order. Now, run!"

Tian Shi Bowa darted off immediately. It took him quite a while to run to that small hill ahead and then run back. Seeing him panting, sweating, face red and throat choked, Liu Wanyi shouted out suddenly, "Quick, shout 'run'."

"Run!" Tian Shi Bowa opened his mouth and spat the character out suddenly.

"Great! Great!" Teacher Liu repeated it a few times. She then picked up a twig and wrote 'run' in the sandy earth. "'Run', now it's your turn to write it."

Tian Shi Bowa took the twig, stared at the one written by his teacher and wrote his down very accurately. He even wrote an extra one next to it. Teacher Liu wiped out the character and said to Tian Shi Bowa, "'run', write it one more time." Bowa wrote it again and this time he was correct again. Teacher Liu said, "Wow, you have done a wonderful job. Can you write 'snake' one more time?"

Tian Shi Bowa nodded his head. He levelled the sand on the ground and wrote the character correctly again. Teacher Liu said, "Well, one more thing. I taught you three characters this morning, 'father', 'mother' and 'me', now, please write the character 'father'."

Tian Shi Bowa tilteld his head and thought about it for a while. 'Father', wasn't it the one he occasionally used to call his dad at home? But it had been quite a long time since Teacher Liu had taught him these characters. What were the strokes of this character? Tian Shi Bowa racked his brains to try to recall but at last he failed and shook his head disappointedly.

"OK. It doesn't matter. I know something now." Liu Wanyi didn't ask him to write any more characters. Instead, she said to him sincerely, "Today you came to my rescue when I was in danger. Thank you very much. I am not going to send you home now. Remember to come to school earlier tomorrow."

Tian Shi Bowa looked at his teacher, nodded his head, turned around and walked away. Liu Wanyi watched his back until he disappeared in the fir woods.

13
THE THIRD LESSON

After the fir woods incident, Liu Wanyi didn't send Bowa home nor did she intend to tell his parents that there was no need for Bowa to go to school. Why? Because Liu Wanyi had discovered that Tian Shi Bowa had a special gift of memorising a character after he had read it. As long as he read and wrote a character soon afterwards, he could memorise the character easily. Liu Wanyi was unwilling to give up any chance of nurturing a child. She remembered a report she had read before. In the report the German anthropologist Benbe David found in his research that the late Moscow biologist Dr Efroimson had once made a statistical study that one in 10 million people was a genius. And as psychologists said, the speciality of these gifted children was often manifested in their childhood and if discovered, nurtured and developed in time, their special gift would be further converted into powerful energy, which meant they would surely excel in their future careers. Otherwise, they would remain in obscurity like ordinary people. Perhaps Tian Shi Bowa's ability to memorise through reading was precisely his special characteristic, a kind of super power or gift. Liu Wanyi secretly resolved that if it were true, she would never give him up and she would redouble her efforts to nurture his talent.

To confirm her guess, Liu Wanyi came to the classroom very early the next morning.

THE THIRD LESSON

Tian Shi Bowa was already quite familiar with his journey to school. When he arrived at school, he found there was no one in the playground, so he went straight toward the back door of his classroom, which was half-open at that time. He pushed it open. The moment he stepped in, he was shocked and his eyes straightened. Teacher Liu was sitting in the back row waiting for him.

"You've come, good." Wanyi stood up and greeted him kindly, "Let's review what we have learned before the other students come."

Teacher Liu took out the small blackboard. She didn't set it up this time but put it on the desk. She gave a piece of chalk to Bowa standing beside her and asked, "Do you still remember your running on the mountain road yesterday?"

Bowa nodded his head. Teacher Liu said, "Good. Now write down the character 'run' for me."

Without any difficulty, Tian Shi Bowa wrote 'run' on the blackboard. Teacher Liu said, "Now write 'snake'." Very soon Bowa had finished, '*wan* (bend)', '*gou* (hook)' and '*dian* (dot)', all perfect.

"Great. Continue. '*Ba* (father)', as in 'mother and father'." Liu Wanyi was secretly very happy. She wanted to strike while the iron was hot so she repeated with emphasis, "*ba.*"

Tian Shi Bowa froze with his hand holding the chalk, staring blankly at the blackboard.

It was as she had expected. Teacher Liu didn't force him any more. She set the blackboard up, asked him to take out his textbook and turned to the text *Quietly*. She pointed at the characters on the lower part of the page and said, "Now we have five new characters here, '*da* (big)', '*mi* (rice)', '*tu* (earth)', '*di* (field)', and '*ma* (horse)'. What I am pointing at is the first character '*da*', please read after me. '*Da*'"

Tian Shi Bowa moved his lips and he choked on something. He glanced at the classroom, hesitating. He didn't read after his teacher.

Teacher Liu looked around the classroom too and comforted him, "There is nobody else but you and me. Relax and read, '*da*'."

Tian Shi Bowa looked around the classroom again, focused his eyes again and stared at the '*da*', his mouth closed tight and cheeks puffed. Suddenly a sound burst out from his open lips, "*da*".

"Wow!" Teacher Liu was startled by the sound, "You do have a loud voice."

Tian Shi Bowa lowered his head, slightly embarrassed. Teacher Liu continued, "Now look at this character. Can you write it down?"

Tian Shi Bowa nodded his head. After glancing at the word, he picked up the chalk and wrote a big '*da*' on the blackboard.

"Write the character 'snake' again."

Bowa was about to put down the chalk when he heard what Teacher Liu said. He therefore wrote the character '*she* (snake)' on the blackboard. Teacher Liu moved her finger to the character '*mi*' and said, "Now read after me, '*mi*'."

Bowa stared at that '*mi*', with his cheeks puffed out, his throat choked and lips parted, but there was no sound at all even though he exhaled a long breath. He wanted to read but he could not make any sound. Liu Wanyi was a bit anxious. She walked back and forth in the classroom, rubbing her hands. She thought of the method she had used yesterday. She said to Bowa, "Let's go to the playground. You try your best to run, three laps."

They arrived at the playground. Tian Shi Bowa stamped his feet on the ground and ran quickly like a race horse.

Although it was in the morning, the temperature was still very high at the time as spring was turning to summer. Three laps later, Tian Shi Bowa was panting and sweating all over. Teacher Liu immediately took his hand and dragged him back to the classroom regardless of how tired Bowa was. She pointed at the character '*mi*' in the textbook and said, "Bowa, quick, read it out loud, '*mi*'."

With a nervous facial expression, Bowa looked at the character '*mi*', puffed his cheeks out and opened his mouth with a sudden effort. Boo… he blew out some air but there was no sound at all except a weak purring sound in his throat.

Liu Wanyi felt she was losing the battle and heaved a long sigh. She had never encountered such a situation and she was full of confusion. How could Tian Shi Bowa be like this?

A group of students were romping along the road to the playground. It was about time for class.

Liu Wanyi went back to her office to fetch her teaching materials while Tian Shi Bowa reluctantly went back to his seat and sat down. He was a sensitive boy. When he saw the disappointed expression on Teacher Liu's face, he thought he had failed Teacher Liu and he hated himself for it. He slapped himself a few times on the throat. *Smack, smack, smack*! Very soon, reddish marks appeared on his neck.

It was three days since Tian Shi Bowa had been coming to school. Perhaps out of a feeling of inferiority, he didn't like to hang out with the other classmates and he didn't greet anyone when he arrived at school, which made a lot of classmates think he was so stupid that he didn't understand what he should do, especially the naughty Xiao Jianbo and Huang Xiaoqiu. They always liked to make trouble and have some fun. This time they decided to give Tian Shi Bowa a generous welcome gift.

Although Huang Xiaoqiu and Xiao Jianbo were naughty, they were the best students in the class. In the final exam of the last semester, they had ranked first and third respectively, which is why they were so popular in class no matter whether their behaviour was good or bad. They summoned a few classmates to a private corner, whispered for quite a while and went back to the classroom at last.

The exercise breaks between classes usually lasted twenty minutes, which was just enough time for them to play some tricks. When the classroom door was opened, students rushed out to exercise in the playground while teachers would go back to their office for a glass of water or a short break.

A lot of students huddled together and chatted noisily, all squinting at Tian Shi Bowa, behaving as if they were looking at an alien.

As for Bowa, he felt inferior to his classmates. He went to school as a first-year student at the age of ten; he wanted to read aloud but he could not; he wanted to remember something but he could not although he had read it already. He quietly hid behind the group and stood in the very last row during class exercises.

The hand-waving dance was performed during class exercises, a local feature indeed. With Huang Xiaoqiu leading in front of the group, all the other students followed her movements, heads shaking, waists twisting, hands waving and feet kicking. They danced for five minutes and scattered to move around freely. Some students went to the toilet, some played ball games and some chased after each other for fun. Tian Shi Bowa alone stood far away from them at the edge of the playground, looking at them. Unexpectedly,

Xiao Jianbo and a few other students ran over to him and chanted very loudly:

> Dumb Tian
> Dumb numb
> Shining forehead
> He looks like a monk

Immediately, all eyes on the playground were on Tian Shi Bowa, who didn't expect it at all and was totally stunned, his face pale and eyes bulging. He just stood there like a puppet, not knowing what to do. More and more joined in the fun and they went wild, shouting and chanting at the same time: *shining forehead, he looks like a monk.*

That was too humiliating! After Tian Shi Bowa came to his senses, he fled as fast as he could amid the mocking laughter around him, hoping to hide in the classroom for a moment of peace.

The back door of the classroom remained ajar, leaving a narrow gap there. Tian Shi Bowa pushed it open and sidled into the classroom. Suddenly, he heard a few crashing sounds overhead. Before he had time to look up, a bamboo basket fell down, followed by a broom and a plastic scoop full of water. Tian Shi Bowa instinctively raised his hands to cover his head and, along with a loud rattling sound, he became a spectacle again. The bamboo basket hit him on the shoulder, bounced and hit the ground; the scoop hit his hands and the water splashed over his head and flew down along his hair, to the forehead, nose and mouth, then to his chin and dropped into the scoop on the ground, tinkling on and on like a melody.

Wet all over and unable to see anything, Tian Shi Bowa was in such an awkward situation!

Xiao Jianbo, Li Zhaoyue, Huang Xiaoqiu and their lot ran into the classroom from the front door in time to witness the poor Tian Shi Bowa's plight. They doubled over with laughter. After that, they began to chant loudly again:

> Silly Tian
> Dreams of studying
> Stealing water to drink

> He has become a drowned rat

At that moment, Teacher Liu entered the classroom. These students immediately stopped making faces and went to their seats. Teacher Liu didn't notice Bowa who was still standing beside the back door until she went to the platform. Looking at his wet hair and then at the mess on the ground, she knew immediately what had happened: a mischief. She walked over to him and stroked his head, asking, "Are you OK? It will get dry very soon these days. Did you get hurt? Are you feeling any pain?"

Tian Shi Bowa shook his head and, as if waking up from a dream, he began to wipe his eyebrows, nose and mouth so that he could see. He glanced at the other students in the classroom and smiled a bit without knowing why. Then he hurriedly went back to his seat and sat down.

In the classroom, the jabbering and jeering of the other students continued for quite a while.

Teacher Liu went back to the platform and stared at the class with a slow and stern look. Gradually the noise faded and disappeared. All eyes focused on her face.

Liu Wanyi opened her teaching plan, turned around and wrote down the teaching objective on the blackboard, preparing for the new lesson. She had a rough idea of what had happened just now, like who had played the dirty trick on Bowa, for what reason and how Bowa felt. She wanted to progress slowly on how to get the other students to accept Tian Shi Bowa.

It was close to evening and the setting sun was moving diagonally towards Tanglian Hill. A slight breeze blew from the lake, comfortably cool. When it reached the peach trees, it failed to stir any noise except as it blew over some slender and swaying leaves, leaving some fine slivers of spots reflected by the setting sun. Willow trees were touched by the gentle wind and fluttered their beautiful hair, rising up quickly and then falling gently. Of course, the night wind would favour the village school as usual. The cement courtyard which had been scorched by the burning sun was now gradually cooling down under the soft kiss of the night breeze.

There were still a lot of vegetables left over that had been sent by the villagers. It was dinner time but Wanyi was not in the mood to cook anything for herself. She had no appetite tonight.

She took a wooden chair and sat outside. She leaned on the back of the chair and sat up straight for quite a while. Then she moved her body a bit, ran her fingers through the tangled hair resting on her face and smoothed it back behind her ears. Resting her elbows on her thigh, she sat in the chair pondering quietly, her chin in her hand. It was not correct to say Tian Shi Bowa could not make any sound because occasionally he could blurt out a character. But when he was asked to say two characters successively, he would appear so anxious that he was ultimately blocked. What exactly was the problem? Was his lung power inadequate which made it difficult for the air to get out? Was there a tumour on his epiglottis that affected sound articulation? Or was something wrong with his other organs? Liu Wanyi was not a medical expert and didn't know the answer. She suddenly remembered she had a classmate who right now worked in the Department of Otolaryngology (specialising in ear, nose and throat ailments) in Chongqing's Linjiangmen Hospital. Wouldn't it be a good idea to ask him to find an expert to conduct an inspection?

14
SUCCESSFUL OPERATION

Tian Fashui went back to Chongqing from Guizhou after Liu Wanyi had contacted him. He accompanied Bowa to Linjiangmen Hospital for the operation for about 20 days. When it was time for Bowa to be discharged from the hospital, Tian Fashui went to check out at the financial office. The clerk there told him the total cost of Bowa's hospitalisation was 37,000 yuan. Tian Fashui had prepaid 20,000 or so but someone else had come to check out the balance for him, and the medical invoice and some other documents had been handed over to the person who paid the bill.

It was of course a good thing that someone else had checked it out for him. Tian Fashui felt that a burden had been lifted off him. He thought it was Teacher Liu who had done this and he was right.

Liu Wanyi had done it but she hadn't come to do it herself because she had already gone back to the village school. When Tian Shi Bowa was still in hospital, she had already contacted the hospital, asking them to phone her first when Bowa was going to be discharged. She later asked her relatives to go through the check-out procedure for her including mailing her the invoice and other documents.

On the day Tian Shi Bowa left hospital, Tian Fashui found that his son looked much better than before and had put on more weight than when he had first arrived in Chongqing. He wanted him to open his mouth and say something but Bowa just moved his lips without saying anything. When he asked him to try again, Bowa stared at him and turned his head away, ignoring him.

That was pretty strange. Before the operation, the hospital had promised that his son would be able to talk within days of the operation. Now he was leaving hospital but it seemed he still could not speak. Could it be that the city hospital was cheating him? Tian Fashui wanted to argue with them but gave up after thinking it over for a while. Why? He didn't have any evidence to argue the point because it didn't necessarily mean that his son could not speak simply because his son didn't open his mouth, nor did it mean he could speak either. Tian Fashui knew his son was a bit stubborn and it would not work even if he tried to force him. He said to himself that his son would open his mouth to talk after he left hospital anyway.

It turned out that Tian Shi Bowa didn't speak on the day he was discharged from hospital.

They took the lift to descend from the 22nd floor and went out of the hospital. Along the base of the tall building was a row of granite stone blocks for people to sit on to take a rest. Tian Fashui plonked himself down on a stone, pulled his son to his face and said, "Bowa, since you have had your throat cured, say something to me."

Tian Shi Bowa didn't even move his lips.

"Say something! You might have felt shy about opening your mouth in the hospital just now, but now that you are here outside, you should feel relaxed enough to say something." Tian Fashui stared at his son's mouth, yearning for some characters to come out. Tian Shi Bowa looked at him, still showing no sign of opening his mouth at all.

"Tian Shi Bowa, tell me, whether you don't want to talk or you are unable to talk? If you are unable to talk, I will go and argue with the hospital at once!" Tian Fashui was quick-tempered. He was about to lose his temper but finally held it back. He urged, "Speak! Hurry up. You could say one character in the past, so now say five characters at once. Quick, say them. OK, OK, look at yourself! Like a fool! Say two characters at one time, two characters, is that OK?"

Tian Shi Bowa pursed his lips tight and narrowed his eyes, which indeed made Tian Fashui very anxious. He firmly believed his son could not speak. He said to his son, to himself as well, "Damned hospital. I have been taken in this time. You could say one character in the past but now you can't even say anything. What a waste of my 20,000 yuan! I have been saving for this for about 10 years!" As he said this, he stood up suddenly, held Bowa's arms and pressed him down on the stone blocks, "You wait here while I go upstairs to argue with the hospital."

When he was about to leave, Tian Shi Bowa stood in front of him.

"What are you doing? Bowa, what do you mean?" Tian Fashui looked at his son in surprise.

Tian Shi Bowa pursed his lips, moved his lips a little bit, but still didn't say anything. He pointed at his lips and then his throat.

Tian Fashui asked "You mean you can speak?"

Tian Shi Bowa nodded his head.

Surprise sparkled in Tian Fashui's eyes at once. He squatted down, held Bowa's arms and shook his arms as he said, "Come on, son, say a few characters for me. Say 'dad'. Or say your own name. Say it."

Tian Shi Bowa took a look at his father and rolled his eyes slowly toward the sky.

From a narrow passage among the trees, spots of shining light could be seen on top of rows of tall buildings. How vast the blue sky was! Hundreds of doves joined together and flapped their wings, flying freely and happily in the sky.

Wow, those were turtle-doves. So many of them in the sky!

Tian Shi Bowa, a rural boy, had never seen doves of the same colour, same appearance and same size as turtle-doves. He might have mistaken them for the turtle-doves in his hometown that had gathered together and flown here to welcome him back to the White Crane Stream, to his village school and to his dear Teacher Liu. Bowa became excited, joyous and very anxious. He had opened his mouth and the vocal cord in his throat began to prepare for a surprising encounter so hurriedly as if it were an impatient child. Wow, turtle-doves; what a huge crowd of turtle-doves. But all these words he wanted to say just stayed in his vocal cords and the air from his lungs finally failed to breathe them out.

Some children begin to speak at about one year old and when they reach ten, one can imagine how much they talk. Tian Shi Bowa, however, began to speak his first character when he was nine years old and what's more, one character at a time. When he was ten, everything he had said was less than what a child of his age would have said within half a month. But as for this rural boy, he might have converted all the words he was unable to speak into thoughts, a kind of intelligent energy that even adults found it very hard to understand.

He was lost in thought. If there had been no difficulty for him to say a few characters, that would have been a great joy. But what if he could not say anything after opening his mouth? His ill-tempered father would surely go and cause trouble with the hospital and no one knew how long it would last. And his father was sure to quarrel with teacher Liu if he could not say anything. He would claim it was Teacher Liu who had urged Bowa to go to school and it was Teacher Liu who had provided the information about the hospital. Such a large sum of money! Teacher Liu might be obliged to compensate his family for the loss.

If so, his going to school was bound to fall through. Besides, Teacher Liu would suffer from being wronged too. But she had done all this just for him…

Yes, he could not speak, at least not now.

Squatting there, Tian Fashui looked at Tian Shi Bowa intently. He was eagerly looking forward to hearing some characters from Bowa's mouth, who however just moved his mouth and turned his head to the other side to look elsewhere. He concluded from this that Bowa could not speak. He stood up and walked toward the hospital. Tian Shi Bowa rushed to stop him again, looked up at him and shook his head like a rattle. Tian Fashui was confused, asking, "You don't want me to go and argue with the hospital, do you?"

Tian Shi Bowa nodded his head.

"Well, say something then. As long as you can say two characters, I will stay here."

Tian Shi Bowa hesitated but nodded again and pointed in the direction of his home at the same time.

"Well, Bowa, I know you want to go home. You just say something, two characters, and we will go back home at once."

Tian Shi Bowa pointed at the hospital, shook his head, waved his hands and turned round again, pointing in the direction of home and nodding his head.

Tian Fashui was really confused. He wanted to clear his head, so he closed his eyes to turn things over in his mind. Tian Shi Bowa wouldn't allow him to go and argue with the hospital, which he was certain about, but what did Bowa mean after he nodded his head but still kept silent?

When Tian Fashui opened his eyes, Bowa was no longer in front of him. He hurriedly looked around only to see that Bowa was already on his way home, walking along the sidewalk on one side of the street. Tian Fashui quickened his pace to chase after him.

It was nearly evening when they reached White Crane Village. Tian Shi Bowa was so concerned about his little white crane that he had left his father behind and run to their house when he saw it. His mother Li Runlan had just finished pouring chopped pig grass into a large wooden tank, walked into the courtyard and untied her apron to flick off the weeds. Her eyes lit up when she saw Bowa run into the yard. Having no time to think of whether her clothes were clean or not, she took a few steps forward and held Bowa in her arms, saying repeatedly with joy, "My sweetheart, you are back. I was worried about you. Let me look at you. How is your mouth? And your throat?" She didn't ask Tian Shi Bowa whether he could speak; right now what she cared about most was her son's body. Nothing is as important as good health.

At this time, Bowa was thinking about something else. He wormed his way out of his mother's arms and kept gesticulating eagerly with both hands, pointing to the blue sky outside the door for a while or spreading his arms flat and flapping them up and down like a pair of wings. Li Runlan didn't care whether Bowa answered her question or not. She felt relaxed when she saw her son capering healthily. She knew her son and understood what he meant. She laughed and said, "Bowa, Mum knows what you are thinking about. You are missing your little white crane and he is missing you too. Your little pal flies off in the morning, flying with those big white cranes, and together pecking grass roots, fish and shrimps beside the White Crane Stream. He flies back alone in the evening and rests on the big banyan tree behind our house to trim his feathers. After that, he lays his neck on his back, sticks his long beak into the narrow passage between his wings and goes to sleep with his eyes closed…"

Before Li Runlan had finished her words, Tian Shi Bowa seemed to understand his mum. He turned and ran towards the White Crane Stream immediately, so eager that he even forgot to put down the luggage hanging on his shoulder.

Grandma, who was sitting inside the room, heard Li Runlan's voice in the courtyard and felt the breath of her grandson. She walked out of the room and happened to see her grandson run down towards the stream. She was worried her grandson might get hungry, so she shouted, "Bowa, my good grandson, don't stay out too long and come back home for dinner."

The White Crane Stream was flowing merrily, water grass swaying in the water as if it was dancing. There was no sign of any white cranes, not a single one.

Bowa stood in the sandstones by the stream, standing straight and completing circle after circle. He looked up at the vast blue sky and looked around at the silent green mountains.

Bowa's eyes flashed and twinkled like bewildered stars in the sky as if they had been transformed by gods. Bowa felt weak and empty, disappointed and frustrated as if his stomach had been emptied; he felt dizzy too, so dizzy that it seemed there were a lot of clouds in his head, blown by whirlwinds and swirling one after another. Bowa couldn't help closing his eyes.

"Croak! Croak!"

It was the call of white cranes. Yes it was, one after another. It sounded as if a lot of white cranes were crying at the same time as they happily flew back to their nests. The sound echoed in his ears. Bowa suddenly opened his eyes.

Ah! In the blue sky, flocks of white cranes formed a few V-shaped formations, flying from afar and soaring leisurely over the White Crane Stream. It was exactly what Bowa had hoped to see in his heart. He was particularly excited. "Little white crane, my little pal must be with them, soaring in the sky. My little fellow, I miss you and I will call you loudly."

"Little white crane…"

What a great miracle it was! Tian Shi Bowa suddenly shouted out three characters from his mouth. He had entered a state of ecstasy, looking up at the cranes in the sky, jumping and shouting:

"Little white crane, little white crane…"

The flocks of cranes in the sky seemed to be startled by Bowa's shouting or they probably didn't hear clearly who Bowa was calling. Their V-shaped formation suddenly scattered a bit and after a while was restored to its original formation and flew away gradually. Seeing the distinctive change of the crane formation, Tian Shi Bowa was full of confidence. He took out a red and yellow handkerchief given to him by Teacher Liu from his pocket and ran in the direction of the crane formation flying in the sky. As he ran, he raised and waved the handkerchief and shouted loudly, "Little white crane, little white crane…"

The miracle happened again. In the flying V-shaped formation, an obvious passage suddenly appeared, from which a little white crane glided down from the passage, croaked and turned back to fly toward White Crane Creek.

"Little white crane, my little white crane, is that you?" Bowa shouted whatever came to mind, the sounds coming out of his vocal cords without any blockage. The more characters were articulated, the smoother the expressions became and the louder his voice became.

The white crane and the teenage boy ran towards each other, moving closer and closer.

"Croak! Croak!"

"Little white crane…little white crane."

The little fellow stopped flapping his wings and glided down at an angle, hoping to land slowly and smoothly beside Bowa. However, he could not stop himself because of the inertia of his descent. When his two long legs touched the ground, he was dragged by the force when his body leaned forward. He could not help running past Bowa to the front.

Tian Shi Bowa hurriedly turned around to have a look while the little white crane that had already run ten metres ahead of Bowa finally stopped his feet and folded his wings. He uttered a cry and ran back lightly towards his young master.

Bowa was overwhelmed with joy. He squatted down to hold the little fellow in his arms, bending slightly to put his cheek against his, and said to him affectionately, "My little white crane! Look, in only a bit more than 20 days, you have grown taller and stronger! It is very nice of you to still remember me."

The little white crane pushed out of Bowa's arms, circled around him and croaked a few times. Then he waded through the stream and ran towards the small road on the hillside.

The two good friends walked and stopped for a while and walked on until they arrived at the edge of the front courtyard in front of Bowa's home.

How could they have known that a fierce argument was taking place inside the courtyard!

"Good heavens! How could the medical charges change like this? Didn't they tell me at the very beginning that we only needed to pay 20,000 yuan for the operation? Teacher Liu, why did the invoice you just brought to me read 37,000 yuan?"

Tian Fashui's voice was so loud that it sounded like thunder, so loud that it could be heard 16 kilometres away. "Teacher Liu, I have to tell you I don't even want to pay the 20,000 yuan. Why? My son was able to say one character out loud in the past but after the operation he could not even do that! Anyway, I accept it. My bad luck! My fate!"

"Fashui, Fashui, what's wrong with you? Why are you getting mad at Teacher Liu? Teacher Liu did this for the good of our Bowa and we can't renege on the debt." It was Li Runlan who was trying to persuade Tian Fashui to calm down and be reasonable.

Tian Fashui however became angrier and shouted, "You damned woman who has made me lose money. I could have felt a bit better if you had kept your mouth shut! How dare you come to persuade me? I have only just learnt that you were bold enough to allow Bowa to go to school without my permission. Look what you have done! Very good! I have lost tens of thousands of yuan for nothing while my son has become totally dumb."

"As the saying goes, keeping clear accounts is what a gentleman should do. I have to make it clear to you that Tian Shi Bowa's medical charges are 37,000 yuan according to the hospital's calculation. At that time, when I knew you were having a hard time and could not afford that much for the time being, I asked my relatives to pay for it on your behalf since Bowa did need this operation." Teacher Liu briefly explained this to Tian Fashui and then asked him calmly, "Tian Fashui, I just want to know if you really don't want to see your son remain like this, do you? And you want him to have a bright future, don't you?"

"Teacher Liu, to be frank, I have been polite to greet you as Teacher Liu. Probably you didn't want to cause us any trouble, but you shouldn't have poked your nose into our business. Obviously Tian Shi Bowa is a fool. Why did you ask him to go to school?" Tian Fashui tried to hold his temper, but he didn't lower his voice. "Put yourself in my shoes. Suppose you were me, a poor countryman, and think about it. Could you have held back your tears when your son was unable to say anything, when you had a 17,000-yuan debt to pay and when everything you had saved for the past 12 years was gone?"

"Fashui, it can't be 17,000 yuan for nothing! Teacher Liu has explained it clearly," said Li Runlan, pulling Tian Fashui's clothes to remind him.

"Stop talking nonsense! Li Runlan, if it hadn't been for you, how could this family have suffered so much?" Tian Fashui pushed away his wife's hand and scolded her, "Listen, if Tian Shi Bowa does become dumb, I will give your bottom a good beating."

"Tian Fashui, I have a question. How do you know Tian Shi Bowa can't speak?" Liu Wanyi was very sensible. She was good at grasping the crux of the problem and wouldn't be misled by others when she listened or when she talked. What's more, she had consulted experts before Bowa had the operation. Again, she asked Tian Fashui, "What if Tian Shi Bowa could speak? If so, how do you explain it and what are you going to do about it?"

"How do I know? How could I not know my own son! When we were still in the hospital I asked him to say something for me, but he didn't. On the day he was discharged from the hospital, I stopped and held him tight at the hospital gate and ordered him to speak, but still he could not. I did the test myself so how could it be a lie?"

"Could it be the case that he was unable or even unwilling to say anything?" said Liu Wanyi as she stared at Tian Fashui.

"Look how sour you intellectuals are! Is there any difference when you say this and say that?" Tian Fashui became very impatient and his anger increased, "I could be polite if you didn't manipulate me like this; if not, let's not beat about the bush. If Tian Shi Bowa could say a few characters at once, I would be more than happy to settle all the medical charges. If he can't, then sorry, I won't pay the extra 17,000 yuan."

Well, it is useless to reason with a rural dweller in this area, so difficult that it seems as if one is unable to fix a tangled fishing net inside Xiaonanhai. But no matter what the problem appears to be, explicit, implicit or hidden, it exists like a knot. It is sure to come to you, become loose, untied and finally disappear.

Before Tian Fashui had finished his words, a head rose from under the steps leading to the courtyard.

It was Tian Shi Bowa who had come back, followed closely by his little white crane.

Tian Shi Bowa had already heard his parents' shouting before he arrived at the yard. He had thought they were arguing about something as usual while, unexpectedly, the moment he entered the courtyard he caught sight of his beloved Teacher Liu.

Tian Shi Bowa felt a clatter in his heart and a flash of light in front of his eyes. The characters that he had been conceiving in his stomach burst out suddenly from his mouth, "Teacher Liu!"

15

THE MAGICAL FOURTH LESSON

Liu Wanyi was unable to sleep that night.

She had asked for it, to be exact. That was to say she had a lot of things to consider and a lot of plans to work out. She even felt it was a good opportunity given by god that she could do something that she had never experienced in the past.

When Tian Shi Bowa had shouted "Teacher Liu", Liu Wanyi's heartbeat had suddenly quickened and she felt the blood course through her veins, which made her very excited. She had been looking forward to this but she had never thought it would come to her so suddenly and be so real. She actually was gambling when she was at the Chongqing Linjiangmen Hospital. Although she had consulted experts who were quite certain about it at the time, she knew she could not take science for granted which should always be proved by practice. On her way back to the village school, she broke into a sweat because she had little confidence in this. If Tian Shi Bowa could not say anything after the operation, it would be a small thing to lose some money for her but the responsibility weighed heavily on her and others would blame her for a lifetime. She was unable to explain clearly why she had made such a decision; it might have been a kind of feeling on her part to do something for this poor Tian Shi Bowa who had a birth defect or that she felt it worthwhile for her to do so.

Liu Wanyi's feeling was right or it was quite worthwhile for her to feel this way. Tian Shi Bowa's later academic performance, like fruit weighing heavily on the branch, validated her feelings.

The day she asked Tian Fashui to write an IOU for 17,199 yuan, Tian Fashui had turned his head away, saying he had no money to hand and no money at home either. Liu Wanyi handed the IOU to him and said, "This 17,000 yuan has been used on Bowa's operation and the 199 yuan was the round-trip bus and train fare when I helped send Bowa to Chongqing. Honestly, tell me directly, are you going to settle this or not?"

Although Tian Fashui was a bit lazy, he basically had guts. After thinking about it for a while, he bit his lip and wrote an IOU to Liu Wanyi.

Liu Wanyi should have been a bit unhappy with Tian Fashui's attitude at the very beginning, but she didn't get mad, which actually was what she had anticipated. If Tian Fashui couldn't afford the money, she initially thought about excusing the debt without any hesitation, but immediately she dropped this idea. She couldn't do this, especially not for Tian Fashui who was such an insolent and unreasonable man. It was not a direct and simple question that a gentleman who desired wealth made it in a good way; it involved the construction of many psychological elements such as personality, morality and ambitions and the reform of the way of thinking as well. If she had been a bit careless, it could have harmed others or even had a huge impact on Tian Shi Bowa's life, which would surely have been a really serious problem.

Liu Wanyi had come to realise that although she had come to teach in this village school, what she had to do was not only to teach a few Chinese characters or a few mathematical formulas to children, but also to give them some spiritual and psychological education to imbue them with a high standard of morality, ambition and personality.

It was good to know Tian Shi Bowa had not been polluted by negative factors in the environment, which comforted Liu Wanyi quite a lot.

Teacher Liu had a very good habit of making predictions and plans for the things she should do, such as what would happen to Tian Shi Bowa's studies, and if something should happen, how would it develop further? Wanyi had long had a prediction in mind: suppose Tian Shi Bowa did have the gift of super-memorising skill after getting to know a certain pronunciation, what would she plan next for him? If so, when he graduated from primary education, he was bound to catch up with Huang Xiaoqiu.

THE MAGICAL FOURTH LESSON

She indeed had foresight. Tian Shi Bowa's academic performance made huge progress the way Chinese trumpet creepers climbed high and bloomed flourishingly. He learned whatever Liu Wanyi taught him well and, unexpectedly, when sometimes Teacher Liu was relaxed with him, Tian Shi Bowa's speed of learning got faster like the flowing spring water of the river that rolled eastward to the sea, which was totally beyond Liu Wanyi's expectation.

As usual, when it was time for the first year's class, Teacher Liu went to the back row in the classroom to give lessons to the only first-year student, Tian Shi Bowa.

According to her teaching plan, they should have started from the initial consonants of pinyin (the romanised sound of Chinese characters). Liu Wanyi thought it might be a bit boring to start with pinyin. Since Tian Shi Bowa was already ten and a half, it might be better to teach him some Chinese characters first to arouse his interest, then they could go to pinyin.

They turned the textbook to the page of Chinese characters, on which three characters were written *ba* (father), *ma* (mother) and *wo* (I or me).

"Tian Shi Bowa, can you speak?" asked Liu Wanyi gently in Chongqing dialect.

"Yes, I can, Teacher Liu."

Tian Shi Bowa spoke six characters at once and in clear, accurate and fluent *putonghua* (the common Chinese language). Teacher Liu was very surprised. She asked, "Tian Shi Bowa, you speak very good *putonghua*. Who taught you this?"

"Television, television reporters taught me this," said Tian Shi Bowa. "I have been dreaming about speaking for quite a long time although I was unable to do so. Television reporters all speak beautiful *putonghua*. When they spoke on TV, I followed them in my heart."

"It's pretty good. I am sure it will help you a lot in the future. Many people choose to learn to speak *putonghua* when they grow up, which actually makes it more difficult for them to speak it well. They often speak a kind of local *putonghua*, harsh to the ears and inaccurate, to be honest." Teacher Liu stopped talking about *putonghua* and went back to the textbook. "Now go back to our task and learn textbook knowledge first. Now read after me, *ba*."

"*Ba*," said Tian Shi Bowa, reading it out while looking at the character.

"*Ma.*"
"*Ma.*"
"*Wo.*"
"*Wo.*"

"Follow me one more time, then do it by yourself," said Teacher Liu.

"No need, Teacher Liu," said Tian Shi Bowa, "I have already memorised these characters."

"Oh, have you? Well, read them again and we will practice writing these characters later." Liu Wanyi thought it was normal to remember these characters after reading them once; who didn't say those characters every day when they were children, after all! She planned to move to the next lesson after Bowa became familiar with those strokes. However, Tian Shi Bowa said, "Write them down? We may skip that too because I can write them."

"How could you do that? Without practicing writing, you can't remember them in your mind."

"I already knew how to write those characters. Teacher Liu, when I read just now, I was practicing writing them on the desk with my fingers."

No wonder, Liu Wanyi said to herself. She remembered she did see him writing something on the desk with his fingers just now but she never thought he was practicing writing at the same time. He was indeed a very considerate boy. But was it possible that he could memorise those characters after a few scratches on the desk? With a kind of puzzled look, Liu Wanyi said to Bowa seriously, "Well, take out your exercise book and write them down first."

Tian Shi Bowa took out his exercise book, opened it and very soon finished writing these three characters with a pencil, perfectly correctly.

The characters he wrote were all in beautiful proportion but with the wrong stroke order. Teacher Liu said, "All the strokes are correct but you have written them in the wrong order. There is an eight-character basic rule to follow when you begin to write, that is, from top to bottom and from left to right. As for the complicated ones, I will teach you in the future." Liu Wanyi taught Tian Shi Bowa how to write *ba*, *ma*, and *wo* in the correct stroke order then she turned the textbook to the next lesson *Quietly*.

Tian Shi Bowa had studied it before he had the operation but hadn't grasped it. Or, to be exact, he didn't have the chance to learn it well. What about this time then?

Teacher Liu read the title as she pointed at it, *Quietly*. Tian Shi Bowa read after her immediately. Wanyi moved to the second and third characters in the title and Bowa repeated what she had said. As Teacher Liu moved on to the text and was ready to teach Bowa one character at a time, Bowa cautiously asked, "Teacher Liu, could you teach me a sentence at a time?"

"One sentence at a time? Ah, such a teenage boy with a small body, you want to get fat and become a strong man in one mouthful?" Liu Wanyi smiled and said firmly, "How many characters do you know? There are many new ones in this sentence, so how could you memorise them all at the same time?"

"Could we have a try?" insisted Tian Shi Bowa.

Seeing his insistence, Liu Wanyi said, "Tian Shi Bowa, you could have a try but if it doesn't work, don't take it to heart and we'll go back to the very beginning and learn one character at a time. Is that OK?"

"OK, Teacher Liu."

Liu Wanyi read a complete sentence, *"Rabbit rabbit bounces lightly.* Now it is your turn."

Tian Shi Bowa read after his teacher. Liu Wanyi said, "Now read it a few times and try and familiarise yourself with each character."

"Teacher Liu, I don't need to read it any more. I have already memorised them. Shall we move on to the next sentence?"

Tian Shi Bowa, you proud boy! A little praise for you has made you stick up your tail! What if I should give you a moon? Would you swallow it as if it were a mooncake? Teacher Liu said earnestly, "Tian Shi Bowa, do you know that learning requires step-by-step efforts, something down-to-earth; you should never be overambitious."

Tian Shi Bowa replied seriously, "Teacher Liu, I don't quite understand what you just mentioned about being 'overambitious', but I get your meaning. You want me to study in a down-to-earth way, one character at a time. I did read one character after another and I could memorise them after I read them. If you don't believe me, you could read a sentence in the text for me one more time and you will know whether I am telling a lie or not."

Liu Wanyi was shocked but fascinated by what Tian Shi Bowa had just said. Of course she knew it would be good enough for a child with such a poor foundation to recognise a few more characters in one lesson. It was totally unbelievable that he could memorise the text after reading it just once. But since he was so eager to learn new things, she as a teacher didn't want to discourage him. Right, give him one more chance. If he should fail to prove it, he would stop on the precipice. With that in mind, she said, "OK, you can have one more try."

One sentence after another, Liu Wanyi read the text to Tian Shi Bowa, who stared at those characters, reading after her very carefully. When they had finished, Liu Wanyi purposely didn't repeat them, wanting to give him a challenge. She said, "Tian Shi Bowa, now it's your turn. There are four sentences in this text. Please read it."

How could Tian Shi Bowa perceive his teacher's intention? He had already been immersed in the great joy of reading and memorising those characters. As he looked at the characters in the textbook, he drew quickly in the air with his forefinger and read out at the same time:

Quietly

Rabbits rabbits bounce lightly;
Puppies puppies run slowly.
Should you step on the grass and hurt them,
I am no longer your friend for sure.

"Tian Shi Bowa, can you remember the pronunciation and strokes of each character if you write these sentences down?" With great joy, Teacher Liu had already forgotten about the idea of challenging him that she had had at the very beginning. Her joy was written on her face. What an amazing thing it would be if Tian Shi Bowa could memorise all the strokes of each character after copying them down once.

However, Tian Shi Bowa's answer once again was unexpected.

"Teacher Liu, I don't need to copy them down. I think I can do that without looking at the text."

"What?" Liu Wanyi could hardly believe her ears. "Tian Shi Bowa, what did you say just now? Did you say you could write them down from memory?"

"Yes, teacher. I want to have a try." As he said this, he closed his textbook and began to write in his exercise book.

After a while, Tian Shi Bowa laid down his pencil. Liu Wanyi couldn't wait to pick his exercise book up and take a look. Sure enough, he had written down all the sentences. Although the strokes were skewed, they were all perfectly correct. There wasn't a single mistake in his practice!

Liu Wanyi blinked her eyes and looked at it again. She didn't believe Tian Shi Bowa, not to say herself. But what had happened in front of her eyes was all real! Was there going to be a miracle in the Qianjiang area? Liu Wanyi bit her lip hard, frowned and thought for a while, picked up the textbook and turned to the next text.

"*A little bamboo raft floating in a painting*; Tian Shi Bowa, have you read this text before?" Teacher Liu seemed to be asking this very casually, but she wanted to check whether Tian Shi Bowa had some other access to the text.

"No," answered Tian Shi Bowa naturally and firmly.

Liu Wanyi felt relieved. She said, "Tian Shi Bowa, let's study another lesson. Do you have any problem with that?"

Hearing Bowa say no, Liu Wanyi placed the textbook in front of Tian Shi Bowa and said, "Listen carefully. After I read it through, you read it again. Is that OK?"

Tian Shi Bowa said, "Let's have a try."

There were six lines of text. Liu Wanyi read it through at normal speed first and then she asked Tian Shi Bowa to read it. Bowa looked through the text from the very top to the bottom and kept drawing something on the desk with his fingers as he looked. When he stopped his finger, he pointed at the character *mi* and asked Teacher Liu to read it again. Then, he finished reading the six lines in one breath, all correct. After that, he asked involuntarily, "Teacher Liu, may I try to write it down from memory?"

Liu Wanyi didn't know whether she had answered him or not. She felt she was in a dream, her ears unable to hear and eyes unable to see. How could she believe what had just happened in front of her! She had been teaching for so many years but she had never met such an amazing student before.

"Teacher Liu, I've finished." Liu Wanyi was still lost in thought, failing to hear what Bowa had just said to her. It was after Tian Shi Bowa grabbed her sleeves a few times that she felt she heard Bowa saying something, "Teacher Liu, I have finished. Please check it."

Liu Wanyi hurriedly replied, "Good, good." She rubbed her eyes and checked it line by line. No mistakes at all, not even a character or a punctuation mark!

A little bamboo raft floats in a painting

A little bamboo raft flows along the water;
Birds sing and fish swim.
Trees grow densely on both sides of the river;
Green are the rice seedlings;
Fragrant is the smell of rice and fish.
A little bamboo raft floats in a painting.

It is said that Fu Rong in the Eastern Jin dynasty had the gift of photographic memory. Was it possible that someone nowadays had that gift too? She put down the exercise book, squatted down, put her hands on Tian Shi Bowa's two small shoulders and began to check it very carefully. Well, it was the child with his bare calves, clean forehead and long, narrow eyes who played with the little white crane in the White Crane Stream. At that time, he seemed to be timid, stupid and dumb, but now how had that wild child suddenly become such a smart, amazing and exciting miracle?

"Tian Shi Bowa, are you for real?" asked Liu Wanyi incredulously.

"Yes, I am, Teacher Liu." Wanyi's question turned Bowa's small eyes into big ones, sparkling with confusion and doubt.

"Are you the same Tian Shi Bowa I took to have an operation in Chongqing Linjiangmen Hospital?"

"Yes, it is me, indeed. Is everything all right with you?"

16

CREATIVE TEACHING METHODS

Liu Wanyi wasn't sure how to write her diary. On the one hand, she was in a state of excitement while on the other hand she was still lost in a dream-like suspicion.

She wrote in her diary:

The progress of Tian Shi Bowa's study, like a radio wave emitted by a radio station, is fast and productive. The visible is transmitted by the invisible while at the same time the invisible includes the visible, no backward motion but moving forward.

It is only about two weeks since Bowa has already memorised all of the text in the first-year Chinese book. The use of the word 'memorise' means not only is he able to read, he also can write them down from memory from lesson one to where he just learned. And he doesn't make any mistakes! These days, I have tried teaching him some year-three stuff and he continues to move forward very fast like a high-speed train. Think about it, he hasn't learned the second-year texts yet. If things go on like this, he will surely be that miracle child, won't he?

Could it be the case that I, Liu Wanyi, am so lucky that I have met a wonder child, a born genius?

Maybe it is a fantasy or maybe everything is possible. In any case, this child has a unique ability that makes me particularly happy.

Mencius said, "The superior man has three things in which he delights, and to be ruler over the kingdom is not one of them. That his father and mother are both alive, and that the condition of his brothers affords no cause for anxiety; this is one delight. That, when looking up, he has no occasion for shame before Heaven and, below, he has no occasion to blush before men; this is a second delight. That he can get from the whole kingdom the most talented individuals, and teach and nourish them; this is the third delight."

Based on my feelings, a lot of people are able to achieve the first two things, the anchor of life and spirit and the pleasure of family bonds and personal stuff. The third one, however, is different, which cannot be achieved by everyone, therefore the third thing is the delight of the soul, a poetic happiness, an ultimate happiness, which is incomparable to family and personal affections.

If, enlightened by my teaching and guidance, Tian Shi Bowa grows up to be a talented person in the future and benefits society, it is indeed an honour for me.

Can Tian Shi Bowa, born with his innate gift, be classified as a genius? Perhaps it is because I have helped him discover his articulation disorder, one of the 'lost children' in his body so that his innate gift that has been hidden for more than ten years finally burst out, which seems more powerful than the IQ of children of the same age as him. Perhaps he will stop half way when he encounters setbacks on the road of learning the way some people do or perhaps...

Although Tian Shi Bowa has a high IQ, he started his learning by memorising numbers and then moved on to maths problems one by one. The only difference between him and the other students is that he is slightly faster than them, although it is much slower than his progress in his language learning. Is maths a bit more difficult? I know it can't be Bowa's problem when I see him finish his assignments easily. Even a genius still needs a mentor to lead the way. As the saying "get from the whole kingdom the most talented individuals, and teach and nourish them" goes, a mentor first must be equipped with knowledge and ability to nurture talent. There is no problem for me to teach Tian Shi Bowa considering my store of knowledge, but do I have the ability to impart knowledge to my students?

Now there is one teacher and nearly 50 students spanning different years in the class and each student is unique. As the saying goes, one key opens one lock. What will happen if you try to open 50 locks with one key? Won't it be the same thing when a teacher teaches their students with one method? Yes, it is. It is necessary to critically practice reverse thinking. Think about it. If a teacher could work out 50 different teaching methods for 50 students, how could students not get good scores?

Tian Shi Bowa is a special lock. If I can find a special key to open this special lock, will that get better results with less work?

Liu Wanyi stopped writing her diary and made a decision. She began to change her teaching methods at school. She arranged her students in groups and made the best use of each student's situation, trying to make sure that every student could learn real knowledge.

As for Tian Shi Bowa, Teacher Liu of course put much more thought into his study. She had a special teaching method for Bowa: using 'fishing' to keep 'fish' alive, teaching senior-year stuff to facilitate the learning of junior ones.

Wandering beside the bamboo forests and lingering beside Xiaonanhai, Liu Wanyi could not drive away the image of this special kid that repeatedly appeared in her mind. Yes, Tian Shi Bowa didn't know a character, but his desire for knowledge was like the one for rain after a serious drought. He used to be Silly Tian who couldn't even speak, but after he was reborn like a Nirvana, he thirsted for knowledge and presented an exceptionally good memory. She thought she should foster his strength and circumvent his weakness and teach him how to fish. 'Fishing' here was not as simple as the dictionary term; it was a way to obtain knowledge, which could help Tian Shi Bowa sail in the vast ocean of knowledge to capture big fish alive left by human civilisation.

Why should 'big fish' be characterised by being 'alive'? Because 'fish' in this context is not used to compare to simple and rigid written answers; it is living knowledge that can be applied flexibly into social practice.

Perhaps Liu Wanyi's creative teaching methods would be accepted and promoted in the field of Chinese teaching; perhaps its uniqueness would bring about quite a lot of controversy and rejection, but it didn't matter because Liu Wanyi didn't think about how these methods would be in the future. She just wanted to start right now, abandon the dogma and proceed from reality, and the demand for better, faster progress.

A good method deserves a good tool. What had to be given to Tian Shi Bowa in time was Chinese Pinyin.

Liu Wanyi settled the matter at once. Instead of buying a *Xinhua Dictionary*, she went to look for a proper one in the town but in vain. She therefore went to Qianjiang city and bought the *Chinese Pinyin Instant Learning Guide* and the *Modern Chinese Dictionary*. At that time she thought about buying a *Dictionary of Modern Idiomatic Chinese*, but she gave up the idea after careful analysis. She felt it would be good enough for Tian Shi Bowa to fully grasp the *Modern Chinese Dictionary* during his primary school time. More haste less speed. The *Dictionary of Modern Idiomatic Chinese* was a six-volume *magnum opus* and if Tian Shi Bowa could not digest it, he would be choked by so much stuff which would harm him for sure. When Liu Wanyi gave the two books to Tian Shi Bowa, she said, "Bowa, let's put our textbook aside for a while. The two reference books I'm giving you are stepping stones for you to enter the hall of Chinese language. If you want to succeed, you are sure to feel tired and worn-out and you will have less time to play with the little white crane. Can you do that?"

Tian Shi Bowa replied without hesitation, "Yes, I can, Teacher Liu."

Within a week, Tian Shi Bowa learned Chinese Pinyin, and learned how to use the *Modern Chinese Dictionary*. Teacher Liu said to him, "You have already mastered the basic methods of Chinese Pinyin and you will gradually understand and grasp those lateral sounds, nasals, front nasals and back nasals in your reading. This term, you don't need your textbook any more; read and copy all the words and expressions in the *Modern Chinese Dictionary* with the Chinese Pinyin you have learned. Come to me whenever you have questions, but you need to start in two steps…"

After she had finished, she asked, "Bowa, as for how to study, how many steps did I just teach you to remember?"

"Two steps, Teacher Liu."

"What are they?"

"The first step, remember and memorise the pronunciation and strokes of words according to the rules of the initial consonants order in the *Modern Chinese Dictionary*. Next, go back to the first word to make phrases and try to recognise and memorise the explanations and sample expressions."

"Great! Ten points!" Liu Wanyi was so satisfied with Tian Shi Bowa's answer that she adopted the words some TV programme hosts like to use in some entertainment competitions to encourage Bowa.

As for Bowa's maths, Liu Wanyi racked her brains for a better way out. She used the 'teaching senior-year stuff to facilitate the learning of junior ones' to teach Bowa maths. She taught him some basic numbers, addition and subtraction, and asked him to learn his multiplication tables by heart. She then creatively skipped the first-year and second-year maths questions and began with third-year maths questions directly when teaching Tian Shi Bowa. Teacher Liu thought that although Tian Shi Bowa didn't learn maths in the first year and the second year, he would surely be able to solve those questions easily as long as he learned third-year maths.

As it turned out, Liu Wanyi was correct.

How did Liu Wanyi do it in practice then?

Multiplication and division were the teaching focus in the third-year second-term maths. Teacher Liu however didn't let Bowa do multiplication; she gave him a series of division directly:

$3600 \div 6 =$

Tian Shi Bowa was bound to be in the dark if asked to do this at once. Yes, it sounded correct, but Tian Shi Bowa knew numbers and could recite multiplication tables. Teacher Liu tried to enlighten him, "Which number should 6 be multiplied by to get 36?"

"Six times 6 is 36," answered Tian Shi Bowa.

"Good, let's learn how to do division and how to write an expression." Teacher Liu wrote a division expression and taught Tian Shi Bowa how to use his knowledge of multiplication into division, explained to him why the result was 6 after division and why it was necessary to keep the remaining two zeros directly as the result after the division. As for questions like this, Teacher Liu usually gave Bowa three examples.

For those that were a bit different, Teacher Liu also gave him three examples.

For example, $82 \div 9 \approx$

"This symbol '$\approx$' is read as 'approximately equal'. Why is it approximately equal? Because it cannot be divided evenly by the divisor." Teacher Liu asked Tian Shi Bowa to calculate the division question above, and he was smart enough to have doubts about the remaining number '1'. "As for '1', a number that cannot be divided, it does exist. How to handle this then?"

Liu Wanyi very much appreciated this question raised by Bowa. She therefore explained to him what decimals are and why we need to calculate decimals. In this way, the basic knowledge that Bowa had to learn had been naturally brought out by his working with relatively difficult maths questions, which was indeed twice the result with half the effort!

For the whole first term of the first year, Teacher Liu asked Tian Shi Bowa to repeatedly do the exercises in the second volume of the third-year exercise book and some auxiliary exercises in volume 1 and 2 of the book she had bought from the bookstore. That was all that Bowa did during his maths classes.

When the semester was about to end, the final maths exam set by Liu Wanyi for Bowa consisted of three parts: first-year maths, second-year maths and third-year maths with each comprising one-third of the total. Tian Shi Bowa scored 96 out of a maximum possible score of 100!

It was good that Bowa had maanaged to master the maths. Liu Wanyi now began to think about how to help him with the other subjects apart from Chinese and maths. As she thought about it, she sighed with relief. Fortunately, Bowa did live up to her expectations. Otherwise, she would have been leading young people astray.

As she reflected on this, she thought of another assignment she had left for Tian Shi Bowa: Chinese Pinyin. Although it took her a week to teach him some basic knowledge of Chinese Pinyin, she didn't have the time to check on it. Besides, he had an assignment to read, memorise and write down words and expressions in the *Modern Chinese Dictionary* and she wanted to know how it was going. Children love to play and probably Bowa forgot about this assignment when he played with the little white crane. She felt she should not slack off and she managed to find some time to go to his home and check on it.

17
A MIRACLE BROUGHT ABOUT BY MISCHIEF

When word of Tian Shi Bowa's maths score spread around the campus, it created an uproar in Huang Xiaoqiu's mind. "Well, it must be a lie. It's just one semester since he came here; how could he do third-year maths questions. Nothing could be as unreal as this. Teacher Liu must have faked it in order to encourage him."

Huang Xiaoqiu always came top of the class, which made her quite proud of herself. It was natural for a student to be a bit proud, not a bad thing anyway, but being too proud was a problem. A proud person would worry that someone might catch up with them, which would easily fill them with envy. Envy meant narrow-mindedness; envy often gave birth to hatred while hatred in turn could lead to unfriendly words and deeds which as a result would harm others and oneself.

As for Huang Xiaoqiu, she wanted to find a chance to verify whether Tian Shi Bowa's score was true or not.

One morning, Huang Xiaoqiu met Xiao Jianbo on her way to school. She wanted to take advantage of Xiao Giant to go and look for Tian Shi Bowa, but she didn't express it directly. Instead, she beat around the bush and said to Xiao Jianbo, "I heard the little white crane Tian Shi Bowa saved has flown away, hasn't it?"

"Yes," Xiao Jianbo replied, "but that little white crane flies back to the big banyan tree in Tian Shi Bowa's home to sleep at night."

"Impossible!" Huang Xiaoqiu argued. "My father said white cranes live in groups. They would never rest alone at night; they all fly in groups to rest in forests of pine and bamboo."

"But Tian Shi Bowa's little white crane indeed flies back to rest on the big banyan tree," said Xiao Jianbo firmly. "My mum heard Tian Shi Bowa's mother say this. She said whenever Tian Shi Bowa waves his hand and shouts to the sky, the little white crane flying overhead flies back to his side."

"Xiao Jianbo, you are good at making up stories. As long as Tian Shi Bowa waves his hand and shouts, the little white crane flies back to him? Have you seen it with your own eyes? Have you heard it yourself? Xiao Jianbo, you are telling lies like the others. I would rather die than believe you!" Huang Xiaoqiu looked at him with disdain.

A bit embarrassed, Xiao Jianbo muttered, "I didn't say I've seen it. My mum told me that."

"Ha-ha, that is acceptable," said Huang Xiaoqiu somewhat proudly. "Words are just hot air while seeing is believing. Xiao Jianbo, how about this? Let's go and test Tian Shi Bowa to see whether he can call the little white crane back to him from the sky or not."

Xiao Jianbo immediately answered, "Hey, great idea. I also want to know whether he has this skill or not."

As they chatted with each other, Tian Shi Bowa happened to walk close behind them. As Bowa walked along the mountain road, he felt a bit uncomfortable. Why? It was the school bag strap that was rubbing his shoulder and making him very uncomfortable. It was a drawstring bag made by his father that he used to carry to the fair. When he first started school, it was very convenient, not at all heavy with some textbooks and exercise books inside, but later more textbooks and exercise books plus the *Modern Chinese Dictionary* Teacher Liu had given him made the bag very heavy. It was bad enough holding it in his hand, but when he carried it over his shoulder it almost killed him. Tian Shi Bowa had to shift the load from his left shoulder to his right and had to stop and rest from time to time. Couldn't he ask his parents to buy him a backpack? He thought about it but eventually didn't open his mouth. His family was already in debt for his operation and his parents were both trying their best to make ends meet. Tian Shi Bowa didn't want to give them any trouble.

In the afternoon after school, Huang Xiaoqiu and Xiao Jianbo waited for Tian Shi Bowa on the winding road through the fir woods to meet him.

"Tian Shi Bowa, we have something to tell you," said Huang Xiaoqiu.

"What's the matter?" Tian Shi Bowa sounded very serious, but he didn't mean to. He was about 11 years old and seldom laughed and even if there was something to smile about, he just opened his mouth or turned up the corners of his mouth while people could not hear any sound from him. When it happened quite often, some people said he was a weirdo or some would say he was deliberately mischievous. So he had to get used to keeping a straight face. Finally few people saw him laugh unless he was compelled to.

"Xiao Jianbo said you like rowing and he is willing to lend you his boat."

"Huang Xiaoqiu, when did I say I would lend him the boat?" Xiao Jianbo asked Huang Xiaoqiu anxiously.

She stared back at him, winked and said, "Didn't you say that? Xiao Jianbo, didn't you say that when you see Tian Shi Bowa, you should invite him to go rowing with you?"

"Oh, yes," Xiao Jianbo pretended to come to his senses, "Tian Shi Bowa, shall we go boating together?"

"Do you mean it?" Tian Shi Bowa did like boating because his family didn't have one. His mother usually borrowed boats from their neighbours when she went to the other side of the lake to farm the fields while Bowa went with her and rowed the oars. Sometimes when he wanted to go boating himself, he would look for a chance to borrow one from his classmates.

"Don't you trust your classmate?" asked Huang Xiaoqiu. "We are here waiting specially for you."

"Great."

Three of them went to the lake and sat in the boat owned by Xiao Jianbo's family. It was a double-swallow boat, pointed at both ends, without an awning but with a board in the middle to sit on and two oars. It was an open boat and rowing it made one feel smooth and refreshed.

"Tian Shi Bowa, rowed towards Niubei Island. Let's play on the island for a while," Xiao Jianbo said to Tian Shi Bowa who was rowing the boat.

The boat moved across to Niubei Island.

Sitting on the board in the middle of the boat, Huang Xiaoqiu looked at

Tian Shi Bowa and said, "I heard the little white crane you saved has flown back to his flock?"

"Yep."

"It is said that as long as you wave your hand and shout, the little white crane flies back to you. People are making up stories, aren't they? I don't believe it anyway!" Huang Xiaoqiu squinted at him, challenging him to say something.

Giving her a look, Tian Shi Bowa didn't say anything. Huang Xiaoqiu's words didn't work on him. Tian Shi Bowa said to himself secretly, "It has nothing to do with me whether you believe it or not. The story between the little white crane and me is personal and isn't anyone else's business."

"It's a lie, isn't it? I said Xiao Jianbo, who was arguing with me just now, was bragging."

"My mum told me this and it is not me who said Tian Shi Bowa could call the little white crane back," said Xiao Jianbo honestly. "Bowa, don't take it seriously. Whether you can do it or not has nothing to do with anyone else. Let's carry on playing as we want."

"It has nothing to do with anyone else?" Huang Xiaoqiu stared at Xiao Jianbo, raising her voice at the same time. "It is a matter of integrity, something to do with morality, a matter of personality. If Tian Shi Bowa cannot call his little white crane back, it just means he is cheating on us. He is a liar."

This really worked. How could Tian Shi Bowa accept such a judgement? He glanced at them and said, "Who said I cannot? You? Him? Or me? Ridiculous!"

"Well, go and call your crane to come back. Come on," Huang Xiaoqiu said loudly. "Big talk is worth nothing!"

"Why should I listen to you?" said Tian Shi Bowa calmly. "Would it be better for my little white crane to live in his world freely? Why should I bother him?"

"Ha…," Huang Xiaoqiu laughed out loud sarcastically. "As we can read in books, it is so funny! It seems you do have a good reason if you're protecting the ecological system. Why do you talk big when you actually do not have the ability to do it?"

In White Crane Village, it is regarded as a kind of contempt and insult to tell someone to their face they are bragging, although sometimes it might be acceptable if it is said behind someone's back. Tian Shi Bowa was of course a bit annoyed. He argued, "When did I talk big? I just don't want to interrupt the little white crane's life."

"Hey, I have seen quite a lot of tricks like this." As she said this, she saw Bowa's drawstring school bag on the seatboard. She hit upon an idea and said, "Tian Shi Bowa, let's make a bet. If you can call the little white crane back to you, I will get you a backpack."

"A backpack? You mean you have an extra one?" Attracted by this, Tian Shi Bowa stopped the oar and asked.

"Of course. My father bought them for me. I still have two at home," said Huang Xiaoqiu proudly. "Are you up for the bet or not? I mean it."

"If you lose, you will really give me a backpack?" Tian Shi Bowa was eager for that. But when he looked up and saw the sun still high above the mountain, he hesitated.

"Well…"

"There is no point in keeping up appearances. If it's not OK then it's not OK. You don't dare to bet, which means you are indeed bragging!"

"It is still too early. The little white crane right now is looking for food."

"Ha…" Huang Xiaoqiu laughed out loud again, laughing heartily. She thought to herself, I knew you couldn't. But I understand you want to make excuses. Who can call a wild bird back from the sky anyway? Go and brag to someone else! Well, your scores in the final maths exam might be faked too. It must be a show the school has put on to win a reputation just like the TV broadcasters do.

As she thought about this, Huang Xiaoqiu didn't envy Tian Shi Bowa any more, but mischievous as always, she wanted to play a trick on Bowa. She therefore changed the topic and asked, "Tian Shi Bowa, I know Teacher Liu praises you so much. But as for this final maths exam, I heard you did the third-year maths questions. You are in the first year anyway, so tell me is it true?"

"Just one-third of the questions were third-year ones," answered Tian Shi Bowa honestly.

"You made no mistakes at all?"

"One mistake. I lost four points."

"You are talking big again!" Huang Xiaoqiu pouted scornfully. "Do you think you could do this in the same way that you brag about the little white crane? You might as well make up stories about cranes that fly in the sky, but as for exams, it is black and white on paper! I only got 92 points; how could you get 96?"

"I did get 96." Tian Shi Bowa answered briefly, in his usual way.

"Good, show me your test paper if you dare!" Huang Xiaoqiu replied distrustfully.

Tian Shi Bowa didn't say anything. He put down the oar, sat on the seatboard and took his test paper out of his bag.

Huang Xiaoqiu was very smart. She finished reading the paper very soon and found out the only mistake on the paper was a second-year one, a mistake of operation order. And he had done all the third-year questions correctly. If it was really true, that was incredible! Incredible indeed! Huang Xiaoqiu wanted to test Bowa herself.

"Tian Shi Bowa, I have a maths question for you. Dare you do it in front of me?" Staring straight at Bowa, Huang Xiaoqiu challenged him.

Bowa didn't look her in the eye and said, "Let's try."

Huang Xiaoqiu took out a stack of papers, a ballpoint pen and wrote down a multiplication question quickly. She handed it to Bowa and said, "Here you are. Enjoy!"

Bowa looked at the question: $321 \times 9 \times 16 \times 0 =$

"No need to calculate," said Tian Shi Bowa.

"What? Tian Shi Bowa, you don't know how to do it, do you?"

"No need indeed. The result is 0," said Tian Shi Bowa confidently, "Haven't you forgotten that 0 times 0 is 0?"

"Haven't I forgotten? How could I forget? I am testing you! OK, a tough one for you this time." Huang Xiaoqiu got another question for Bowa, a pretty difficult one for a third-year student.

$403 \div 4 =$

Tian Shi Bowa picked up the pen, but he knew the result before he wrote anything down. "The result is 100.75."

Huang Xiaoqiu took the pen and did it herself. It was indeed 100.75. Should she continue testing him? Her eyes widened like a pair of table tennis balls, Huang Xiaoqiu could not believe that this Bowa in front of her was the one she used to know. Was it real? If so, there could be only one explanation: Tian Shi Bowa had a teacher who had been teaching him since he was a child. If so, that was also cheating. She decided to check Bowa's drawstring bag.

"What's this? *An Instant Guide Book of Chinese Pinyin*. Ha…I finally caught you! Look, a *Modern Chinese Dictionary*! A reference book used by senior students! But you Tian Shi Bowa have one!" As she thought about this, Huang Xiaoqiu stood up and flipped through the two reference books, making them rustle. Very angry and very proud as well, she said to Xiao Jianbo and Tian Shi Bowa loudly, "Look, isn't this a kind of cheating? The *Modern Chinese Dictionary* is a reference book used by senior students, but you Tian Shi Bowa have turned the pages over and over again like this until they have become dog-eared, which means you have had it for quite a long time, and that you have been learning since you were young. Now you come out and pretend you've just begun school, saying that a year-one student can handle year-three courses. It is definitely a show to curry favour and to win a false reputation! There are too many reports on such kind of frauds on TV! Tian Shi Bowa, you are cheating us, you are a liar."

"Xiaoqiu, Xiaoqiu, put the book down!" Tian Shi Bowa was worried that Huang Xiaoqiu might lose her grip on his *Modern Chinese Dictionary* and drop it into the water. He stood up to remind her, "Xiaoqiu, what are you doing? Be careful!"

"Me be careful? What a joke! You should be the one to be careful!" Huang Xiaoqiu said scornfully, as if she had something on him. "I tell you, Tian Shi Bowa, you are gaining fame by deceiving everyone and you should be careful about this."

"No, no, I mean…" Tian Shi Bowa was a bit anxious, "I mean put down my *Modern Chinese Dictionary*!"

"You are so changeable! Yes and No by turn! Ha…you want me to put it down? You are feeling guilty, aren't you?" Huang Xiaoqiu slapped the book and said in a tone as if to announce something, "Stuff that you have used to cheat! Is it worth keeping? Better throw it into the lake!"

She did mean it. Huang Xiaoqiu held the book high with her hands and threw it forward wildly. The poor *Modern Chinese Dictionary* turned a few times in the air, was blown open by the wind, and flopped into the water.

"Oh, no! My *Modern Chinese Dictionary*!" Tian Shi Bowa screamed out in agony. When he saw that his book wasn't swallowed up by the water but floated on the surface because of the inside pages blown open by the wind, he was overjoyed. Immediately, he took off his sweatshirt but when he was about to take off his trousers, he realised there was a girl inside the boat, so he stopped at once. But he dared not jump into the lake with his trousers on because he was used to swimming in the lake naked and with his trousers on, he might sink into the water. He was so anxious that he kept turning around on the boat. "What should I do? What should I do?"

"Row the boat, row to get the dictionary," Xiao Jianbo reminded Bowa, who at that time realised this and prepared to grab the oar. Huang Xiaoqiu however was faster. She held the oar with her hands and paddled in the opposite direction of the book.

"Hurry up, Bowa, call your little white crane to help you."

The little white crane? Yes, he could help with it. Bowa stopped thinking about anything else but shouted at the top of his voice, "Little white crane, little white crane, come! Little white crane…"

"Ha…" Huang Xiaoqiu laughed crazily as if she were mad. She could not even hold the oar, leaving the boat circling in the middle of the lake. "People are not always reliable, let alone a bird. You cannot cheat me. Go on, shout louder!"

Bowa took the yellow and red handkerchief out of his pocket given to him by Teacher Liu, held it high and waved, shouting, "Little white crane, little white crane…"

Wow, then a miracle happened. It did happen! From the sandy beach on the other side of the lake, a little white crane suddenly flew up, appearing small and then gradually looming large. He flew above the three teenagers very soon, his long beak moving from left to right, changing the angle as his eyes searched. The inner layer of black feathers of his wings contrasted sharply with the white feathers all over his body, making him look much whiter.

"Little white crane… little white crane…" Bowa continued waving his handkerchief to greet his pal who, at the same time, hovered and approached the boat slowly.

Huang Xiaoqiu at that time was so stunned that she plonked herself down on the seatboard!

Seeing the approaching little white crane, Xiao Jianbo knew his mother hadn't been telling lies. He was very happy too and jumped around, "Hey, little white crane, we are here; Bowa is here."

Looking at his little white crane descending slowly, Bowa immediately pointed in the direction of the *Modern Chinese Dictionary* with the handkerchief and shouted, "Over there, the reference book, the reference book…"

The little white crane really knew how he felt. He followed Tian Shi Bowa's instructions as to where to go and what to do. He watched, hovered twice above the reference book and descended quickly, using his long beak to pick up the hard cover of the book and soaring high into the sky. However, the little white crane had not grown into an adult and he was not strong enough to hold it for long. When he flew up, he had tried his best to flap his wings but the reference book had become heavier after getting soaked in the water. Gradually the little fellow was dragged back to the surface of the lake.

The little white crane was very clever. Even when he was dragged back to the surface of the water, he didn't let go of the book. He paddled and flapped his wings to swim backward with the help of his body's buoyancy. Slowly, and with everyone staring at him, the little white crane dragged the *Modern Chinese Dictionary* ashore.

18
REAL TALENT

Tian Shi Bowa was in floods of tears, eyes swollen, sobbing, not loud but continuous.

The *Modern Chinese Dictionary* in Bowa's hands was soaking wet and dripping on the way home. After Bowa arrived home, he opened the dictionary, put a hemp rope in the middle of the book and hung it around a wooden beam of the house on stilts, some pages sandwiched with newspaper in the middle. But many pages were so wet that they stuck together and could not be pulled apart. What if he couldn't pull them apart after the pages had dried? What if he tore them when trying to do so? Bowa was crying over this but he forced back the tears in case someone could hear. Fortunately, his mother was not back yet, otherwise he wouldn't have known how to explain this. Crying was a sign of sadness that he had failed to put out of his mind while he was worried about being heard in case his grandma might feel upset too when she heard it.

Huang Xiaoqiu was indeed very thoughtless. How could she have thrown Bowa's reference book into the water in such a careless manner? The next day after school, she was kept behind by Teacher Liu.

"What did Tian Shi Bowa do to annoy you like this? Huang Xiaoqiu, tell me. Why did you throw his reference book into the water?" Teacher Liu questioned Huang Xiaoqiu directly.

"Tian Shi Bowa is a liar! He deserved it," replied Huang Xiaoqiu brazenly. "You know, in fact he has been studying hard since he was a child and those reference books prove it. Like a spy, he pretended he could not speak and went to study at school at ten and a half years old. He wants to create an image of being a wonder child and to astonish the world."

"Ha... is that the way you envy your classmate?" Teacher Liu couldn't help laughing, "Even if Tian Shi Bowa had done something wrong, there was no reason for you to throw his dictionary into the water."

"His reference books? I could buy a dozen as simply as opening my mouth," said Huang Xiaoqiu in a very indifferent manner. She continued, "My father has a lot of money. I could buy one for him as compensation. He is a nobody! How dare he report me to you! He deserved it and I have the money to pay for that."

"Oh, you are truly a young local tyrant! Is your family really very rich?"

"Huh, much richer than Tian Shi Bowa's family!"

"Huang Xiaoqiu, think it over. Is Tian Shi Bowa inferior to you just because his family is poorer than yours?"

Huang Xiaoqiu dared not answer this question, lowering her head. Liu Wanyi didn't push her to say anything. Huang Xiaoqiu after all was a teenager who still needed years to discover the world. It was better to stop at that; it might be another good means of education. "Let me tell you the truth and it's better for you to think about what you should do after you've listen to me." Teacher Liu continued, "Tian Shi Bowa didn't come to report you to me. It was Xiao Jianbo who told me you had thrown away Tian Shi Bowa's dictionary. Xiao Jianbo said he was very shocked and angry at your behaviour. He said you are all in one school while you have chosen to bully Bowa, which is quite unreasonable. He also said good always prevails over evil and he just wanted to report you, and is not afraid of the consequences."

Huang Xiaoqiu was really shocked, and her eyes widened so much that only the whites of her eyes were visible.

"Huang Xiaoqiu, you have overestimated Tian Shi Bowa's intelligence by saying he is a spy. You must have watched too many spy TV dramas, have you? Tian Shi Bowa could not say anything before he was ten and a half years old. He didn't pretend to be like that; it was a physical defect. I helped arrange an operation for him in the hospital. Yes, his family is poor at present and is still in debt, but Tian Shi Bowa has ambition, ideals and a strong will to work hard which, of course, has enabled him to get good scores." Teacher Liu patted Huang Xiaoqiu on the shoulder and continued sincerely, "Xiaoqiu, you are a smart girl but sometimes you are a bit too emotional which often leads you astray. As for Tian Shi Bowa at present, it is the very time for you to help him but you tried to tease him and make fun of him instead. This won't do you any good either. Make a comparison in your heart: do you want to be better than others in everything while being unwilling to see others do as well as you? Tian Shi Bowa on the contrary wants to better himself while he is willing to treat others with kindness and help others to do well too. This is the difference. You two will both be excellent students, even if the gap between you both is narrowed."

"Teacher Liu, I am in the wrong," muttered Huang Xiaoqiu. "I want to write a self-criticism or a letter of guarantee to you."

"It is good enough to know you are wrong. No need to write any self-criticism or a letter of guarantee," said Liu Wanyi. "The key point is you must be the master of your heart. If you could concentrate more on study, and on helping others, you are sure to be appreciated by more people and your academic performance is sure to be much better. I won't say any more and I believe you know what you should do in the future."

Liu Wanyi left home shortly after Huang Xiaoqiu left school.

She wanted to make an immediate visit to see whether Tian Shi Bowa still had his heart on studying.

Walking along the mountain road, she imagined where and how Tian Shi Bowa read books. He must be sitting on a small stool using a wide bench as a desk under the roof, writing his assignment quietly. Or maybe he was inside the courtyard, with his textbook or a dictionary in his hands, walking back and forth, reading and reciting loudly.

As these thoughts ran through her mind, she began to go downhill, where the White Crane Stream was located at the end of the slope. After crossing the stream and climbing up another slope, she arrived at Tian Shi Bowa's home.

Blue mountains, green grass, water flowing slowly, a white crane stalking about in the stream, stretching out its long beak into the reeds in the shallow water, pecking from time to time for tender reed roots or small fish and shrimps, or who knows what? On the other side of the river, a teenager wearing a short yellow jacket was crawling on the sand beach and no one knew what he was doing over there.

Liu Wanyi took a close look. Ah, she was extremely upset and annoyed at what she saw. She could barely drag her feet forward, feeling that she had lost power all of a sudden, and that her feet and legs were too heavy. And involuntarily, she uttered a sigh, stood to take a rest for a little while and walked on.

Obviously, the teenager was Tian Shi Bowa. How could he not know what he should do? How could he not know that he should cherish what he had right now? Why hadn't he stayed at home working hard but come to the stream to play with the little white crane? Liu Wanyi decided to give him a good scolding when she was face to face with him, although she seldom reprimanded her students.

When she reached the riverside and rolled up her trousers, ready to cross the creek, she raised her head to take a look ahead and uttered a little cry of surprise. She was so startled she froze right there.

Crawling still, the teenager was holding a book, his head tilted back slightly as if reading something in the book.

Wanyi suddenly felt light on her feet. She rolled up her trousers and waded through the stream in a few strides.

The noise of her crossing the stream was loud, but the teenager didn't notice it at all, his eyes fixed on the thick book and lips moving and muttering something. Seeing that, Liu Wanyi walked softly, approaching the boy quietly from behind.

It was indeed Tian Shi Bowa with the *Modern Chinese Dictionary* in his hands. Teacher Liu's heart was overflowing with relief.

"*Xie huang* (crab roe), the ovary and digestive gland inside a female crab, shiny orange in colour, delicious, steamed buns stuffed with crab roe…"

"Bowa," Liu Wanyi called him sweetly and gently.

Tian Shi Bowa didn't hear her, still lost in the joy of reading, "*Xie meng* (Crab-eating mongoose)…"

Teacher Liu had to raise her voice and called him again, "Tian Shi Bowa!"

The boy turned round and saw his teacher standing there. He panicked and hurriedly put down the dictionary, and with his hands on the ground, he sprang up, glanced at her and said shyly, "Teacher Liu, sorry, I didn't hear you."

"I know. I tell you, I am very happy," said Teacher Liu, gently dusting the grass and sand off Tian Shi Bowa's short jacket. She looked around and said to him kindly, "It is a good place to read books, fresh air and a quiet environment. But why don't you study at home and come all the way here instead?"

"I didn't plan to come here. When I took my dictionary and flipped through it, I walked along and eventually found myself here. I don't know why."

"Ha… I understand. You are missing your little white crane, aren't you?"

"Heh…" Tian Shi Bowa smiled and didn't know how to answer.

"When you arrived here, the little white crane was playing in the stream, wasn't he?" asked Teacher Liu curiously.

"No, he was not here when I arrived. I didn't call him and I just sat on the beach and took out my dictionary to read." Bowa said to his teacher, "As I read, I felt a gust of wind blowing from above. I looked up and saw my little fellow fly down of his own accord and stalk around beside the stream airily."

Teacher Liu chuckled and recited a couplet:

> The boy and the animal live together harmoniously;
> The sound of reading aloud echoes with the flowing river.

"Bowa, even at such a young age you are spending your time like a celestial being! How admirable it is! Come and sit down. Let's have a chat."

Bowa was very thoughtful. He hurriedly ran to grab some clean dry grass from beside the stones, spread it on the ground and asked Teacher Liu to sit on it while he himself squatted down on the sand diagonally opposite where Wanyi sat. Teacher Liu smiled and sat on the grass, saying, "Tell me how you read the dictionary, will you?"

"How should I say this? Teacher Liu," Tian Shi Bowa looked straight at Wanyi, not knowing where to start.

"Think about it and tell me what you have already done," Teacher Liu tried to encourage Tian Shi Bowa to think positively.

"Well," Tian Shi Bowa said, "I started with syllables determined by the order of 23 initial consonants…"

"What? What did you say just now?" Teacher Liu stopped him, "Chinese initial consonants are arranged in the order of the English alphabet - 26 letters from A to Z. Why did you say 23? It's not correct. You have made a mistake at the very beginning!"

Tian Shi Bowa rolled his eyes a few times, thought for a while and said, "Teacher Liu, you are right. It goes from A to Z. I haven't learned English so I don't know that, but there are indeed 23 Chinese initial consonants."

"Wrong! Tian Shi Bowa, you are wrong." Teacher Liu said very firmly but her habit of checking things carefully developed over years made her pick up the dictionary, and turn to the page of syllables and initial consonants to count. Ah, it was 23! She could not believe her eyes and counted it again. Yes, 23 initial consonants indeed. Wanyi blushed at once. It was the first time she had made a fool of herself in front of her students. She had always remembered characters in the dictionary were arranged in the order of the 26-letter English alphabet since she had been educated from elementary school to college. In the past, she might have been careless or misinformed while today a student had corrected a teacher's mistake, and a year-one elementary student at that! How embarrassing!

"Teacher Liu, a lot of knowledge at the very beginning of the dictionary is beyond my understanding so I skipped the radical index system, the table of old and new character forms and some others." Tian Shi Bowa didn't notice his teacher's facial expression; he followed his thoughts and continued, "I started directly from the initial consonant A until I read to the last word 'zuo' on page 1689 of the *Modern Chinese Dictionary*."

"Oh, it's good for you to study selectively." The calm tone Tian Shi Bowa adopted when he talked about his method of studying concealed Liu Wanyi's embarrassment. Her thinking immediately turned to Tian Shi Bowa's narration, "You mean you now know all the characters listed in the index?"

"Yes, Teacher Liu, basically, but I still could not remember all the strokes of some characters and some strokes in the dictionary are not clear enough, such as the character *cuan*, referring to the word for burning wood to cook."

"Well, it is natural that you can't remember the strokes of some characters or that you can't totally understand their meaning. It is amazing that you have managed to read the whole dictionary in such a short time," continued Liu Wanyi. "Let me test how your study is going. Is there another way for us to read the character *zuo*?"

"*Cu*, Teacher Liu."

Liu Wanyi went on tentatively, "Do you know what *zuo* means?"

"It means a toast to hosts offered by guests. As in the expression *chou zuo*."

"What does this character mean when it is read *cu*?" asked Liu Wanyi.

"It equals *cu*, (another character meaning vinegar)." Tian Shi Bowa memorised it based on the dictionary definition. He asked Liu Wanyi curiously:

"*Cu*? Teacher Liu, is it the vinegar we have when we eat noodles?"

"Yep." Pondering for a while, Liu Wanyi asked, "On which page is the character *hong* which meant school in ancient times? How many strokes does it have?"

"Page 524, the last character on the left column." Tian Shi Bowa drew the character in the air and when he had finished, he said, "Teacher Liu, it has 16 strokes."

"How about *liu* (flow), the *liu* in the expression 'White Crane Stream is flowing', on which page does it appear in the dictionary? What does the expression *liu jin shuo shi* mean?"

Tian Shi Bowa turned it over, closed his eyes for a while and said, "Page 810, the last one on the right column. *Liu jin shuo shi* means heat intense enough to melt stone and metals, used to describe extremely hot weather. It comes from *Summoning the Soul of Chu Ci*, also pronounced *shuo shi liu jin*."

Liu Wanyi remembered the expression *liu jin shuo shi*. This character just came out when she saw the flowing water. She was not sure whether Tian Shi Bowa's answer was correct or not, so she took the dictionary and turned to page 810 to check. He was right. *Liu* was the last character on the right column! As for the definition, Tian Shi Bowa explained it very accurately according to the dictionary. Did he understand the notes given in parentheses as well? Liu Wanyi went on with her question, "Do you know what *Summoning the Soul in Chu Ci* is about?"

Tian Shi Bowa replied immediately, "No, I don't know, Teacher Liu. There is no explanation in the dictionary."

"Oh? How do you know there isn't?" Liu Wanyi turned to the page with the character *chu* and indeed there was no explanation about *Chu Ci*.

Liu Wanyi was secretly overjoyed. How could the boy be so excellent in such a short time? That was so amazing! How did he do it? Why could he do it? Was it real? Like Paoding in the fable of dissecting cattle, Liu Wanyi wanted to find the answer from a scientific perspective.

Before she had figured out how to ask him or how to know more about the boy, Tian Shi Bowa asked her a question first, "Teacher Liu, there is something I cannot understand. You know, when I read a character out as I look at it, I can memorise it without any problem, but if I do not read the character out loud, I cannot recall it the next day even though I looked at it at the time and felt I had already memorised it."

"Well, in your case, I remember an educator once did some research saying it is a gift of memorising by reading aloud, that is to say, some people are born with this outstanding skill while some are not born with it and have to acquire this ability through hard practice in the future," explained Teacher Liu seriously. "It is said that a person blessed with this special gift peaks before the age of 21 and after that this skill gradually fades. Bowa, you are very motivated and I am very happy for you. But the acquisition of knowledge is a process, the deeper you go into it, the more difficult it is and the harder it feels. Can you cherish and persist in it for a long time?"

"Yes, I can, Teacher Liu," said Tian Shi Bowa firmly. Meanwhile he told Wanyi about some of his feelings, which had made him very confused. He said, "When I am doing maths questions, reciting a formula, reading the dictionary or copying something down from the dictionary, I can only concentrate on it for an hour or at most two hours. Then I allow my thoughts to wander. I don't want it to happen and tell myself that I should study hard to catch up with the others, but I still become absent-minded. As a result, even if I try to read it out loud, I forget some of it the next day. When this happens, I slap my face and pinch my arms, but it doesn't work. My memory doesn't come back until the next day after I have played with my classmates for a while. Teacher Liu, I know it is playfulness in my body that has been causing trouble. Can you give me some suggestions on how to overcome this shortcoming?"

While Liu Wanyi listened to him attentively, she was lost in thought. Had she led her student into a blind alley of studying mechanically?

19

OUTDOOR ACTIVITIES

The end of the semester was around the corner, but Huang Xiaoqiu had not made up her mind whether she should send Tian Shi Bowa a backpack or not. No, it was not 'send'; it should be 'give'. Why? Because they had had a bet on the boat that if Tian Shi Bowa could call the little white crane back to him from the sky, she would forfeit a backpack for this. The result was she had lost. A bet was a bet. She was a good loser and would give the backpack to Bowa. Also, she was definitely wrong to have thrown Bowa's dictionary into the water, for which she had been harshly scolded by Teacher Liu. Yes, it was indeed her fault. Huang Xiaoqiu at that time knew she was wrong. Why did she behave so arrogantly and treat others so contemptuously? She ought to make an apology to Bowa, which was also what Teacher Liu wanted her to do. But how could she afford to lose face like this? Making an apology to Silly Tian? All her classmates would definitely laugh until their noses ran. A backpack? She didn't care about a backpack at all. Even if she only had one herself, she was willing to give it up, whereas in fact she had a few at home. But she cared about face. If she gave one to Bowa, it would be such a shame. She hesitated; she was confused. Bothered by this feeling, Huang Xiaoqiu could not concentrate on anything, whether reading, reciting or doing her assignments. In the final assessment test, her maths score dropped by five places and her Chinese score turned out to be below average!

Liu Wanyi had a good eye for this emotional instability in the process of growing up. She thought of the day when Tian Shi Bowa had confided to her all his worries beside the White Crane Stream and then something clicked for her. She wrote in her diary:

> *Maria Montessori described her findings in the educational process in her book Secrets of Childhood. She said, "Activity is the basic element of intelligence development. The bridge between the human mind and the outside world is built through physical activities, which is the sole access to building relationships between a person and the outside world. People get in touch with the environment through it, which not only helps people express themselves but also helps human beings develop their consciousness."*
>
> *Yes, development or improvement of students' consciousness, emotions and thoughts through activities gradually helps them get to know the outside world, teams and themselves so that they grow up naturally. As for the emotional worries and confusion common to both Bowa and Huang Xiaoqiu, there are some educational and cognitive reasons, and some physiological ones as well and proper group activities in nature might be one of the best ways to solve their problems.*

On Thursday afternoon after school, Xiao Jianbo ran to Tian Shi Bowa's home and happened to run across him reading the *Modern Chinese Dictionary*.

"Bowa, good news for you. Guess what?" Xiao Jianbo wagged his big head, joyfully keeping Bowa in suspense.

"How should I know what the good news is?"

"Guess, it's about our school."

"About our school?" Bowa tilted his head and thought about it, "School, news, it must have something to do with us students. I think it is about practicing folk dancing, am I right?"

"Wrong! Bowa, we are going to have an outdoor activity!" said Xiao Jianbo very proudly. "When school was over today, Teacher Liu asked me to stay for a while. Why me? Because my family is close to Bandengyan. Teacher

Liu asked me whether Bangdengyan is steep or not; if we climb it in groups, how much will it take? She told me we are going to have a group activity this coming Saturday. An award ceremony will be held at the foot of the mountain. We will be divided into small groups and we will bring cooking pots, bowls and chopsticks, and some vegetables, rice and corn flour. A picnic!"

"A picnic? How wonderful! But I don't know how to cook."

"I can teach you, Bowa."

"You're bluffing! Jianbo, you don't even know how to cook yourself."

"Hey, I have seen my mother do it."

"Well. If so, I have seen my mother do it too. Can I teach you?" Tian Shi Bowa said seriously, "We may not be in the same group. I need to think about it."

When Xiao Jianbo ran to tell Huang Xiaoqiu the news, she pulled a long face, squinted and said, "Xiao Jianbo, you are flattering me, aren't you? Is there nobody else except you who can tell me the news? Don't you love to tell the teacher on me? I remember that."

"Hey, Xiaoqiu, you are still holding a grudge against me? It was quite a long time ago!"

After Xiao Jianbo left, Huang Xiaoqiu snorted, "Mountain climbing competition? What's to be afraid of? I am sure to win."

Tian Shi Bowa was somewhat anxious after he got the news from Xiao Jianbo. He worried about being laughed at for not knowing how to cook so he didn't go to the White Crane Stream to read books but stayed at home waiting for his mother. When his mother went back to cook, he followed her like his mother's tail, helping her and at the same time familiarising himself with how to cook. Li Runlan said, "A boy won't achieve greatness if he learns girls' stuff. Bowa, why do you want to learn how to cook? It is much better for you to improve your academic performance and get admitted to college. It's not a big deal that your class will have a picnic the day after tomorrow. Your father will be back home tomorrow from Guizhou to Xiaonanhai for the nectar source. He could help you with the picnic food."

"Mum, your thinking is very outmoded. The reason why Teacher Liu is arranging outdoor activity for us is to give us the chance to think and do things independently, to learn from each other and learn to cooperate. In this way, our ability to integrate will be improved and we won't be at a loss when encountering difficulties."

The outdoor activity organised by Liu Wanyi was to be held on Saturday morning.

The mountain where Bandengyan is located is in the middle of the Bamian Mountains. It was named Bandengyan by local villagers. As one climbs along the Xiaonanhai, the mountain road winds north and south, and the farther one climbs, the steeper it is. When one gets close to the top of the mountain, there is a section of road that is as smooth as a long bench, on both sides of which however are bottomless cliffs.

There is a small hill, lower than Bandengyan, named Shuangyan Hill which is relatively flat. The two roads, although used by only a few people, wind straight to the summit, some sections flourishing with quite a lot of moss, shrubs and grass. For safety's sake, Teacher Liu finally chose Shuangyan Hill as the place for the mountain climbing competition.

A few frail students were left at the foot of the mountain. Two students were selected in advance to climb the hill and raise two flags on the top, red and yellow.

By casting lots, mountain climbers were divided into two groups with 20 members or so in each group. Tian Shi Bowa was the captain of the first group and Xiao Jianbo captained the second group.

Teacher Liu cheered her students up before the competition, "Each group must choose one road to climb the hill and the person who climbs to the top and gets the red flag first will be the winner of the singles and the team which arrives first and gets the yellow flag will be the team winner. All champions will get a certificate with a school seal and for team champions, all team members' names will be written on the certificate, and every team member will have one. They will be issued once you have finished next week."

Wow! Everyone had a chance to stand out. Teacher Liu's words lit the passion of these climbers, all rolling up their sleeves ready to go. Some students joked, "It's OK to lose as well; the worst is still the second place anyway."

"Ha...there is no such thing as runner-up or second runner-up," said Teacher Liu. "After the competition, we will have a picnic together beside the Bandeng Stream at the foot of Bandengyan. The losing team will pay for it by taking care of collecting dry wood and grass for the winning team."

Raising his head high, Xiao Jianbo said, "It's not worthwhile! Too much for the losing team. Losing a game itself is depressing enough while the losing side has to prepare firewood for the winning one! Too much!"

"Xiao Jianbo, you are smart this time to know you are going to lose," said Huang Xiaoqiu ambitiously. "Look at your round body! Walking for you is like rolling. Stop thinking about climbing the mountain! The mountain will climb you instead! You were born to collect firewood for us."

"Hey, Xiaoqiu, your tongue does have a nasty sting! Your words are hurtful!" Xiao Jianbo was fat and also he didn't have any experience of competing in a mountain climbing game. He didn't have enough confidence.

"Honestly, it is not a bad thing to lose the game," said Tian Shi Bowa as he looked at them sincerely. "It seems the losing team gets punished, but in fact it is a good chance to learn how to adjust one's mentality and exercise one's body during the punishment."

"Tian Shi Bowa, you are such a goody-goody! Come first, if you can!" Huang Xiaoqiu ended up in Tian Shi Bowa's group after drawing lots and of course she was not convinced about that. She said to herself, "Be my team leader? How long have you been in this school?"

Huang Xiaoqiu had prepared for this mountain climbing. She knew climbing the mountain would mean a steep ascent, so high-heeled shoes would help her climb faster. She therefore wore a pair of sturdy high-heeled shoes her father had bought her in the town. Although she was a girl, she had an excellent physique. Since she was a child, she had chopped firewood and cut grass like boys and was never considered to be inferior to others. She had a pair of high-heeled shoes and there was nothing for her to be afraid of. She planned to be the first to climb to the top and be the champion. Teacher Liu once educated her to learn to help others by doing things. OK, when Tian Shi Bowa could not hold on, she could give him her hand and when they reached the top, she could jeer at him as much as she wanted, "Well, aren't you the team leader? Why did you fall behind me? Why weren't you the champion?"

When the two teams lined up on their respective roads, Liu Wanyi whistled and all the climbers rushed off like tigers out of a cage. Why were they running so fast? It was not a 60-metre race but a mountain-climbing competition. Sure enough, both teams, without exception, were tired out within a minute, some holding onto tree branches, some grabbing grass, some leaning on stones and some crawling like dogs. Teacher Liu burst out laughing and sat down in the meadow. But the good thing was that no one stopped, they all tried to adjust their breath and pace, waiting for the best time to speed up again when they felt refreshed. During this kind of recess, those in good physical condition and with prior experience gradually climbed ahead of the others. Huang Xiaoqiu in Tian Shi Bowa's team was the fastest.

Huang Xiaoqiu didn't try her best at the beginning; she just followed the others climbing. When the other climbers panted, walked and stopped to take a rest halfway, she speeded up and ran proudly to take first place. Tian Shi Bowa was at the very end of the climbing team at first. When he saw Xiao Jianbo's team fall behind his, he was very satisfied with Huang Xiaoqiu who was far ahead. He felt more strength from under his feet, climbed bravely and followed close behind Huang Xiaoqiu.

Either Huang Xiaoqiu's heart was bursting with energy or she had a good constitution, or perhaps both. She was also very smart, climbing forward without looking back. She grabbed the grass, or got some help by holding onto some tree branches so that her high-heeled shoes could step firmly on the solid soil and stones, one step after another, very fast. The climber who was closest to her was more than eight metres away.

The top of Shuangyan Hill was getting closer and closer. The overall climbing speed of the two teams was almost the same, with only a few team members left behind. Xiao Jianbo was in the first place in his team but four team members in Tian Shi Bowa's team were leading far ahead. Tian Shi Bowa knew that only by helping the team members who had been left far behind to catch up with those who were in the middle, could their team possibly take the lead as a group. He slowed down, waited in any low-lying rocky places that required more effort to pass, and stretched out his hand to assist those members who came last. In this way, those who were left far behind followed up quickly and joined those who were in the middle. The whole team had a good lead over Xiao Jianbo's team.

"Victory is in the bag. If I am not the champion, who is?" Huang Xiaoqiu was full of ambition, leading all the way. She was only about 20 metres away from the mountain top but it was this 'but' that made Huang Xiaoqiu's championship dream slip away.

The road leading to the top of the mountain however was covered with green grass. Huang Xiaoqiu's high-heeled shoes could not step firmly on the soil or stones under the grass. Whenever she put her feet on the grass, she slid down and when she stepped forward again, she slid down again. She thought of making use of tree branches but it happened there were no small trees on this part of the small path. A lot of climbers climbed past her. Huang Xiaoqiu was very anxious. On all fours, she tried her best to climb up part of the way but unfortunately she slipped a long way down when she failed to find her footing. Tian Shi Bowa, who was bringing up the rear, was anxious too when he saw what had happened to Huang Xiaoqiu. He hurriedly climbed in front of her and grabbed her hand to drag her upward as he tried to hold onto the grass with the other hand. Then he held her high-heeled shoes steady with his hands to enable her to move upward a few steps and when Huang Xiaoqiu had maintained her balance, he rushed in front of her again, turned and stretched out his hand for her. They climbed to the top at last after a few attempts.

They were still happy to climb to the mountain top but happiness is not victory. As they sweated and stopped to take a look, Xiao Jianbo's team had already bagged two wins: the individual and team championships.

During the picnic, Huang Xiaoqiu sat under a tree sulking, her mouth pouting. Xiao Jianbo walked over and said, "Huang Xiaoqiu, there's no shame in losing. It's your turn to find us some dry wood."

"To hell with your dry wood! If you can, let's do it again."

"You have already lost the competition. When a duck is cooked in the pot, only its beak is hard," answered Xiao Jianbo, who had won the championship, in a very hurtful tone.

"Huh! If it had not been for this pair of high-heeled shoes, how could I have lost?" Huang Xiaoqiu was getting angrier as she talked. She took off her shoes, stood up, raised her hand high and threw the shoes far into the wild grass. "Am I to blame? Am I? It's all these damned shoes' fault!"

Tian Shi Bowa and a few of his other team members brought some dry wood they had found to Xiao Jianbo's team. He and his team members said, "A bet is a bet. We found a large stretch of woods at the foot of Bandengyan. There should be a lot of dry wood there. We will get some more."

Xiao Jianbo chuckled and said, "Thank you guys for the dry wood. We, as the winning team, are generous too. We are willing to give you enough stream water."

A lot of team members laughed. Who needed water? They were having a picnic beside the Bandeng Stream from which water was to hand all the time.

They began preparing the picnic, laughing, talking, fetching water, washing vegetables and making a fire to cook. Teacher Liu Wanyi didn't interfere or participate, leaving everyone to make full use of their skills.

To get dry wood, Tian Shi Bowa went deep into the woods. As he came out with a bundle in his arms, he suddenly heard someone calling "Help! Is anyone here?" Sensing something strange, he stopped to listen but heard nothing. As he started walking again, he seemed to hear a weak call again, "Is anyone here?" He squatted down for quite a while but the sound disappeared. He slapped his ears a few times, "You silly boy! You must have been watching too many TV series!"

As they were having their picnic, the sound Tian Shi Bowa had heard in the woods came to his ears from time to time. He felt it was a bit strange and began to set his heart on it. When the picnic was about to end, he sneaked into the woods quietly and quickly, took a few turns nearby and when he was ready to walk back, a faint voice reached his ears, "Help!"

It was a weak call for help! But nothing could be heard later except this one. The voice was a little hoarse and he felt it was that of an old man who was trying his best to utter such a faint and hoarse cry. It was real and Bowa trusted his feelings. Bowa didn't know he had developed a super-strong listening ability because he could not speak when he was a child. Within a certain range, he could hear some minute sounds and distinguish their features, which other people could not do. But what if what he had just heard today was not real but an auditory hallucination?

He stood there, turning his ear in the direction of the sound, and calmed down to listen to it carefully but still there was no sound at all.

He wanted to go deeper into the woods but Teacher Liu's whistle came and all the students needed to gather together.

20
LOOKING FOR A WEAK SIGNAL FOR HELP

Tian Shi Bowa sat under the roof. When he felt tired after reading aloud for a while, he began to read silently the explanations of expressions in the dictionary. In the past, he could not memorise what he had read in silence but as his memory grew, the meaning of many expressions he had come across in his silent reading gradually lodged in his mind.

The rosy glow of sunset shone brightly on Bowa and the air was still scorching. He grabbed the hem of his sweatshirt, ready to wipe the sweat from his face as his father Tian Fashui was stepping into the courtyard, as his mother had told him to yesterday. Tian Shi Bowa took a look at his father and greeted him with a "Dad".

Generally speaking, when the youngest son saw his father come back home from a long journey, he would either look forward to some gifts from his father or run to him for some cuddles or help his father carry his luggage into the house. Tian Shi Bowa however didn't. What first went through his mind was a kind of surprise instead. "Yes, if the faint call for help at the foot of Bandengyan was real, is it the best time for my father to come back home?"

Some outsiders might have giggled if they knew this. Wasn't he either looking for trouble or overreacting? He was just a boy after all! They were right in a sense. Perhaps for some other outsiders, they would say Bowa was indeed looking for trouble and was indeed overreacting. But was it wrong for him to be so sensitive and to look for trouble like this?

Well, we don't need to pass judgement on whether it's a good thing or not. Let's try and find out what Bowa wanted to do.

"Dad," Bowa greeted him again.

His father had already entered the courtyard. He took a close look at his son who could not tear himself away from the book in his hand, looking so healthy with a ruddy complexion. He felt greatly relieved and was very satisfied too, although his reply to his son was a seemingly impatient "what?"

Hearing their voices, Li Runlan came out of the room to meet Tian Fashui, "You are back?"

"Emm." As simple as his reply sounded, it delivered his assuredness and satisfaction with his wife.

Li Runlan took the bag from her husband's shoulder and the straw hat from his head, entering the house behind her husband. Bowa put the dictionary down on the bench and walked into the living room.

Li Runlan went to brew the tea the moment she put down the luggage while Tian Fashui greeted his mother sitting in the living room. Then he sat down in the wooden chair, took the tea bowl his wife handed to him and swallowed a few big mouthfuls.

He breathed out a long sigh of relief and leaned back in the chair.

"Dad." The present Tian Shi Bowa was different from the one who didn't go to school in the past. Gone was the fear he used to have and likewise the anxiety and embarrassment when he was unable to express himself. Looking at his father, he took the opportunity to say to him, "Dad, you are back just in time."

"Ha… Bowa, it's very interesting. What do you mean by saying I am back just in time?" Tian Fashui asked his son with a smile. Li Runlan was also attracted by Bowa's words and stopped her feet to listen what would follow next.

"I heard a sound," Bowa said very seriously, "a sound of someone calling for help."

"What? Bowa, don't scare me, will you?" Tian Fashui sat up straight, asking with nervousness and surprise, "Calling for help? Who was calling for help?"

"Today, Teacher Liu took us to have a picnic at the foot of Bandengyan…" Bowa recalled what he had found in the woods to his father.

"Oh, child's play." Tian Fashui felt at ease, "You must have watched too much TV, ringing in your ears."

"Ringing in my ears? How could a child have that?" The hearts of mother and son were always linked together, as were their thoughts and feelings. Li Runlan believed in Bowa's hearing but she wanted to make things clear. She cut in and asked, "Bowa, did someone hear it and tell you this or did you hear it yourself?"

"I heard it myself, more than once. But later it disappeared."

"If someone did call for help, he must have fainted since at first his voice was weak and then there was no sound at all from him."

"Nonsense! Did you see that person black out with your own eyes? You sound like you're telling a story," Tian Fashui said carelessly. "And even if someone did have an accident and pass out, what's that to you anyway!"

"Fashui, life matters. You are a man past middle age and you can't talk like this." Tian Shi Bowa's grandma interrupted.

Tian Fashui shut his mouth.

"I want to go and check in the woods," Tian Shi Bowa said, as if telling all the elders in the house or saying this to himself. "Think about it, suppose that person were my grandpa, could I find peace in my heart? Would I not choose to go and check on that?"

"The point is that person is not your grandpa," continued Tian Fashui, taking up the conversation. "Moreover, it is hard to find anything in the dark. Let's wait until tomorrow."

"It's getting dark. If that person did have an accident, the chances of someone going and saving him are zero. He might die tonight. I agree with Bowa. We should go and have a look," said Li Runlan after putting herself in that person's position. "What if someone did have an accident? Such as falling down from Bandengyan? Fashui, do you think…"

"Such as? 'Such as' is not a fact. I have no such 'do I think'. Such as I came all the way back home and my stomach is empty, but you haven't even said you are going to cook something for me."

Tian Fashui stopped his wife and muttered, "Even if someone fell off the cliff, what's that got to do with us? Is it your uncle or your uncle-in-law? You are all looking for trouble."

"Dad, Teacher Liu and we are not relatives either but she helped me go to school and brought me to have my vocal cords cured. Can we say she was looking for trouble?"

Tian Fashui leaned his body forward, staring at his son in a daze, eyes bulging, as if he had never seen him before.

Li Runlan was shocked. How dare her son ask his father questions like this? She looked at her husband's facial expression, worrying that he might do something to her son out of anger. She hurriedly walked over to fill his tea bowl.

There was a few minutes' silence. Tian Fashui closed his eyes and thought for a while. When he opened his eyes, he looked apparently calm. He rose from his chair, walked over to his son, stroked his ears and shoulders, squatted down and suddenly took his son in his arms. He said very emotionally, "Bowa, my good son. Even though you are so young, you have posed a very good question which has woken me up and enlightened me!"

"Fashui, monks in the temple say saving one life is better than building a pagoda." Bowa's grandma said, "Bowa wants you to go and check it with him. Do you think…?"

"OK, Grandma, I will go. I promise." Tian Fashui at this time was very decisive, "Bowa, bring a torch with you. Let's go."

"Wait, I want to go with you too. Perhaps I can help a little," said Li Runlan.

"You want to go with us?" Tian Fashui thought for a while and said, "All right. Bring a hatchet and two strong ropes in case we need them."

As they were about to leave, Bowa's grandma thought of something and said to them hurriedly, "I'll go and fetch some wheat flour buns steamed at noon for you and a mineral-water bottle of cold tea so that you can fill your stomach on the road."

The woods at the foot of Bandengyan were part of the ancient forests of Bamian Mountain. Not very far from the entrance, there was no path at all, towering trees, flourishing shrubs and tangled vines and thorns; total chaos. Tian Fashui made certain of the place where Bowa had heard the call for help. He led the way by cutting off errant branches and thorny vines with his hatchet while mother and son followed behind. It was getting darker and gradually everything inside the woods was barely visible. Li Runlan switched on the torch for Tian Fashui walking ahead and she shouted a few times after walking for some distance, "Is anyone here? Is anyone in the woods?" Unfortunately there was no answer. No matter whether there was such a person or whether they could find him or not, they didn't show any sign of complaint or any tendency to blame Bowa at all. What they wanted was to give Bowa an explanation or an answer. The three of them shared a common goal, a very definite one although they didn't have a discussion or an agreement, that is, to continue searching until they reached the foot of Bandengyan.

It was indeed a blessing in disguise. As they felt their way and arrived at the foot of Bandengyan, the strong beam of Li Runlan's torch was fixed on a human body a few steps away.

It was indeed a sudden surprise, although they had already imagined that before. Their eyes all focused on that human body for quite a while, to calm themselves down or to make sure it was really a human body. Perhaps both. Although they were prepared for that, they were still shocked when they cautiously walked to one side of that body.

The torch shone on that body for a while but there was no response at all. When they came closer, they found a man battered to a pulp, black and blue all over. Obviously he must have fallen off Bandengyan. A streak was visible from the top down to the foot of the cliff when the torch was shone at an angle on the side of the sandy cliff. It was a man of about sixty years old, with a thin face lined with wrinkles but still looking strong and healthy. In front of his head lay a large denim backpack. The blue-black jeans on his body and the canvas hiking shoes on his feet had both been torn to shreds by tree branches and stones. One of his calves was bent into a V shape, a fracture apparently. One of his arms was bare and had a deep cut scraped by something unknown; a blood clot had formed a small island around the wound.

Li Runlan and Bowa both held their breath and didn't dare to move while Tian Fashui who was well travelled and had seen the world took the torch from his wife's hand and shone it on the face of the injured man. He put two fingers under his nose to check for a while and said, "He is still alive."

"Hello, Hey, Mister, can you speak?" In White Crane Village, people usually greet strangers as mister, not sir or boss. Seeing there was no response, Li Runlan felt the man's neck with her hands and said to Tian

Fashui, "His body is still warm and there is hope. Bowa, bring me the bottle. It's better to feed him a few mouthfuls of tea."

"Here you are," replied Bowa as he unscrewed the bottle cap and handed the bottle to his mother. He then took the torch from his father to provide light for his mother.

Tian Fashui straightened the man's head, pinched his cheeks and squeezed his mouth open while Li Runlan immediately fed the tea from the bottle into the man's mouth; he swallowed it like a knee-jerk reaction of his body. Tian Fashui gently patted his face and called out, "Hey, wake up! Say something, can you speak?"

It was strange that the injured man just could not open his eyes and say anything, although he did drink some tea. Li Runlan asked her husband, "He has lost consciousness. What should we do?"

"Take him to the hospital in town," answered Tian Fashui decisively. He then turned to Bowa, "Bowa, hold the torch for me, I need to cut two strong pieces of bamboo and find a few millettia to make a stretcher with the rope we have brought with us."

21
GOOD DEEDS LAST

Many days passed. The bet on Huang Xiaoqiu's mind was becoming a burden and she at last decided to put an end to it. One afternoon, she thought Tian Shi Bowa might be reading books under the Chinese oak tree beside the White Crane Stream. She walked there, holding a backpack in her hand.

Under the Chinese oak tree was mostly fine sand washed clean by water. Tian Shi Bowa lay on his stomach, two bare feet rising and falling towards his bottom in turn like a seesaw, head leaning back, eyes fixed on the dictionary in his hand, reading word by word excitedly.

"Hey! Wagging your head like this while reading? It seems we are going to have a number-one scholar soon," said Huang Xiaoqiu loudly behind him.

Tian Shi Bowa turned over and sat up immediately, "You scared me to death! Huang Xiaoqiu, you scared the hell out of me and I almost had my heart in my mouth."

"Well… very talented. No wonder Teacher Liu always gives you special treatment." After a holiday, Huang Xiaoqiu's jealousy had softened somewhat but she was still fond of making sarcastic remarks, "That's a bit of an exaggeration! How could a girl's voice scare the hell out of you? Are you still a man?"

Bowa wanted to ignore her because of her interference with his study. He stood up and found some black stones to play with. He struck them against each other, which created bright sparks occasionally. Huang Xiaoqiu was attracted by it and said, "Hey, stones can make fire! What's the use of it?"

"What's the use of it?" replied Tian Shi Bowa a bit disdainfully. "Suppose you need to make a fire in a special situation when you are out, it will help ignite firewood and dry grass."

Huang Xiaoqiu giggled, "We have lighters and matches. Who needs those ancient methods you just mentioned?"

"I'm not talking with you any more," said Bowa, wanting to get rid of her. "What did you come here for instead of staying at home doing your homework?"

"What for? To pay my debt." Huang Xiaoqiu took the backpack off her shoulders, threw it to Bowa and said, "A bet is a bet. This is your backpack now."

Holding the backpack in both hands, Tian Shi Bowa stared at her and said, "You said it without thinking at the time. It is not a real bet. How could I accept it?"

"Take it! Do you think I am unwilling to lose the bet? I have extra ones, two more at home." Huang Xiaoqiu curled her lips and said, "You know, I did throw your dictionary into the water anyway. I should pay for it."

"I have already dried it out and it's still usable now," said Tian Shi Bowa, patting the dictionary. "I can't accept your backpack. There's no reason to at all. Don't make me feel so uncomfortable, will you?"

"Hey, Bowa, stop being so aloof! Just like it says in books, your pride will trap me in unrighteousness and make me feel uncomfortable as well. A bet is a bet and I can't be a deadbeat. Otherwise, our classmates at school are sure to laugh at me when they find out about it," said Huang Xiaoqiu. "It will be more disgraceful if I don't keep my word. Who wants to do that?"

"I am not keeping myself aloof. I also accept things when I am in difficulty, but it depends on whether it is given to me sincerely."

"You mean I am not sincere?"

"Ask yourself, wasn't it in a fit of pique that you took a bet with me on this? You won't be happy if I accept your backpack and neither will I. Why bother then?" said Tian Shi Bowa. "What's more, my drawstring bag is good. I don't believe books put inside will become weeds when taken out."

"Well, I have to admit I am not sincere as you just said," said Huang

Xiaoqiu, "but can you accept it when I put things right and give it to you with all my heart?"

"Well, we'll come back to this later," replied Bowa.

After Huang Xiaoqiu left, Tian Shi Bowa got down to reciting explanations of some expressions in the dictionary. When the sun began to go down, he waded through the stream and walked home. Before climbing up the steps leading to his house, loud noises and laughter came to his ears from the courtyard. Curious as a child would be, he quickened his step and walked up the stone steps along the edge of the yard. Ah, quite a lot of strangers inside!

The square table in the living room had been moved out into the yard, around which were high stools all taken by many people - Grandma, his father, and Grandpa Li, the chubby village director. He recognised them all except the other three. Who were they?

"Come over here, Bowa, come on," said Tian Fashui when he saw Bowa, waving him to the table. He gestured toward an aged guest sitting at the table, "This is Uncle Qu."

Very politely, Bowa greeted him with "Hello, Uncle Qu."

The gray-haired Uncle Qu was about sixty years old. His square face looked a little pale. He moved his body a bit and the two young men standing beside him hurriedly supported him by the arm and helped him stand up on his crutches. He looked at Bowa kindly, "You are Bowa, aren't you? Good, nice to meet you, Bowa."

Grandma stood up at once when she saw Uncle Qu standing up with the crutches under his arms, "Uncle Qu, come and sit down. You are his elder and also your legs haven't totally recovered. Come and sit down."

Uncle Qu smiled and said, "Sister, I should stand up when I talk. If it hadn't been for your son and daughter-in-law who risked their lives to save me, how could I have had the chance to stand here?"

"Don't mention it! They were supposed to do that. Come and sit down, please," said Grandma, gesturing Uncle Qu to invite him to sit down.

"This is Grandpa Li. You should know him. Uncle Qu was transferred to a big hospital later. Today he went to the town hospital to look for us and Grandpa Li brought them here. Otherwise, they couldn't have found the way," said Tian Fashui, pointing to the village director. He then pointed at the two young men, "The two elder brothers have come from the city to take care of Uncle Qu. You should learn from them and work hard."

"Hello, brothers," greeted Bowa, smiling at the two young men.

Listening to the adults' conversation, Bowa gradually came to understand what had happened.

Uncle Qu was the boss of a large company in the city. For his extraordinary achievements, he was awarded an honorary title as the Deputy Director of the Standing Committee of the District People's Congress. His hobby was travelling alone. After he was 60 years old, he left the company to his children while he himself decided to travel in the mountainous area on the border between Chongqing and Qianjiang. He didn't expect that he would fall off the cliff at Bandengyan in the Bamian Mountains in Qianjiang.

"Grandma Tian, I am very grateful to your family for saving my life," said Boss Qu earnestly. "If it had not been for your son and daughter-in-law, I would have been a bag of bones by now."

"Brother Qu, you are blessed," said Li Runlan who happened to hear this when she went out of the room holding the tea pot. She continued as she filled their tea bowls, "Brother Qu, I should say you are indeed very lucky. You should thank Bowa, honestly speaking."

"Thank Bowa?" Boss Qu said with confusion, "Do you mean Bowa went out with you two in the dead of the night to save my life?

"More than that! It was not he who followed us but we who followed him up the mountain to save you."

Li Runlan told the whole story of how Bowa had heard the faint calling when he was having a picnic, how he had asked Tian Fashui repeatedly to check it out and how he had helped his parents take Boss Qu to the hospital.

Before Li Runlan had finished her words, Boss Qu was already tearful as he looked at Tian Shi Bowa's innocent face.

22

A TURNING POINT IN HER TEACHING

In the new semester, White Crane Village elementary school was to have a new female teacher.

Liu Wanyi got the news in Chongqing at the end of the summer vacation. She was very happy. A person should try their utmost but it would have been kidding herself to struggle to keep up appearances with people saying that Teacher Liu Wanyi was so great that she taught so well in the school all by herself which, in her opinion however would definitely harm young students and was also a self-deception in a sense. What if teachers were robots who never got tired and didn't need rest? Although there were not so many students at the school, it was almost impossible for one teacher to teach well since there were students of different levels. Liu Wanyi was not a woman who wanted to make a reputation for herself. At the end of the last semester before the vacation, she was interviewed by newspaper reporters who praised her for not only taking care of the whole school, but also for discovering a young genius. Their leaders said they would make it into a good report. She smiled and said, "They are making up stories. Why do you take it seriously?"

On the bus back to the village school, she felt a bit relieved.

The village school enrolled six first-year students this semester, which meant there were three different levels at school: first-year, fourth-year and sixth-year. Tian Shi Bowa came to school in April and there was only one semester left until the summer vacation in July. They wondered whether to put him into the fourth year or the sixth year? If he were to move on step by step, he should have begun year two. But there was no year two. He had no choice but to follow up with the fourth year. Could he handle it? Liu Wanyi couldn't help but laugh out loud as she walked along the mountain road thinking about this. As for Bowa it was not a question of whether he could handle it or not but whether or not he would be satisfied. What about putting him into the sixth year? Considering his age, it was feasible. He was about 11 years old and when he turned 12 the next year, that was the proper time for him to begin middle school. But he needed a careful study plan. He hadn't attended school for long, after all, and what if he could not keep up with his studies? That would be much more difficult to make up if he didn't make a good start.

Or there might be another possibility. Liu Wanyi stopped when she thought of this. She herself was shocked by this bold idea. Would it be too fast and too soon? What was she thinking just now? She was wondering that if Tian Shi Bowa was indeed a born genius, it might be OK for him to learn some middle-school subjects in advance one semester later, such as physics and English.

That would give him one and a half years to finish all the sixth-year subjects and begin middle school in advance. Tian Shi Bowa, could you do that?

For the new semester assessment test, two teachers had a discussion. They finally agreed maths would be done according to the requirement of the school district while Chinese would consist of essay writing, the same topic for fourth and sixth-year students.

A lot of students did well in maths. Huang Xiaoqiu, Xiao Jianbo and Tian Shi Bowa all took the third-year test. Huang Xiaoqiu lost her leading place in the class and was below the average this time, Xiao Jianbo took second place. Who won the first place? It was Tian Shi Bowa!

Although Teacher Liu was a bit mentally prepared for the result that Tian Shi Bowa would probably enter the top ten in the class, she hadn't expected he could take the first place!

The essay topic was 'Early Morning', with an 800-word requirement. It was a topic providing students with plenty of freedom to write anything they wanted, which gave them quite a lot of scope for imagination and to choose any style they liked. They could write an exposition, a narration, an argumentation or even a poem, each of them having the opportunity to fully demonstrate their wit and imagination.

The two teachers, however, were both very disappointed with the results. The quality of students' compositions was generally poor. In terms of content, most of the compositions were narrative journals; some were like lectures given by critics or scientists. No one wrote a poem. The common problem was inadequate knowledge accumulation, poor imagination and little connection with real life. Some students' compositions were even full of spelling errors!

What disappointed Liu Wanyi most was Tian Shi Bowa. Obviously he didn't know how to write an essay. He did write a lot of words but there was no content at all, all empty expressions and idioms he had copied and pasted after racking his brains, rather far-fetched and incoherent, to be frank. Liu Wanyi scolded Tian Shi Bowa for this.

Back home, Bowa covered his head with the quilt and wailed for quite a long time. When he finally stopped, he went out of his home, sat by the White Crane Stream, and slapped himself twice on the face in an attempt to calm down and figure out what the problem was but he didn't manage to work it out until it got dark.

"Where does the problem lie?" Like Tian Shi Bowa, Teacher Liu was thinking about the same question at the same time. She read Tian Shi Bowa's composition again and found it was rich in idioms and descriptive adjectives but most of them were used in the wrong places and were incoherent too. Liu Wanyi felt Bowa's head was like a huge warehouse filled with all kinds of goods which required a perfect and intelligent distribution mechanism to coordinate a reasonable and harmonious output. Tian Shi Bowa hadn't established such an intelligent system in his mind yet.

The next morning, Tian Shi Bowa went to school very early as usual. Liu Wanyi asked him to come into her office.

"Bowa, what came into your mind when you began to write 'Early Morning'?"

"At first, I didn't know how to start. After I picked up my pen, so many words and expressions in the dictionary floated before my eyes again and again," recalled Tian Shi Bowa. "Since it required 800 characters, I wrote down everything that I felt was suitable for this composition and, as a result, it has exceeded the character limit."

"You are indeed making a forced marriage! Tian Shi Bowa, do you know what a forced marriage is? You don't know, do you? It is a story from ancient times, concerning a girl who was so eager to get married for some special reason that she sent matchmakers out on the street at random to find a husband for her." Liu Wanyi pointed at Tian Shi Bowa's composition and said, "The expressions you used here are just like a man found casually on the street to meet the bride, regardless of whether he was suitable or not, making up the numbers, to be exact. Tell me, do you understand the meaning of those expressions you have used?"

"I could memorise the explanations of those expressions but I could not fully understand the connection between expressions and between expressions and sentences."

Right! That was the problem, gulping down knowledge without digesting it and force-feeding ducks to speed up their growth. After Tian Shi Bowa had gone back to the classroom, Liu Wanyi thought about it carefully. Many years ago, some universities enrolled a group of teen college students, all young geniuses. They did a follow-up investigation and a few years later, they found that most of those young geniuses didn't make great achievements in their important posts. Those teenagers were born with some endowments, had been crammed with textbook knowledge and established cultural heritage like machines. They did have excellent performance in the *Gaokao* (the national college entrance examination) or some stereotyped competitions but that knowledge had not been digested by these young people at all.

How could there be transformation of knowledge without digestion? And how could there be any outcome without transformation of knowledge? She made up her mind that she would never repeat such mistakes when teaching students like Tian Shi Bowa.

The division of work at school was as follows: the new teacher Chen Min was in charge of the third year and Liu Wanyi took care of the teaching and management of the sixth year. She had a sixteen-character teaching plan for the sixth-year Chinese: to read extensively, think critically, select good sample essays and teach them how to write.

The last three-character policy was particularly important. After students had read extensively, many characters and expressions, essay content and their doubts would be digested and mutually understood in reading. If teachers should fail to provide them with a set of effective writing methods on a timely basis which in a sense would equal learning Chinese while being unable to write in Chinese, there would be no point in talking about the purpose and meaning of learning.

No doubt this plan not only worked for the actual learning situation of current students, it worked especially well for Tian Shi Bowa.

Liu Wanyi made a report to the higher authorities for some funds to buy extracurricular reading materials for senior students in the village school. They told her they could not resolve the situation for the time being due to a shortage of funds. Liu Wanyi was a little angry. With her own money, she bought *The Wonderful Adventures of Niles, Nobody's Boy, The Straw Hut, Girls' Diary, Boys' Diary, Chinese Myths, Lifetime Commitment, The Heart of a Boy, Chinese Children's Literature Series* and *Chinese Contemporary Teenager Fiction Series*, a lot of after-class reading books recommended by the country for elementary school senior students. Liu Wanyi placed a few book storage areas inside the classroom for the convenience of all students to borrow and read. She even had the series a *Syllabus of Elementary Senior Students Extracurricular Reading Guidance Courses* used by teachers when they prepared for class copied and distributed to students to read and discuss.

Liu Wanyi stood on the podium, glanced at all the students and said earnestly, "Students, a traditional motto says if one works with a sustained effort, one can grind an iron rod into a needle. Now, none of you were able to write a good composition but as long as you work hard, you are sure to get to the forefront of students in the same year as you in the town and the county."

She gave one copy of *Syllabus* to Tian Shi Bowa in particular, saying to him eagerly, "Bowa, you are beginning the sixth year directly from the first year. There is quite a lot of stuff in this skip. I put some fourth and fifth-year stuff into this for you to study at the same time, which means it will be harder for you to study than for the other students. But I trust you and as long as you work hard, I will be glad to be your bridge to success."

Liu Wanyi didn't sacrifice in-class teaching time but was smart enough to make an appropriate amount of time available for composition. She was well versed in Mr Ye Shengtao's teaching method that treats books and textbooks as nothing but examples. Teachers should make good use of good examples to teach students how to learn first, then give them a lot of practice because only through practice could students consolidate and improve their ability.

Liu Wanyi gave up her idea of making the rice shoots grow by pulling them up. She changed the one-and-a-half-year plan to end Tian Shi Bowa's primary school curriculum into a consecutive consolidated study plan spread over three consecutive semesters.

When Liu Wanyi found her students were having a lot of fun reading and were full of passion and eagerness to demonstrate their writing skills, she selected some award-winning compositions in the national competition as samples and together they appreciated the excellent expressions, paragraphs and positive ideas, and discussed why authors were able to write so well. After learning each sample essay, students would get a similar topic as the sample essay to write a composition. Peer-to-peer reading and evaluation were done after each draft, mutually pointing out each other's good and bad points and doing the rewriting later. In each semester, she would require her students to write at least 12 essays. This semester Bowa's compositions, compared with the ones he did at the very beginning, were worlds apart.

Especially the one 'Early Morning' which Tian Shi Bowa rewrote, which had made Liu Wanyi and Chen Min overjoyed when they read it. This composition vividly depicted a series of images the author had seen with his own eyes.

> *Under the first rays of the rising sun, the atonal crowing of roosters had just started inside a corner of a village garden, reeds were dancing in the wind beside the White Crane Stream, the little white crane was stretching its long beak into the water, croaking and looking for food in the shoals, the mid-morning sun burst out from behind the Jigong Mountain against the glow of clouds, and beams of colourful bright sunlight from the sun, like a spotlight, illuminated the school boy who was walking along the mountain road and the white sail drifting away with the flowing water of Xiaonanhai.*

Meaningful expressions, good content, rich imagination and smooth coherence. The images under his pen imparted a kind of spiritual thinking. There were no characters such as *mei* (beautiful) and *ai* (love) in his writing, but one could discern the harmonious beauty of nature and the true love the author had for nature.

The village school happened to receive a notice about the *Hope Cup National Middle School and Elementary School Composition Contest* from the school district. Liu Wanyi and Chen Min immediately filled in the application form, selected two other excellent student essays and together with Tian Shi Bowa's 'Early Morning', they submitted all the materials.

23

A TEENAGER WITH A NOBLE CHARACTER

Suddenly one day, Tian Shi Bowa didn't come to school. The next day, he was absent too. What was wrong with the child? Did he forget to go to school? Liu Wanyi felt she had to put the screws on him when he came back. To her surprise, Tian Shi Bowa didn't show up on the third or fourth day either, and this continued for more than a week! Had something happened to his family like his grandma passing away because of old age? She asked the other students about it and they all told her Bowa's grandma could not have passed away because if she had, the noise of firecrackers to ward off evil would have been heard in the village and the adults would also have gone to help with the funeral arrangements. Liu Wanyi was all at sixes and sevens. What on earth had happened to the child? She could not wait and set out immediately for his home.

Liu Wanyi climbed over the mountain ridge of the fir woods and through the trees in the woods; she could vaguely see the White Crane Stream under the hillside.

It was beside the stream that Liu Wanyi had got to know the White Crane Boy and it was beside the stream that she had accidentally discovered the boy was so fond of reading books. She was wondering if Bowa was a child who truly loved to learn, so maybe at this time he was lying beside the stream, holding a book, reading and reciting. Yes, at this time when the setting sun was just hidden in the woods on top of the mountain and when it was still not dinner time yet. The boy, who was once laughingly called Silly Tian and Stammering Tian, but was now known as Tian Shi Bowa endowed with a special gift for learning, should be there and must be there, beside the stream where water flew and water grass flourished.

She had more time in the afternoon. Bowa's little pal, that beautiful little white crane, would fly to look for food in the White Crane Stream if he knew Bowa was there. She laughed at herself as she walked. Why did she have the feeling that Tian Shi Bowa was there? Was it because she could not forget the beautiful scene of the White Crane Boy she had seen for the first time? Was it the second time when she had found Tian Shi Bowa studying so hard by the stream? Or was it because she worried Bowa was too hardworking so she had hoped he could play for a while beside the stream? Well, maybe all these options were possible.

Preoccupied with her thoughts, she arrived at the White Crane Stream unwittingly. To her disappointment, Bowa was not there. She looked around and saw colourful clouds hanging on the tip of the mountain, bamboo forests on the hillside bowing and smiling at her, and gently flowing water singing a lyrical song for her. But under the shade of the Chinese oak tree, on the clean and flat sandstone and inside the stream glittering in the golden sunlight, Tian Shi Bowa was nowhere to be found, neither was his good companion the little white crane.

A bit disappointed, Teacher Liu Wanyi kept turning back to look as she walked along the mountain road to Tian Shi Bowa's home. Tian Shi Bowa couldn't be at home. Something must have happened that had made Bowa leave home. For example, his father working outside needed his help or his mother had to go to visit relatives and wanted him to go with her. If not, how could Bowa have any reason not to go to school but to stay at home?

"Bowa, Bowa, Tian Shi Bowa!" Teacher Liu shouted loudly under the roof of Tian Fashui's house. It was very quiet inside the courtyard, so were the rooms. The door of the living room was partially closed. She called a few times but there was no response.

Teacher Liu pushed the door open.

"Goodness!" She uttered a cry of surprise.

She was surprised because on the right side of the living room stood a wooden bed on which a person lay motionless. She uttered a little cry because she saw a teenager sitting in a wooden chair beside the bed, facing the door. His head leaned back against the back of the chair, breathing evenly with his eyes closed, his hands resting on his legs and an open sixth-year maths book in his hand.

Teacher Liu walked over to him softly, took a glance and found it was Tian Shi Bowa.

She could not recognise the person on the bed but knew that must be a patient. Covered with a thin quilt, the man lay there with a food cover mesh net on his head to ward off mosquitoes and bugs perhaps. Who was the patient?

Teacher Liu didn't wake up Bowa. She noticed an open exercise book on a square desk next to him. She picked it up and found some characters and Arabic numerals written on it.

A line was written on the very top: Debts must be paid and one must remember to return a favour when one is helped. She read on and saw some names and numbers written on the lines. She was very surprised to find her name there when she read the first line:

Teacher Liu Wanyi: operation fee, 17,199 yuan

Teacher Liu Wanyi: Modern Chinese Dictionary, 65 yuan

Teacher Liu Wanyi: Chinese Pinyin Instant Learning Guide, 32 yuan

Teacher Liu Wanyi: Selected Excellent Compositions of Primary and Secondary School Students, 28 yuan

Li Chaosong: 80 kilograms of rice

Xiao Chuangzhang: 2 old ducks

Zhang Guize: 260 yuan

Guo Zhaotai: 260 yuan

Zheng Liping: 260 yuan

Uncle Qu: medical fees, 63,359 yuan

Uncle Qu: transportation fee, 2,600…

Liu Wanyi sighed silently, "He has so much on his mind!"

The sound of a wooden barrel touching the ground came from the courtyard. Liu Wanyi went out of the living room and over there in the pigsty, Bowa's grandma was stepping into the courtyard with her head down, carrying a pig food bucket in her hand.

"Grandma, you are feeding pigs?"

Bowa's grandma raised her head and saw Liu Wanyi. She put down the bucket and said, "Teacher Liu, it's you. Please take a seat. I will be back as soon as I've got the pig food and fed the pigs."

Liu Wanyi was lost in thought. Why hadn't she discovered this in the past? Why did Grandma still need to feed pigs at such an old age? Had something happened to their family so that she had no choice but to shoulder the burden? She went over to Grandma and said, "Grandma, let me help you."

"How could I let you do this for me?" replied Grandma but finally she didn't refuse Liu Wanyi's offer and let her hold the bucket to fetch the pig food already cooked in the kitchen.

Liu Wanyi took the pig food to the pigsty, fed the pigs and went back to talk with Grandma, "Grandma, how can you do this work? The bucket is so heavy! Where are Bowa's father and mother?"

Grandma didn't answer immediately. She shook her head, sighed deeply and said with a bit of sadness, "Well, I hate to bring it up. Teacher Liu, misfortune has befallen our family!"

"What happened?"

"Do you know who is lying on the bed in the living room?" Grandma asked as she answered immediately. "Bowa's father. He was very happy when he saw Bowa study very hard. So he decided to save some money for Bowa's future study and pay the debt at the same time. In the past few months, the price of meshima mushrooms was on the increase and a lot of vendors came to buy them. He therefore often climbed cliffs to collect these mushrooms. More than half a month ago, together with a few other villagers he went out to collect mushrooms again. When he was busy working, he slipped and fell off the cliff head-first. He fainted on the spot and was sent to hospital immediately. Bowa and his mother attended to him day and night and half a month later, he was still in a coma while the whole family had already run out of money. The hospital said he would be in a persistent vegetative state and it would be better to take care of him at home. Look, he just got back yesterday. The breadwinner of our family has collapsed but we, including Fashui himself, have to live on. Bowa's mother has to work in the fields and she will bring back a basket of pig grass while Bowa stays at home taking care of his father. As for me, I manage to share some of the housework since I can still move around."

"Oh…" Hearing this, Liu Wanyi didn't know what to say. It was truly a disaster! How difficult their lives must have been since the breadwinner had been lost! How would they handle the large amount of medical fees?

Grandma seemed to see through Teacher Liu's doubts. She said, "It is impossible for our family to collect enough money for the treatment fee, you know, it's quite a lot. Luckily Bowa's Uncle Qu knew about it and he paid off the rest for us."

"Uncle Qu? Oh, yes, Grandma, I saw a notebook of Bowa's where he wrote that Uncle Qu spent more than 60,000 yuan. Was there a story behind it?" asked Liu Wanyi.

"Hey, yes, fate!" Bowa's grandma then explained how they happened to have saved Boss Qu's life. With deep emotion, Liu Wanyi said, "So that's it! Bowa never told me this. Your family saved Boss Qu's life who in return offered to pay for the bill. He won't ask you to return it."

"Right, Boss Qu said in front of a lot of people that he had given this to us and there was no need to return it to him. Bowa however is stubborn. He insisted we should be grateful while the debt must be paid off. He will work hard when he grows up and pay off all the debts," replied Bowa's grandma. "It's good for a person to have principles! I feel I can rest assured knowing that Bowa thinks like this."

Well, Tian Shi Bowa not only had ambition but also had a noble character. Liu Wanyi praised him in her heart on the one hand and sighed on the other. God was unfair to him. He had suffered from an articulation barrier since birth and when he needed family support, such a disaster had befallen his father! The whole family was experiencing hard times now. Could he still go to school?

"After Fashui suffered this mishap, Bowa insisted on fulfilling his filial duty and decided not to go to school. His mother and I both wanted him to go back to school but he just wouldn't listen, saying that if it had not been necessary to pay for his operation debt and save more money for his future education, his father wouldn't have fallen over the cliff. He was prepared to stay at home and take care of his father for a lifetime." As if she had noticed some of Teacher Liu's concerns, Bowa's grandma stopped for a while and added, "While he was still in the city, Boss Qu asked the hospital to keep Tian Fashui in hospital for further treatment, particularly after he knew that Bowa was unwilling to go back to school. He said he would pay for all the medical expenses so that Bowa could feel at ease and concentrate on his studies. Bowa is good at numbers, you know. When he made a rough estimate of the cost of three years of medical care, he was scared stiff. He is only a child, after all, a child under 13 years old! Poor child! A rough estimate scared him stiff!"

"Bowa, why do you have things on your mind like adults?" wondered Liu Wanyi, who was truly worried about him.

"When Bowa consulted the doctors, they told him that as for his father's case, it wouldn't make much difference whether he was taken care of in hospital or at home. The cost of medical care in hospital however is very expensive and Bowa was worried he might not be able to pay for it after he grew up. I know my grandson has his filial love and wants to see his father every day," Grandma continued. "But Boss Qu is very stubborn too. He said to Bowa, 'Your family saved my life and I am responsible for looking after your father too. Unless you promise me you will go back to school, I will try my best to keep your father in hospital.' Bowa at last gave in and agreed to go back to school, but things like feeding food through a tube, cleaning his father's body, massaging him, and assisting with his bowel movements at night had to be left for him before and after school."

24
LONG WALK TO THE MOVIE

Huang Xiaoqiu did meet her Waterloo! She broke her leg when she was dancing their local dance at school. At that time, she felt very miserable and absolutely frustrated. Fortunately the doctor said it was not a big problem but a tiny bone between the two bones in her calf had a fracture. At most it would take a month for her to recover using a medicine bag and a splint. But she might not be able to walk normally for a while and might limp a bit.

Huang Xiaoqiu however suffered a sudden emotional decline, feeling she was done for. Tian Shi Bowa couldn't help worrying about this all day long, thinking it would be a big issue for Huang Xiaoqiu's future. An opportunity arose. This morning he heard that a documentary would be shown on the lower pier of Xiaonanhai, so he decided to invite Huang Xiaoqiu and Xiao Jianbo to go and watch it together.

As the sun was setting on the mountain, Tian Shi Bowa finished his sweet potato rice dinner in a few mouthfuls and ran to look for Huang Xiaoqiu.

Huang Xiaoqiu's home was inside the bamboo forest in the Huang Family's place. Bowa shouted over the bamboo forest, "Huang Xiaoqiu! Huang Xiaoqiu!" No one answered. Bowa then went into the bamboo forest.

Next to the main building of Huang Xaoqiu's family was a house on stilts.

Downstairs were a pigsty and a toilet. Some farm tools that used to hang under the crossbar beside the toilet were now gone.

Standing at the foot of the house, Bowa called Huang Xiaoqiu. Still, no one answered. He looked up at the crossbar and found the hoe was not there any more. He knew they must have climbed up the hillside. He ran up toward the hillside.

Yes, Huang Xiaoqiu was there helping her mother dig sweet potatoes.

A few years ago, Huang Mingfu, Huang Xiaoqiu's father, went to work as a carpenter in the city. He would always send money back home every one or two months. Later her mother opened a bank account and had a bank card so her father would directly transfer money to the card, saving a lot of trouble indeed. Her family lived an affluent life in the village. Huang Xiaochun and Huang Xiaoqiu had almost never had to do farm work since they were born because they paid others to do it for them. But unexpectedly, Huang Mingfu suddenly didn't transfer money to his wife's bank card and he often was not available on the phone either. Time slipped by and more than half a year passed. Huang Xiaoqiu's mother became impatient and went to look for him in the city. She stayed there for more than a week but couldn't find her husband. What she heard was that her husband might have gone to work in a large city. "Might?" This 'might' was truly horrible! But she had no choice but to go back home and wait. Another three months passed and still no news came. Money was a big problem for her now. All her savings ran out quickly. How was she to manage with thinning and threshing? What about picking corn and digging up sweet potatoes? Hire someone to do it? No payment? She had to pay for that, didn't she? Without any choice, Huang Xiaoqiu's mother had to do it herself. The two sisters, Huang Xiaochun and Huang Xiaoqiu, had to go to school on week days, especially Xiaochun who lived on campus and was unable to help a lot with the housework. But after their family suffered from this unforeseen event, the two sisters suddenly began to understand things. When weekends and holidays came, they started to silently help with farm work but Huang Xiaoqiu became very preoccupied and she always buried her head low as she limped on her way.

"Huang Xiaoqiu!"

When dug out from the field, sweet potatoes would always have some fresh dirt on and some leaves hanging on them too. They needed to be cleaned before being carried back home. Huang Xiaoqiu was squatting in the field, cleaning the sweet potatoes her mother had dug up. She raised her head when she heard Tian Shi Bowa shouting. She took a look at Bowa, walked down the slope, went up to him, puckered up and said, "What's the matter? Can't you see we are digging up sweet potatoes?"

"Stop digging up sweet potatoes. Let's go and watch a movie."

"A movie? Where?"

"On the lower pier! Doesn't the film company come to show a movie on the beach in our village once a month? The postman handed out their notice to a few villages and I took one - here." Tian Shi Bowa took the notice out the pocket of his short-sleeved shirt. "The movie may not be worth watching, *Hero* by Zhang Yimo, but the short documentary shown before the main film is very instructive. It is about Michel Petrucciani!"

"Petrucciani? You mean the dwarf Teacher Liu once told us about in class?" Huang Xiaoqiu asked with some surprise.

"Yes, it's a story about him," said Tian Shi Bowa, sounding a bit annoyed. "But can't you stop calling him a dwarf?"

"He was a dwarf anyway," retorted Huang Xiaoqiu disapprovingly.

"You are making fun of people's physical defects; that's kind of ironic. Petrucciani was a person worthy of special respect," said Tian Shi Bowa solemnly. "What if someone called you Crippled Huang? How would you feel then?"

"Me?" Huang Xiaoqiu wasn't born with a crippled leg so her memory still related to the time before her accident. She was a self-respecting and rational girl anyway, so when she heard the question by Tian Shi Bowa, she suddenly remembered her legs. She blushed and said with embarrassment, "Well, I am sorry. I shouldn't have said that."

"It's OK, really," said Tian Shi Bowa hurriedly when he saw Huang Xiaoqiu was so willing to mend her mistake. "It is usually those people with physical defects who truly know they should work hard and work their best. That's why I want to invite you to see this documentary together."

"I am still digging up sweet potatoes. My elder sister didn't come back home this week and it is not good to leave my mother alone on the hillside," answered Huang Xiaoqiu hesitantly.

"Opportunities do not wait. It is impossible for us to see him on the screen any time we want. I have already invited Xiao Jianbo to go with us." Tian Shi Bowa thought for a while and continued, "What about this? Ask your mother to quit work earlier today. I can come and help with the work tomorrow, a whole day. What do you think?"

"Are you serious? Will you keep your word?"

"Definitely! I mean it. I could also ask Xiao Jianbo to do it together."

Seeing him so affirmative, Huang Xiaoqiu was very happy. She climbed up the hillside, said a few words to her mother and ran down the slope quickly.

Xiao Jianbo had already prepared the boat at the lakeside. But when Bowa and Xiaoqiu got in the boat, Xiao Jianbo said he could not make it because some of his family's piglets had run out of the pigsty and into the woods; his mother asked him to find them and bring them back at once.

A small boat therefore carrying a boy and a girl sailed on the surface of Xiaonanhai.

Boats sailing in Xiaonanhai had many styles, brightly decorated motorboats for tourists, flat-bottomed boats with canopies, long and narrow sampans sailing as fast as a needle for only one passenger and still another one, smaller than a flat-bottomed boat while larger than a sampan. Rowing this kind of boat was a lot of fun. Without a canopy in the middle, a slightly pointed and slanted bow, and a tapered tail, it looked like a slender beauty but not really thin. At the boat's stern hung two oars. Bowa and Xiaoqiu held one each, rowing the boat forward with their bodies leaning forward and backward. The boat sailed on, parting the waves at a very fast speed. From a distance, it looked like beautiful dancing swallows soaring above the green water and that's why it was called a double-flying swallow. This kind of boat could be used to carry small goods like pack baskets, mushrooms, kiwis and tea; it could also take five or six people to the fair in the town. Sometimes, some tourists in a carefree mood also loved to take this boat out to sea.

The boat Huang Xiaoqiu and Tian Shi Bowa rowed was a double-flying swallow.

It was a pity that this boat couldn't fly. The boat had been in a state of disrepair and its bottom and bulwark plate had not been re-painted with tung oil, so it collected water easily while the drainage was poor. It sailed very slowly.

The evening sun had just sunk in the west behind Jigong Mountain, leaving a few bars and patches of red and yellow clouds shining on top of the mountain. The lake looked like a mirror, and red maple leaves on Niubei

Island, age-old but vigorous pine trees in Laoguanpin, tall and straight blue bamboos and dark green drooping willows on Chaoyang Temple Island dancing and smiling in the breeze, all reflected some misty intoxication on the surface of the lake. Seen from a distance, reflections on the lake, together with multi-coloured clouds on the mountain top in the west, opened like a scroll of a colourful Chinese painting on the vast and smooth mirror.

The boat steered by the two teenagers began to sail in the painting. Compared with such a gorgeous and splendid painting, the journey of Bowa and Xiaoqiu perhaps was very unimportant and insignificant, but it might bring some meaning to their future lives.

Without much experience, they struggled to face the world, innocently and hopefully. As for hope and reality, they were unable to conceptualise them. Some people, therefore, were inevitably at a loss or depressed when encountering setbacks, but they all instinctively had a dream of life and looked forward to the realisation of their dreams.

Bowa was rowing the boat. Children living near the lake all know how to row a boat, even Huang Xiaoqiu could do it very skillfully. There was no wind on the lake except for the rhythmical squeaky sound of the oars made by Bowa.

"Bowa, your father needs someone to be with him. Won't it be improper for you to accompany me just to watch a movie?" said Huang Xiaoqiu with some concern.

"I have given him a massage and fed him some mashed potato soup. I will do the rest when I get home after the movie." Bowa answered with a peaceful mind, "It feels good to row the boat tonight in mild weather, quite different from the past when it was getting dark. You know, wind usually comes when night comes."

"Honestly, I am worried about it," said Huang Xiaoqiu, looking at the bright glow that was getting dark gradually and she said a bit anxiously, "Bowa, row the boat a little faster. There can't be no wind before and after it gets dark usually. Didn't you feel that? It is very stuffy now, isn't it? I am afraid something will happen later if there is still no wind at this time."

"You are right, but it's OK even if something happens later. The movie starts at 8:30 and one and a half hours later we should be sitting in the playground watching the movie." Bowa rowed the oar a little harder as he spoke to Xiaoqiu.

The boat splashed on while the chirping of birds suddenly came from the pine woods on the other side of the lake: *jug, jug, jug…*

The birdsong was very pure and melodious, pleasing to the ears. In a short while, the birdsong rang in the sky above their heads from time to time. Huang Xiaoqiu said, "The birdsong is so sweet!"

"Yes, it is," agreed Tian Shi Bowa, stopping the oar and listening to it attentively. "It sounds sweet, but a bit strange."

"Oh? That's interesting. How does birdsong sound strange?" asked Huang Xiaoqiu disapprovingly as she glanced at Tian Shi Bowa.

He continued, "Do you know what kind of bird it is?"

"I heard this kind of bird lurks silently during the day and sings when night falls. It has a wonderful voice like a beautiful song. Adults all call it the night bird so we call it the same thing. I had not seen it with my own eyes until now," answered Huang Xiaoqiu.

"It's normal you don't know what kind of bird it is because we haven't heard it in the past. It has flown to our place in the past two years. Ha…" Bowa laughed, "Honestly, I didn't know about it either."

"You mean you know about it now?" asked Huang Xiaoqiu, a little surprised.

"Of course!" replied Bowa, keeping her in suspense. "If not me, who else then?"

"Look, how proud you are!" Huang Xiaoqiu retorted with some disbelief. "Where are we? In the mountains! Our teacher hasn't taught you and it is impossible for you to know that."

"Hahaha… Xiaoqiu, it was precisely Teacher Liu who told me," chuckled Tian Shi Bowa. "One afternoon after school, when Teacher Liu was helping me with my maths in the classroom, a few bird cries suddenly burst out in the pine woods behind the classroom. Teacher Liu stood up and went out to check, and so did I. We saw a brown bird slightly larger than a thrush fly out of the pine woods, still chirping. Teacher Liu told me it sounded strange and I asked her your question and she said, 'Normally, this kind of bird will start to tweet long after it gets dark and usually it has a very natural and calm song, pure and sweet, very pleasing to the ears. Also it ends its singing with a special closing sound that fades away just as an accomplished female singer does during a performance. You want an encore when it is finished.' Teacher Liu imitated the bird's cry and said, 'Did you hear it? It didn't have that special closing sound and obviously it sounded like a quarrel between birds, very annoying and unhappy. I guess it must have been disturbed by some large birds or a wild beast.' When she saw me become interested in it, she asked, 'Do you know what kind of bird it is?' I told her I didn't. She said, 'I guessed you didn't. It is a nightingale. There are dozens of species, chiefly in Europe while in our country they are mainly in Xinjiang and Yunnan. The species one finds in Yunnan are usually forest nightingales which love to live inside forests beside lakes. Forestry experts used to say that nightingales never appeared in Wuling mountain areas in the past but now, since the forest vegetation is getting better and better, some nightingales have migrated from Yunnan. That's why we can hear nightingales singing in Bamian Mountain.' Xiaoqiu, your Brother Bowa has made some progress, hasn't he?"

"Wow, more than that!" Huang Xiaoqiu was indeed amazed. She opened her mouth, ready to say, "Who agreed to call you Brother Bowa." But eventually she buried her head low and said nothing, feelings of inferiority pervading her face. Two years ago, Tian Shi Bowa was quite insignificant, wasn't he? He could not even articulate two characters, let alone go to school. But the one who used to be as thin and weak as a clothes prop was now as strong as a musk deer. And his academic performance that had lagged far behind her in the past, was extraordinarily good at present. He even had such a wide scope of extracurricular knowledge! What about Huang Xiaoqiu then? Not only did she break her leg, but her academic performance took a nosedive. She didn't even know how to make up for it! Classmates often looked at her contemptuously when they saw her. What should she do?

Tian Shi Bowa glanced at Huang Xiaoqiu as he rowed the oar and found that her face, which used to be round and joyous, had now become long and straight.

"Xiaoqiu, I have a question for you," said Tian Shi Bowa, as he thought for a while. "If right now a sudden storm hit us and a roaring wind blew our oars into the water, what would we do?"

"Tian Shi Bowa, what sort of a question is that?" Huang Xiaoqiu shouted disdainfully. "Reach out your hand to pick it up!"

Tian Shi Bowa continued, "In a storm, oars could be blown far away from the boat. Without oars, the boat can only spin around in the water. One should first figure out a way to bring the boat close to the oars. But when we approach the oars, lean out and reach out our hands to grab them, the boat will lose balance and might capsize. We are both done for then."

"Ah, sounds very dangerous! I can't figure out a way around it, anyway."

"It isn't that you cannot; you are lazy. Xiaoqiu, in the wind and waves, you would really be in danger!" said Tian Shi Bowa solemnly, like an adult. "We should first calm down, observe carefully and work out a way."

"Tian Shi Bowa, aren't you nagging a bit like an old woman? We are not in the wind and waves now, are we? Why bother to think too much?"

"Don't you think life would be boring if we didn't think? Teacher Liu once told us when we think, a lot of interesting and colourful pictures appear in our mind; thinking helps us do things better and faster; thinking also makes our life goals more correct and our lives more enjoyable." Tian Shi Bowa took a look at the still water, stopped the oars and let the boat slide forward freely. Sitting on the board at the bow, he looked at Huang Xiaoqiu and said, "I guess you must feel depressed. Yes, so many classmates who danced the lion dance with you were all fine while Huang Xiaoqiu was singled out to be the one to break her leg? In fact, it could have been another normal thing. Why do I say so? For example, you know the earth is relatively round. In our imagination, it should be smooth, but when we look around we find mountains, valleys, lakes and rivers. Why? Based on what we have learned, there is an expression called an 'accident'. If there were no accidents in our lives, there would not be such an expression in our textbook. If you could really enjoy and appreciate this expression in your heart, your life perhaps could be a bit more enjoyable than the others."

"Hey, you are talking like Teacher Liu! How annoying you are!"

"Ha… that is in fact what Teacher Liu told us. You should remember it." Tian Shi Bowa laughed. "Why are we going to watch the movie? For fun? Yes and no! We both know we are not only doing it for fun. What a hard life Michel Petrucciani had! But he still lived a wonderful life. He was born with *osteogenesis imperfecta,* known as 'glass bone disease'. Teacher Liu says people with this disease easily get bone fractures because their bones lack enough calcium and are very fragile, as brittle as glass. Unable to grow like a normal person, Petrucciani was very short, about three feet tall, with bowed legs, palms and wrists. He could not move freely without help. It was with the help of his father or other people holding him up that he was able to sit on the piano seat. His legs were too short and he could not step on the piano pedals at all, so his father installed a special aid that connected to his feet to control the pedals. With a strong faith in his mind, he endured the pain and practiced playing the piano for at least eight hours a day. Later, not only did his musical achievements shock the world, but the whole world remembered one sentence he said: if I were truly tall, I owe it to my tininess. You see, Xiaoqiu, it is not how brilliant his words sounded, but how he lived his life that mattered. Compared with him, your crippled leg is indeed nothing! Not to say it is just a temporary setback."

"Teacher Liu told us something about Petrucciani during the class. I admire him but playing the piano well doesn't happen overnight. Is it hype to call him a world master? Did he truly have such a strong will?" asked Huang Xiaoqiu suspiciously.

"I understand your doubt. That's why when I heard that the short film before the main movie is a documentary about Petrucciani, I came to tell you right away. Compared with him, you might know what to do next. It is such a rare opportunity in our village. I am very much looking forward to watching a history of the indomitable struggle of a disabled person, which should be very touching and inspiring. We will be grateful for this trip."

Without noticing, night fell and the distant mountains gradually faded into curves.

Bowa rowed the boat steadily and smoothly, without making a splash when the oar touched the water. He paid special attention to rowing technique and often watched veteran rowers when they rowed boats: oars touch the water at a slanted angle; one exerts more effort when the oars are in the water and shifts the force to the rear when raising the oars out of the water, at a slant, and with no sound of water at all. Huang Xiaoqiu also had a feeling that Bowa was rowing the boat very smoothly. She observed very carefully and found four small whirlpools appeared on the surface of the water after each of Bowa's strokes. She was very surprised and wondered why Tian Shi Bowa could do everything so well? Even Xiao Jianbo who had a boat at home could only make two whirlpools after each oar stroke, whereas other students in the class not only failed to make a whirlpool when they rowed but also left a mess on the surface of the water after one stroke of the oar.

As for Bowa, someone who always feels there is room for improvement is never satisfied. Take rowing a boat, for example. He hoped he could row with the oar the way an excellent veteran sailor did. When a stroke was completed, eight whirlpools appeared on the surface of the water in the blink of an eye like flowers in full bloom when spring comes. What a boy Tian Shi Bowa was! He always wanted to do his best but it was definitely beyond his capability because to make eight whirlpools at one stroke not only required technique but also the power of an adult.

Driven by the oars, the boat sailed on.

Huang Xiaoqiu suddenly felt a push of waves from under the boat. She said to Bowa, "Why did I feel waves are pushing our boat below?"

"Yes, I felt it too," said Bowa, who stopped rowing immediately to watch the surface of the water. No wind! And the water surface still looked as smooth as usual. Could it be they had been mistaken? Just at that time, Bowa felt clearly that the side of the boat was silently being pushed again and the hull swayed to the left. He looked at the water in the distance and found slight waves ruffling the surface of the lake.

"Oh no! A storm is coming!" Tian Shi Bowa shouted nervously and immediately bent over to row the boat quickly. He remembered once he took the boat out, an elder had said when waves come before the wind, a storm is on the way. It was in fact not accurate to say waves came before the wind. In Xiaonanhai, before the arrival of a big storm, due to ultra-low air pressure, usually a strong wind pressed closely against the surface of the lake and pushed waves forward. At first it was hard to notice the waves and the wind because the hull of the boat was the first to feel the effects.

Huang Xiaoqiu sensed it too and wanted to help Tian Shi Bowa although, in fact, she couldn't do anything. She looked up at the sky and shouted suddenly, "Hurry up, Bowa, storm clouds are coming!"

In just a few minutes, storm clouds gathered towards them and the sky suddenly darkened. Huang Xiaoqiu and Bowa could not see each other clearly already, one trying their best to row with the oar, the other shouting eagerly, "Hurry up! Row quickly!"

There was a thunder clap and lightning! The two teenagers went pale. A heavy rain rustled and rattled, enveloping the small boat with the two teenagers in it. Within about a dozen seconds they were drenched, the rain streaming down their necks, across their bellies and along their thighs.

"Bail out the water! Xiaoqiu, hurry up." At her wits' end, Huang Xiaoqiu hurriedly grabbed a water ladle to bail out the water.

The gusting wind began to show its true colours, opening its giant net-like claws to seize upon them. Their small boat was blown around uncontrollably no matter how hard Bowa tried to stroke the oar to balance the boat. Amid such a roaring wind, the slightest mistake would have capsized the boat immediately. Bowa stroked the oars, wanting to turn the boat straight against the wind, but the wind was so strong that he could not manage it. And if he continued to haul onto the wind, he would surely be exhausted and the boat would turn turtle at any time. An inspiration suddenly hit him that he could retreat in order to advance. He stroked the right oar backward and with just two strokes their boat was pulled straight.

The moment the boat righted itself a huge wave rolled up again with the strong wind and jumped at them. With a loud splash, they were engulfed by the wave. After the wave retreated, the boat was tossed wildly in the lake. Huang Xiaoqiu, not in the mood to say anything, held the crossbar in the small cabin tightly with one hand as she frantically bailed out the water with the other. Bowa laid the two oars flat on both sides of the hull, trying his best to keep the boat steady. Against the violence of the thunder claps and the dazzling lightning, Bowa saw a huge wave gathering strength and charging toward their boat. He hurriedly stroked the oars, steering the boat to pierce the wave head on. In a split second, their boat was pushed erect clinging to the wave like a puppy climbing a high fence. What was he to do? Climb over the high fence or be buried by it when the wave broke? Bowa chose the former. He pulled the oars hard and steered the boat using the wave to climb to its very top. When the huge wave broke, the boat fell safely on the surface of the lake.

"Chirp! Chirp!" In the stormy darkness, they accidentally caught two bird cries from the water next to their boat. When lightning lit up the sky, a bird suddenly flapped its wings and rose from the water, hoping to fly away from the sea of bitterness. The rain however was so heavy and so rushed that as the bird flew above their heads, it was hit by the rain and fell into the boat. It fluttered a few times but was unable to take flight again. Perhaps it was too tired or perhaps the deck was so hard that when it fell onto the deck, it got hurt. Huang Xiaoqiu picked up the water ladle, trying to pat it while Bowa said to her immediately, "Put it under the forward deck quickly." Following Bowa's instruction, Huang Xiaoqiu felt the bird with her hands at the same time. "It is a little smaller than a turtle dove. Quite a fat one. I don't know what kind of bird it is."

"It chirped like a nightingale. It might be the one we heard before," said Bowa as he held his oars tightly. "It was probably disturbed by some kind of big bird or like us, it had its own things to handle."

"What a damned thing to happen? If I had known there would be a storm, I wouldn't have agreed to come with you," complained Huang Xiaoqiu.

"Stop talking nonsense since you are here anyway. There is too much water inside the boat now. Go and bail out the water; the bow is up already. Watch out! The wave is coming again." Bowa held the oars tightly, laid them flat first, then stroked hard twice and climbed over another ferocious wave.

"What bad luck! I've got water in my ears and my eyes too. I can't even open my eyes!"

"Take it easy, Xiaoqiu. If the god of thunder sings first, there is unlikely to be much rain. The rainstorm will gradually fade away. Let's hurry up and take a break in Laoguanping then."

"Do we have any choice!" said Xiaoqiu. "I'd better hurry up with the bailing work."

Tian Shi Bowa checked the direction by the dazzling lightning. Then he bent every sinew to pull the oars and drove the boat squeakily on.

After a while, the wind and rain did lessen and the waves were no longer as overwhelming as they had been but it looked a bit changeable, tossing the boat up and down, right and left, swaying in the lake like a fallen leaf. Bowa nearly broke his neck in order to row the boat as it bumped along. It was probably not far from Laoguanping, Bowa paddled harder, using his hands and body. Splash! Splash!

A crisp 'bang' burst out.

"Oh, no! Huang Xiaoqiu, the rope that ties the right oar to the boat has broken," shouted Bowa.

"Tie it up again, quickly."

Bowa groped inside the boat for a while. "It's gone. It has fallen into the water."

"What should we do?"

"I have no idea."

"Use your belt, Bowa."

"My belt is perishing; it is a strip of cloth belt my mother didn't have any further use for. It will break with a little force. Use yours, Huang Xiaoqiu."

"Trust you to say that. I am a girl. How can I untie my belt?" said Huang Xiaoqiu, scolding him.

"Oh, yes, I forgot. I am very sorry," said Tian Shi Bowa, embarrassedly.

"How about this? We each hold an oar, paddle as hard as we can barehanded, and find a vine as a substitute for the rope when we reach Laoguanping." Before Bowa could reply, Huang Xiaoqiu had already sat beside Bowa, grabbed the left oar and was paddling hard.

Luckily, the second round of the rainstorm restarted after they had stopped the boat and safely tied it up at Laoguanping.

Laoguanping was a small island in the lake. Dense ancient forests in the middle of the island looked like a majestic Marshal's House or a General Hall, surrounded by thickly woven shrubs and vines. Looking at the dark images in front of her eyes, Huang Xiaoqiu was a little afraid and dared not move her feet. Bowa said, "Xiaoqiu, don't be afraid. I have come to this island many times during the day. There are no snakes, no badgers, not even wild rabbits. Xiaoqiu, you take the lead to find the vine we need and I will protect your back."

Xiaoqiu reached out her hands to grope in front of her. She groped for quite a while and then suddenly shouted, "Found it. Here you are." Bowa took it from her and put it under his nose to smell it, then he said,

"No, this is stinkvine, very crisp." Xiaoqiu went on groping, a stinkvine again. She tried one more time, a handful of kudzu this time. Bowa shook his head and said, "Xiaoqiu, we need to be careful and we need to think before we do anything. Take this kudzu for example. We feel it's OK when we pull it straight but actually it will break when we twist it." As Bowa said this, he began to grope in the darkness himself. In this way, Bowa had to walk in front to look for the perfect vine, which unexpectedly made Huang Xiaoqiu a little scared. She grabbed Bowa's clothes tightly while standing back-to-back. A few deafening thunder bolts suddenly exploded and Xiaoqiu trembled with great fear,

"Goodness! It is much louder than firecrackers in the New Year celebrations. I hope it won't scare my hair out of my head! It is indeed so scary!"

"Afraid? Feeling afraid can't solve our problem. We have to go on looking for it if we want to row our boat." It seemed Bowa had found one, "Got it. Millettia! It is very strong, very durable!"

Tian Shi Bowa twisted the vine into a rope at once. He then wiped the rain off his face, took Huang Xiaoqiu's hand and said, "Let's go. The weather might improve after we fix the oar rope and we can continue our trip."

"Bowa, shall we go back home now?" A corner of Huang Xiaoqiu's mind had retreated, "Look, we are both exhausted. And it is very dark now and even if there are no wind and waves, it will still take us an hour or so to reach the pier."

"The arrow that leaves the bow never returns. Besides, it is the best chance to temper one's will."

"To temper one's will? We are all drowned rats now! I want to quit."

Tian Shi Bowa thought about it and challenged her on purpose, "You don't really want to go? Well, wait for me on this island and I will pick you up after watching the movie."

"No way! It is so dark here and I would be scared to death."

They talked as they made ropes, put the oars back in the boat and fixed the ropes to the oars. The wind however was still very violent, with the rumbling sound of huge waves rolling over from time to time. They had to squat ashore waiting.

Finally, the thunder receded into the distance; a huge wind rose high and slowed down; raindrops turned into drizzle and finally stopped; the clouds paled and dissipated. In the night sky, the shimmering light intensified.

The small boat sailed on the lake again. Around the corner of Zhaoyang Temple Island, lights given off from schools, stores and small work units on the pier suddenly leapt out in front of their eyes. Bowa was uplifted by what he saw and Huang Xiaoqiu's depression and frustration seemed to come to an end as well. Bowa opened his mouth and shouted a few lines of a song, 'Sister, walk on boldly, walk on…', although in fact he didn't really understand what these lines meant, he himself just felt they fit the context perfectly.

They both felt relaxed when they stopped the boat, ready to go ashore. Bowa asked Huang Xiaoqiu as he tied up the boat, "Xiaoqiu, where do you think the movie will be shown tonight?"

"It rained so heavily just now, so it couldn't be shown in the playground. It might be…" Huang Xiaoqiu stopped for a second. "It might be in the auditorium of Haikou Elementary School."

Bowa replied, "That makes sense. If the movie is shown there, I know a place where there are a few cement bricks and I will fetch a few for us to sit on."

They arrived at the elementary school as they chatted. But there was no movie there nor did they hear any noise. "Hurry up, it must be in the auditorium."

They rushed into the auditorium.

The moment they were in, they were both dumbfounded. It was empty; not a single person was there. A small light bulb flickered dimly over the platform; the screen had already been tucked up and put aside. In front of the platform were strewn a few rows of random cement bricks; a lot of cigarette butts from rolled tobacco leaves, filter-tipped ones, torn newspapers, skins of boiled sweet potatoes and melon seed shells were scattered here and there. A few rows of wooden chairs stood in the middle of the auditorium quietly, waiting.

"Oh, no! How could the movie have been shown already?" said Huang Xiaoqiu sadly with a long face.

Bowa was very disappointed too, "Well, we were paddling very fast, weren't we?"

Poor kids. They had both forgotten about the delay on their way and they were seized only by one thing: the idea of watching a movie.

"Well, it's over!" sighed Huang Xiaoqiu. Bowa fought off his disappointment, thought about it and said,

"Let's go and find a film projector."

In the restaurant on the ground floor of Xiaonanhai Hostel, several people were sitting at a table playing Golden Flower, a poker game.

"I've got three sevens. I will win this time," a rough voice shouted.

"Wait, I have three queens! What's the use of your three sevens! Lucky money. Five yuan, each of you. Quick!" shouted this rougher voice as it came out of the door.

"Excuse me," Huang Xiaoqiu asked politely as she entered the door. "Are you the film projectors?"

"Yep," answered one of them with a baseball cap on. "What's the matter?"

"Why have you shown the movie already?" asked Bowa boldly without thinking too much about the consequences.

"Hey! Child! Talking so big! Is it necessary for us to wait for you kids?" shouted the one who had three queens with an awe-inspiring righteousness.

Huang Xiaoqiu explained hurriedly, "Uncle, we are asking why you showed the movie ahead of schedule?"

"Ahead of schedule? Look at the clock. Who showed it ahead of schedule?" argued the guy in the baseball cap, pointing at the electronic clock on the wall. The two teenagers looked at the clock and couldn't help sticking out their tongues. The hands of the clock pointed at 11:30pm.

"Uncle, how about this?" Tian Shi Bowa didn't care about how much work it was for other people; right now he was thinking only about what he wanted. "We came all the way from the upper pier to watch the documentary but we were delayed by a rainstorm halfway. We were wondering whether you could show us the documentary of Petrucciani again? Please!"

"What did you say?" It seemed the harsh voice who had three sevens but lost the game was still upset. He went over to Tian Shi Bowa, patted him on the forehead and sneered, "Child, you think you are too important! Look at your big, bright forehead, you should be very smart; look at your shabby plastic sandals, you are indeed a frog in a well. Let me tell you, you each pay three yuan and fifty cents every year but the government requires us to show you a movie every month. We as the film team get the short end of the stick! Now you want us to show a movie just for you two? No problem! The cost of showing a movie is at least eight hundred and five yuan. Eight hundred yuan is OK too. Hey, not to say eight hundred, as long as you produce eighty yuan at once, only eighty yuan, we will show you a movie."

The two teenagers were shocked rigid, staring straight at them, mouths half-closed, tears ready to burst out. Was it due to the way they had been humiliated by Three Sevens who had put them down by implying they had no money? Was it due to the sudden realisation that they were a bit brusque because of their innocence? Was the blame theirs for not arriving in time for the movie? Would their ambitions be dashed from now on after being humiliated? Were the tears water or gold? Maybe there was no accurate answer to these questions for the time being, but at least the tears were real and the tears were flowing out of the bottom of their hearts.

"Let's go back home, Bowa. No need to pay any attention to them." Huang Xiaoqiu seemed to have grown up suddenly. She continued, "The trip was much more eventful than watching a movie. Very worthwhile!"

In the late autumn, a crystal moon squeezed its way out through a narrow passage between large chunks of clouds after the rain, peeping at the two teenagers on the small boat. Huang Xiaoqiu stood beside the two oars, waiting for Bowa's decision whether to sail back or not. Tian Shi Bowa however sat quietly on the bows, his chin in his hands and elbows resting on his knees. Against the faint moonlight, his broad, smooth forehead reflected a bit of shimmering light.

With a few flapping sounds, the nightingale gradually dried its feathers. It popped out from under the deck where Bowa was sitting and fluttered to Huang Xiaoqiu's feet. She grabbed it immediately and said, "Hey! It is a nightingale indeed. Very fat. Well, Bowa, my mother is not well. Could I find a thin rope, bind its feet and take it home? I want to make a bird soup for my mother. It will be good for her."

Tian Shi Bowa took a look at her and then walked over to her silently to take back the nightingale, holding it in his hands. It was one that had just learned how to fly independently, whose toe skin was still quite tender, and whose wings and tail feathers were still brownish gray. Only its eyes were particularly bright. Bowa patted its moist feathers gently with the hem of his clothes and protected it carefully with his body warmth. He said to himself, "Nightingale! Nightingale! Why did you come out at night when it was raining so heavily?"

The nightingale flapped its wings a few times and took a few steps on Bowa's palm with its dexterous feet. Its feathers had basically dried out. When it jumped from Bowa's palm, trying to flutter its wings again, it finally rose into the air. Although the flapping of its wings looked a bit awkward, it struggled to fly toward the light emitted by the autumn moon through the clouds.

25

VILLAGE SCHOOL BOY COMES TOP

On the morning the new semester started, Wanyi and Chen Min spoke almost at the same time of Tian Shi Bowa's composition 'Early Morning' in the teacher's office. They both hoped this one would win an award. If a student did win an award, his teachers would receive Distinguished Teacher Awards at the same time, which in fact was an honour for them as well. They however felt it was rather improbable, as unbelievable as tales from the Arabian Nights. They were both struggling with the idea, slightly hopeful although feeling that it was not very likely. They knew if it did happen, White Crane Village elementary school would surely take on a new look: school building reconstruction, library construction, computer room construction, faculty improvement and so on. After all this competition was co-organised by the Professional Committee of Chinese Language Teaching, the Guangming Daily Publishing House, the Language and Linguistics Newspaper Agency and Sina Educational Channel, all well-known authorities nationwide.

Coincidentally, as they talked about it, the phone on the table rang. Chen Min picked up the phone and it was a call from the county education committee. Chen Min pressed the speaker-phone button so that they could both hear. It was from a deputy director in charge of school education on the education committee. He asked, "Did a student named Tian Shi Bowa in your school submit a composition 'Early Morning' for the Hope Cup Composition Contest?"

"Yes, a sixth-year student," answered Chen Min.

"I heard Tian Shi Bowa has only been at school for two years or so. How could he be a sixth year student? Are you faking the news?" The voice continued on the phone.

"No false news. It is real."

"That's your side of the story. But you know, it is not a subject to be joked about."

"Hello, dear leader, shall we come to the point directly," said Liu Wanyi, taking over the phone. She asked, "Please tell us has Tian Shi Bowa won an award in the composition contest?"

"He has indeed and reporters know it too. But it's hard to believe."

"Hey, what do you mean by saying this?"

"Competing with so many talented young writers all over the country, how could a student with only two and a half years' school education win the first prize of the Senior Group? Do you believe it?" questioned the voice seriously.

"It has nothing to do with whether I believe it or not; it is the truth."

"The truth? You must be Teacher Liu Wanyi, right? We want to know whether that student of yours would dare to take part in an on-site proposition composition test."

"Why wouldn't he dare?" replied Liu Wanyi immediately. "He would accept any test."

"Great. That's just what we want," said the voice, "The two people from the organising committee in Beijing have already arrived and reporters from the newspapers and TV stations are waiting too. You bring the student here in the morning the day after tomorrow and we will do the test that very afternoon."

What was going on? They exchanged looks without any clue. Chen Min said, "I'll ask an acquaintance first." She made a few calls and got some news. It turned out that Tian Shi Bowa had won the first prize in the preliminary contest for his composition 'Early Morning'. When the Education Committee received the notice, they were very surprised. How could it have happened? They had organised primary and secondary school students to participate in this contest many times and never had a student ever won a prize, let alone the first prize. They immediately verified this with the Xiaonanhai school district and found that Tian Shi Bowa only had two and a half years' school education. They thought the two teachers must have helped the student with the composition and that was the reason for the phone call just now. Chen Min's acquaintance kindly suggested that if it had been some kind of show, it would be better for them to stop right now and not to go and take the test. The education committee would try their best to smooth things over. Otherwise, it would be more shameful when the fake news went viral.

"They have so many reporters there too. They want to make a spectacle of us by taking this opportunity to crack down on false news, don't they?"

"Whatever! Fire proves gold. We will go, no matter whether it is a chasm where dragons hide or a cave where tigers have their lair," said Liu Wanyi.

On that day, Teacher Liu Wanyi took Tian Shi Bowa there on time.

Fortunately, it was a place without distractions, a quiet classroom. The only ones allowed in the classroom were the two experts from Beijing, two working members of the education committee and the media. In order not to distract Tian Shi Bowa, they all sat in the row behind him. Liu Wanyi proposed that she should be in the classroom but her proposal was politely rejected.

The test paper was in a sealed manila envelope. On the cover of the envelope was printed *Hope Cup Elementary School Finals for Senior Group*. Six people opened and inspected the test paper on the spot. The title of the composition was *Evening*, and needed to be finished within 90 minutes.

Tian Shi Bowa read the paper for a while, then looked back at the adults behind him, patted his big forehead, and chewed the pen in his mouth for quite a while, showing no sign of writing anything down. Seeing this, the two reporters exchanged a smile, as if to say they were going to see some fun.

At the moment when smiles were going to disappear from their faces, Tian Shi Bowa began to write.

Sixty minutes! Only 60 minutes. Tian Shi Bowa stood up with the paper in his hand and looked back at the adults, as if asking to whom he should hand in the paper. Experts from Beijing asked, "You got stuck? It's OK, go on thinking about it. You've still got half an hour left."

"I am handing in my paper," said Tian Shi Bowa as he placed the paper on the desk.

He was required to write 800 to 1,200 words and Bowa wrote 1,100 words.

The two experts walked over to him and so did the other four, all huddling together to read Bowa's paper. When they finished, the two reporters couldn't wait to take photos of the paper. Very excitedly, they praised him saying, "What an excellent composition!"

In the evening, with the high blue sky as a screen and the clear lake as a painting pallet, painted shades of the evening glow hanging on the tree tops on the mountain beside Xiaonanhai and reflections of the evening glow on the lake that were refracted again onto the white sails were projected onto the huge screen of blue sky. A V-shaped flock of white cranes later flew onto the screen, crying to echo each other harmoniously, amusing each other at the same time. All of a sudden, a little white crane emerged from the flock of cranes, parading its beautiful wings in sharp black and white and flying like a dancer to its dream land.

"The composition shows an extraordinarily novel approach, with rich imagination, pure artistic conception, smart and accurate use of new words, and vivid and incisive description without wordiness."

With unconcealed joy on their faces, the two experts from Beijing finished the above comments after discussion and went out of the classroom with the paper. One of them announced to the crowd outside the door, "Ladies and gentlemen, we are the judges of the Hope Cup National Primary and Secondary School Composition Contest. We are here today to give Tian Shi Bowa a special live final test. After reading his composition written just now, we announce that his first prize in the national preliminary contest is valid! The excellent teacher award for Teacher Liu Wanyi and Teacher Chen Min are valid. Tian Shi Bowa's composition in today's final test is excellent. As for the result of today's test, 51 judges will give their final vote after we bring the composition back."

A group of reporters surrounded Liu Wanyi for an interview and voices expressing praise burst out among the crowd, "Amazing! Incredible! A kid in the village school! Well done! This boy has won honour for us!"

The local TV station made a special report on Tian Shi Bowa's composition contest that evening. *Wuling City Daily* also had a story entitled *Young Boy Stands Out and Wins a National Prize for His Excellent Composition* on the next day's educational page plus the full text of the award-winning composition *Early Morning* in the preliminary contest.

A few days later Teacher Liu received Tian Shi Bowa's award certificate from the post office. She opened the certificate, read the words inside and said to Bowa with joyous surprise, "Wow, you won the first prize again in the final!" As she said it, she found there was a notice from the Contest Committee, "Bowa, you also won a monetary prize of 1,000 yuan! You will get it in a few days."

Upon arriving home, Tian Shi Bowa put the certificate into Grandma's hand while he himself rolled over in bed excitedly, turned somersaults in the courtyard and giggled so hard that his cheeks shook uncontrollably.

Grandma Tian was happy at the beginning but when she saw her grandson laugh so hard that he almost could not control himself, she was a bit worried. She thought for a while, then took her grandson's hand, walked to the edge of the courtyard, stood there and pointed at a flowing cloud in the sky, saying, "Bowa, look at that, what is it?"

Tian Shi Bowa answered after a glance, "A cloud."

"What kind of cloud is it?"

"A white cloud."

"What does the white cloud do?"

Tian Shi Bowa took a careful look and said, "It is walking in the sky."

"Yes, Bowa," Grandma Tian continued. "Why can it walk in the sky? You watch it carefully and then tell me the reason."

"The cloud is a little thin, and a little long and narrow, as if floating on the water," said Tian Shi Bowa while observing. "It floats as the wind blows."

"Right, you are a good observer. It is a floating cloud, long and thin and it floats when the wind blows." Grandma reached out her hand to push back her silvery hair, then she squatted down and pointed at the sky, saying to her grandson, "It seems you are very happy to have won the first prize, but in fact it is just an empty name, the same as the floating cloud. You know, there is still a long way to go when a cucumber just grows a tiny bit long. The book knowledge you have learned is little and shallow just like the floating cloud.

When a gust of wind blows by, it will be blown to a place hundreds and thousands of miles away. What do you think?"

Tian Shi Bowa stopped smiling immediately. Although he could not fully understand the profound meaning of Grandma's words, he knew floating clouds thin and shallow like this would not bring much rain or no rain at all. Tian Shi Bowa stared at the floating cloud that was gradually drifting away, his eyes looking straight ahead.

26
DIRECTIONS HIDDEN IN A POEM

On the way back after school, Huang Xiaoqiu had a glum face. She said to Tian Shi Bowa, "Bowa, could you do me a favour? I don't know where my elder sister has gone! You know, she didn't tell me. My mother is sure to commit suicide if she gets to know about it."

"Did your sister jump into the river? Or did she go and lie on the railroad track?" asked Bowa deliberately.

"What are you talking about? My elder sister would never kill herself. She is not a coward and always looks on the bright side of things. She has a favourite line: cherishing life is a success while committing suicide is a failure."

"Oh? Then she might have hidden herself somewhere," said Bowa as he stared at Huang Xiaoqiu's big eyes. "Think it over, where could your elder sister have gone and hidden herself?"

"She wouldn't dare stay in White Crane Village and it is even more unlikely that she would have hidden in the city. We don't have many relatives, you know. I have no idea where she might have gone."

"How long has she been away?"

"About three days. No, more than three days. To pay for my school education, my sister went to work in the city. I know she planned to find out what happened to my father at the same time. She wanted to report to the police after secretly collecting some evidence of my father's disappearance. But before she found anything, someone who had noticed her plan threatened her, forcing her to leave the city. When I went to her for some living expenses, she was gone. I heard she left there three days ago. It has been more than a week until now."

"You heard it? From whom?" asked Bowa very alertly.

"The guard of Runlan Garden Community. Oh, one more thing," added Huang Xiaoqiu, fumbling for something in her pocket. After a while, she took out a piece of paper obviously torn from an exercise book, waved it in her hand and said, "She gave this to the guard telling him to give it to me when I came to look for her. I thought it might be something precious but to my surprise it was a poem she had written. How pretentious! What kind of poem could she have written? She didn't even finish middle school!"

"Let me have a look."

"It's not worth looking at. Better to throw it away."

"No, give it to me. I want to know what your sister wrote." Bowa reached for the piece of paper and yes, it was a poem, four lines.

> Veiled in dust, young lotuses shed tears,
> For Qianhui, spring greenness set out on its journey.
> Behind the woods lies Gaolu Village,
> A long flight, startled birds await.

"It is really a good poem!"

"Good for what? She must have copied it from a book."

Bowa read it a few times, staring at the four lines, frowning and thinking. Huang Xiaoqiu was a little impatient, "You are still in the mood to read this? Throw it away! I am worried to death. I need your suggestion."

"The poem seems to leave you some hints," said Bowa as he pointed out the poem to Huang Xiaoqiu. "Do you see what we can get when we put the first character of the first two lines together?"

"Xiao... chun! Ah, that is my sister's name."

"Isn't it interesting? Your sister had to be very careful about her whereabouts and she must have been suggesting something in this poem." Bowa tried to remind Huang Xiaoqiu of something.

"Yes! Yes! She seemed to. Bowa, you are so smart! I will read it again carefully." Huang Xiaoqiu read it a few times more and shouted excitedly, "I know where my sister has gone! Bowa, look at this. The last two characters in the second line: Qianhui! It reads Huiqian when changed round, which in fact is the famous high mountain Huiqian Ridge, far far away from here. In the line '*Lin hou cun gao lu*', isn't '*gao lu*' Gaolu Village?

Two years ago, my aunt was married. Do you still remember you volunteered to perform a fantastic dance 'delivering the embroidered silk ball' during the banquet night and hand-waving dance show on her wedding day? The home of my aunt's husband is in Gaolu Village in Huiqian Ridge, a place that is very difficult to reach! I haven't been there before but I've heard a road has been built up the mountain but I don't know whether it is open to traffic now. I would never have dreamt she would go there! Look, Bowa, what did my sister want to say in her last line?"

"*Jing niao dai yuan fei*, '*dai*' means wait and get prepared. She might be trying to tell us she is waiting for the chance to go to a place far away or very likely she meant she is waiting for you to go and find her, or maybe…"

"Enough, so many 'maybes'! My mother has already thought about ending her life and if something should happen to my elder sister, she is sure to knock herself dead against the wall."

Huang Xiaoqiu bit her lip, thought for a while and said, "Even if she went there to work, she also would have needed money at the beginning. I will try and borrow some money and then go and look for her."

"Forget it, Xiaoqiu, you don't have any relative who is able to lend you any money. Since you know your elder sister is not going to end her life, just let it be. Think about it. A-whole-day bus trip is just one thing but there are still a few days of hard travelling through forests, valleys and mountains ahead of you. It is sure to be a hard journey and you are a little girl still; who could save you if something should happen to you? If so, how about your mother?" Bowa persuaded Xiaoqiu as he looked at her.

"Forget it? I can't do that. It is after all your speculation. I won't feel at ease until I see my sister with my own eyes. What's more, what if my sister is waiting for me now? She can't hide herself in Gaolu Village for a lifetime, right? I need to know what she wants to do next." Xiaoqiu looked at Bowa, then turned to look at the mountains in the distance, saying, "The difficulties and dangers you just mentioned might be there, but I am not afraid and I will go. I have already written an excuse for my absence from school."

"Xiaoqiu, I know you are telling me you are brave enough to do it, and you dare to do it," said Bowa, waving his palms, "but it is not a question of whether you dare to do it or not. The trip is sure to be a very difficult one: wild animals, difficult terrain, weather, and bad people, so many dangers! Who can predict? And Huiqian Ridge is very high and steep, and I don't know whether you have the ability to reach the top of the mountain?"

"Bowa, don't underestimate me. No matter what kind of difficulties and dangers there are and no matter whether I have the ability or not, I believe in one thing: I must go!" How could Huang Xiaoqiu have considered giving up so easily? She was so impatient that she turned around and left as she said so.

Seeing her moving away gradually, Bowa was lost in thought, his eyes fixed on her back. He was not the Bowa who could only say one character nor was he the one who only cared about his own stuff. In his mind, a few stacked images appeared: in the extended range of mountains, Xiaoqiu gets lost, standing beside a fork in the road with a clueless look on her face, not knowing what to do; a rolling mountain flood blocks her way and she looks so terrified; she makes a few attempts to jump over it but becomes afraid and gives up. However, she has to jump over it because it is the only way to continue her journey and she has no choice. She takes a few steps backward, takes a running jump and, with a loud flopping sound, she falls into the torrents and disappears in a flash; in dark, pitch-black forests, gusts of wind roar through from time to time. Clusters of treetops are blown to stoop down suddenly and then straighten up at once, wailing with the feeling they have been wronged. All of a sudden, the strange shape of some beast riding on the back of the roaring wind jumps out at Huang Xiaoqiu…

"Ah!" Tian Shi Bowa couldn't help crying out. He rubbed his eyes, tossed his head, looked around and his senses became cleared. He said to himself, "No! I will talk with my mother. I should help Huang Xiaoqiu to find her elder sister."

Bowa hurriedly rushed back home, telling his mother he was going to help Huang Xiaoqiu find her sister. With an awkward expression on her face, Li Runlan eventually didn't give her permission. Grandma Tian came over to see what was happening when she saw her grandson run back home sweaty all over to say something to his mother. Bowa explained everything to his grandma in a loud voice. Li Runlan said to her mother-in-law, "I'm already stuck doing all the work, in the fields and at home. Tian Fashui must be taken care of by Bowa every day. How could Bowa leave home? What's more, I worry about him; after all it is such a long trip."

"Our ancestors told us we should help people when they are in danger. Huang Xiaoqiu is just a little girl and it is indeed a big problem for her to go out alone without anyone's company." Grandma thought about it and continued, addressing her daughter-in-law and her grandson too, "A human being is quite similar to the banyan tree behind our house. When it is blooming, nectar is dedicated to bees while fruit is left on the tree. People who have been to the fair say the road to Huiqian Ridge has been opened to traffic and nothing will happen. Runlan, I think we should let Bowa go. I can take care of Fashui for a few days."

27

RIVERSIDE ADVENTURE

With Grandma and Mum's support, Bowa resolutely accompanied Huang Xiaoqiu on the bus to Huiqian Ridge. Uexpectedly, the bus stopped at Fengjia Town beside the Apengjiang (Apeng River). They were told large areas of subsidence had occurred on the road ahead.

Wandering by the Apengjiang, Bowa and Xiaoqiu had no idea what to do. At that time, a motorised passenger ship sailed from downstream of the Apengjiang here, blew a long whistle and slowly stopped by the side of the river. A long gangplank stuck out from the bows and landed on the river bank. A middle-aged male crew member held a long bamboo pole and plunged the sharp iron tip into the ridge on the shore while placing the other end on his shoulder, to make a temporary railing. A lot of passengers carrying packs of luggage held on to the temporary railing and walked along the gangplank to the shore.

Bowa had a brainwave and ran over to ask, "Uncle, there has been subsidense on the road to Huiqian Ridge. We want to know whether there is another road that goes there."

"You kids want to go to Huiqian Ridge? That's quite a trip," said the middle-aged man as he pointed at the upper reaches of the Apengjiang, "Our ship is from Zhuoshui Old Town to Zhoubai Town. We can take you as far as Shuizhai in Guandu Gorge. When a ship passes by, get on the ship and you will pass by a small valley called Yixiantian. After getting off the ship, cross Pengdong County, climb up a mountain, and you'll be there then."

"Got it! Thank you uncle." The two boarded the motorised ship at once.

They got off the ship when it reached Shuizhai Mountain.

There was a small platform at the landing place, small in size with nothing worthwhile to look at either. Bowa and Xiaoqiu began to climb up the mountain. After climbing for about 20 metres, they saw a relatively spacious open square, in the middle of which close to the mountain stood a small temple of the Earth God. The temple looked quite local, not big, half a person high and half a metre wide, with two slates standing respectively on the right and left and another lying on the top.

In the middle of the top slate lay a fire-stone like a rectangular strip of stone, on which some black tiles lay silently. A few black tiles were lying back on both sides of the long stone strip, swooping up and down with a well-proportioned effect, a bit similar to the upswept eaves usually seen in a real temple. An Earth God with white hair and a long beard carved out of pear wood was placed for worship inside the temple, and already looked quite old and shabby. In front of the temple was a rectangular incense burner made of clay, with dozens of bamboo holders of unburned incense sticks inside.

As Huang Xiaoqiu watched, she suddenly dropped to her knees and kowtowed.

"Xiaoqiu, what are you doing?"

"My father said we must pray to gods in a temple whenever we encounter one." Appearing very pious, Huang Xiaoqiu had her palms together, closed her eyes and murmured, "Great Earth God, please bless my father and my elder sister. Let them be safe and healthy and let everything be alright."

She made another three kowtows and said, "Bowa, come and kowtow to make a wish. It works!"

"It works? Since you believe in it, why did such a big thing happen to your father and your elder sister?" asked Tian Shi Bowa.

"Well… I don't know either," replied Huang Xiaoqiu. "Bowa, you don't believe in Buddha and their blessings, do you?"

"It's hard to say whether I believe in it or not. You know, without any knowledge about this, I know very little about it." Tian Shi Bowa thought about it and said, "I think we should firstly believe in science, believe in ourselves and try to do our best. It's better to put these unreal things (nihilism) aside. For example, you think Buddhas are powerful and you pray to them and ask them to bless your elder sister. If all this works, do we still need to come such a long way to look for your elder sister?"

"Well, your words sound reasonable," said Huang Xiaoqiu with her fingers in her mouth, beginning to think about things.

Bowa said, "OK! We can't play here long because we need to go down to wait for a boat."

The boat had not come yet. They looked ahead at the river.

The river was flanked by towering mountain peaks and dense forests. On the surface of the river, mist and waves stretched far into the distance, with white cranes flying across from time to time. Xiaoqiu asked, "Bowa, is your little white crane among them?"

"Xiaoqiu, you are telling jokes! There are quite a lot of similar white cranes in this world! How could my little fellow be here?" said Tian Shi Bowa. "But I know white cranes are very intelligent birds. Whenever one of them is in trouble, they can sense it and send messages to each other very quickly."

A white crane flew over and rested on a boulder on the riverside. It flapped its wings, folded them, bent its neck and stretched its long beak into the water, eyes fixed on the water surface.

"Bowa, what in your opinion does the big rock over there look like? The one the white crane stood on."

Bowa took a look and said, "Like a turtle."

"Right, quite possibly. It reminds me of that huge miraculous turtle in Tongtian River." Huang Xiaoqiu said pretentiously, "I guess you don't know this, do you? A long, long time ago, a Tang priest and his three disciples went back to the Tongtian River after they had obtained Buddhist scriptures from the West. When the huge miraculous tortoise carried them to the middle of the river, he stopped and asked the Tang priest, 'Have you asked the Buddha when I will make a fortune? Have you done it?' The Tang priest looked surprised and didn't say anything because he had totally forgotten. The huge tortoise was so angry that he threw them off his back into the river. Ha… The Tang Priest and his disciples must have looked like drowned rats! The big miraculous tortoise was great!"

"It was not some kind of miraculous tortoise, Huang Xiaoqiu. You are wrong," said Bowa.

"I am wrong? How could I be?" Huang Xiaoqiu was a little annoyed. "Tian Shi Bowa, stop thinking you know everything. I've just finished *Journey to the West* that Teacher Liu bought for our class and I remember clearly that it was indeed a huge tortoise that threw the Tang priest and his disciples into the river."

"It was a softshell turtle, not a tortoise," said Bowa, very sure about his answer too.

"A softshell turtle? What's that?" Huang Xiaoqiu sounded a little short of breath.

"The softshell turtle is a Chinese softshell turtle," explained Bowa, looking at Huang Xiaoqiu and saying with a smile, "It is also called *tuan yu* in Chongqing."

"Oh, it's a *tuan yu*!" Huang Xiaoqiu cried out, as if she had suddenly realised something. "It seems to be a softshell turtle in the book."

"Xiaoqiu, you are right to say it is from *Journey to the West*, but do you know in which chapter this story occurs in the book?"

Huang Xiaoqiu thought for a while and said, "I can't remember."

"It is in chapter 99, the last but one chapter: *Nine times nine ends the count and Māra's all destroyed; the work of three times three done, the Dao reverts to its root.*" Bowa continued, "Xiaoqiu, you are not very careful when you read. You said the softshell turtle asked the Tang priest to do him a favour by asking the Buddha when he could make a fortune, didn't you? You are wrong again. Don't stick to the idea that everyone wants to become rich just because you do. The softshell turtle felt he was getting old and he wanted the Tang priest to make one thing sure from the Buddha, namely, how many years he could live." Bowa said as he made a gesture, "Think about it. What did the softshell turtle need money for?"

"Wow, Bowa, you are truly amazing! I really admire you!" Huang Xiaoqiu couldn't help observing him for quite a while and sighed, "Bowa, I am wondering how much knowledge there is in your head?"

At that moment, dark clouds gathered above them and the sky suddenly turned black, so black that things became invisible in the near distance. From west to east, gusts of wind whistled by and the branches of a few big trees beside the cliff bent over and then bounced back. After a few times, they finally were blown down and fell into the river.

They were walking through the woods and suddenly felt the darkness in front of their eyes; they could not even see the road clearly. They looked up at the sky, almost without the slightest bit of light.

A loud rumbling sound burst out! It all happened suddenly, deafening thunder claps riding on the roaring wind and the roaring wind driving pouring rain.

"Hurry up! We've got to find a place to shelter from the rain!"

They felt their way along the rock walls searching everywhere for somewhere to hide. They searched everywhere but in vain. In a little while, they were both drenched by the heavy rain.

It rained heavily and the stones became very slippery. Bowa feared that Huang Xiaoqiu might slip and fall into the river. He shouted, "Xiaoqiu, squat down, protect your head with your bag. I'll go and find shelter."

Tian Shi Bowa went on searching along the riverbank. He saw a hollow in a rock wall at a bend in the river close to the riverbank. He walked in and was overjoyed by what he found. It was a good place indeed, perfect as a shelter and convenient for them to board a passing boat as well. He turned back to call Huang Xiaoqiu to come over and sit down on a dry stone inside the hollow.

The rain showed no sign of stopping. Rainwater washed down from the top of the mountain, twisted itself like a hemp rope, formed streams, slipped along Bowa and Xiaoqiu's feet and rushed into the Apengjiang.

"Luckily we have this place! I am not afraid as long as we're not caught in the rain," said Huang Xiaoqiu.

With a serious look on his face like a young adult, Bowa watched the pouring rain and said anxiously, "Although we're sheltered from the rain here, boats may not come either. If so, we have no way of crossing the Yixiantian and we'll be unable to reach Huiqian Ridge."

Hidden inside the dark clouds, a lightning flash suddenly ripped through the sky, scorched a dazzling tree branch and was followed by a long string of rumbling thunder. The rainstorm became fiercer and fiercer. A lot of treetops were broken by the wild wind; many flying birds were knocked by the raging rain down into the river; the rain, like arrows, shot into the river and made a lot of bubbles. The wild wind swept across again and again, making the surface of the river rough and misty.

Suddenly Bowa felt his toes were cold and wet. He looked down and surprisingly found his feet had already been flooded by the water. His rubber-soled canvas shoes had filled with water like small boats. He cried, "Damn it! The water is rising!"

Huang Xiaoqiu stood up with a small cry too. They looked ahead. In the middle of the river, turbid yellow currents rose high one after another. Foam, fallen twigs, leaves and other unknown objects washed down into the water, twisting and tangling, forming rows of huge waves, beating against the cliffs again and again, fiercer and fiercer. The hollow where they were hiding from the rain was a target of the waves too!

"Xiaoqiu, run!" Bowa got ready to run, but the small path leading to the hollow had already been washed away. In front of them was a rock wall about the same height as a person so they had to search among the rocks beside the river for a place where they could climb up.

Huang Xiaoqiu was very sharp-eyed. She found a crack in the cliff where there were some protruding stones, grass and some small tree branches too, although the moss on the stones was pretty slippery. They stubbornly grabbed hold of the branches, inch by inch, and struggled to climb up to the platform where the temple stood at last.

When they looked back, they found that huge waves had surged over and immediately engulfed the hollow where they had just been standing. And the huge waves were still relentless; they rolled up clouds of waves, roared and beat constantly against the cliff, throwing up spray nearly ten metres high, some splashing all over Bowa's face. They stared at the scene, shuddering and stupefied.

"How could any boat come here? Let's climb higher to see whether we can find a place to shelter from the rain," said Tian Shi Bowa as he took the lead to climb up the mountain. There was no chance for Huang Xiaoqiu to display her strong personality. What else could she say? Better follow Bowa!

The mountain top was covered with luxuriant vegetation, striking green pines and cypresses, tall and magnificent hemlock and purple poplars, stooping masuri berries and crawling vines, all verdant and vibrant. Inside a broad-leaved forest, a pile of toppled walls and broken tiles came into sight. They guessed it might be the ruins of Shuizhai built by ancient people of legendary renown. To their surprise, in a corner of the broken wall lay a relatively complete small cabin, whose herringbone-pattern roof was made of pine wood covered with thatch; the materials were not very old. Obviously, it had been built recently by people for hunting or some other purposes.

Inside the cabin were a few crude wooden stools, a simple wooden bed covered with thatch, and an old iron cooking pot resting on a fireplace supported by three stones.

Bowa's stomach was rumbling when he saw the iron pot. He was incredibly hungry. He glanced at Huang Xiaoqiu's bag. What a smart girl Huang Xiaoqiu was! She giggled and said, "Look! You are hungry, aren't you?"

She pulled out a handful of grass, flicked the dust off the stools and said, "Come and sit down! I will share out the food."

Share out the food? What a pompous attitude! Tian Shi Bowa thought Huang Xiaoqiu had brought a lot of delicious food but it turned out to be a pack of biscuits.

"Why didn't I remember to buy some food at Fengjia Town?" Bowa recalled with regret. He said, "I've got to eat less."

"Eat less? These are salty crackers with honey, sweet and crisp. We'll share them half and half."

Huang Xiaoqiu said quickly, "Bowa, we don't have any soup to go with the biscuits. Can you use the plastic wrapper of these biscuits to get some rain water to drink?"

Biscuits with rain water, it was a meal of sorts anyway.

After lunch, it cleared up. Bowa went out of the cabin to observe the surrounding mountains for a while and said to Huang Xiaoqiu, "Luckily it is summer now otherwise we would be frozen with our wet clothes on. We must leave here. I checked this area and the top of the mountain is connected with the neighbouring ridge. Perhaps we will arrive at Pengdong County if we continue walking along the mountain ridge. When it gets dark, we can find a hotel there for the night or ask people how to get to Bamian Mountian. What do you think?"

"OK, Bowa. It is sunny now in the afternoon. Let's go. When the wind blows, your T-shirt and my short-sleeved shirt will soon dry out." Huang Xiaoqiu handed her bag to Bowa and continued, "Wait for me for a second. I need to do my business behind the cabin."

After a little while, just a little while, Huang Xiaoqiu suddenly screamed behind the cabin, "Help! Bowa, I need your help."

28
BREATH-TAKING MOMENT

"Good heavens!" Tian Shi Bowa turned pale with fright when he rushed behind the cabin and saw that Huang Xiaoqiu was in danger.

A huge cloud of wild bees had surrounded Huang Xiaoqiu, flying around and making a terrifying droning sound. Like crazy, Huang Xiaoqiu was swaying her head, swinging her hands and jumping up and down, as if she was scared stiff. "I've been stung! I've been stung. Help me!"

For a while, Tian Shi Bowa was in a panic too, freezing nervously, not knowing what to do. When a few wild bees rested on his T-shirt, he fixed his eyes on them for a better look and suddenly his nervous tension relaxed.

"Don't move!" Bowa shouted. "Huang Xiaoqiu, squat down and don't move."

Bowa saw clearly that it was a cloud of wild honey bees, not wasps. But wild bees are not domesticated, so aren't they very fierce and dangerous? For a layman, they are felt or perceived to be but Tian Shi Bowa knew they are not because his father once taught him that, by precept and example, there is a very slight difference between domesticated bees and wild ones in China. The former, in fact, are in the habit of just being put into bee barrels and raised together for the convenience of managing and collecting their honey. The stings in their tails are not very poisonous and a few stings would never kill a person.

As young as Bowa was, he knew these bees hadn't picked Huang Xiaoqiu as their target in particular once he had glanced at them. It must have been that Huang Xiaoqiu had disturbed them and, at the same time, they had smelled the sweet and salty crackers with honey they had eaten just now, so they had swarmed towards her. Bowa recognised it was a new group of bees that had broken away from the old bee colony; they were looking for a new home.

Hearing Bowa's shout, Huang Xiaoqiu followed his instructions obediently but she couldn't help crying out, "Bowa, hurry up and help me. I've got a few stings on my back, and I'm burning with pain!"

"Take it easy! Take it easy! Xiaoqiu, they are wild honey bees," said Bowa as he walked to her side and comforted her. "It won't last long. As long as you don't move, they won't sting you any more. I am thinking about how to help you."

"Hurry up!"

"Alright! Alright! Don't move."

The bees clustered around Huang Xiaoqiu's neck, bulging like a stone drum or a ball. Bowa softly put his hand into the bee swarms and gently turned his hand over. Disturbed, quite a few bees flew up and buzzed around. Huang Xiaoqiu still hadn't recovered from her panic and cried, "Bowa, what are you doing? Do you want to scare me to death?"

"Hold still! Don't move," said Bowa as he took out a large handful of bees from the bee swarms, inside which was a yellowish brown one, especially fat with a long belly, about two or three times larger than an ordinary bee. He quickly held its wings gently and slowly put out his hand. Amazingly, the bees buzzing around Huang Xiaoqiu all suddenly flew up, left her immediately and rested on Bowa's hand, surrounding that big bee tightly, forming a big ball again.

Huang Xiaoqiu was safe now. With her eyes wide open, she was puzzled and felt it was rather magical. So many bees were resting on Bowa's hand and so gently that none of them ever tried to sting him! "Bowa, what's going on here? Why don't they sting you? And why do they listen to you so obediently?"

"They don't listen to me; they listen to the queen bee," said Bowa with some pride. "The queen bee secretes a kind of smell that attracts this group of bees to follow her closely. I caught the queen so the other bees find her through the smell. This is how I got these bees to swarm on my hand."

Xiaoqiu asked, "What are you going to do next?"

"Don't worry. Look at me," said Tian Shi Bowa as he walked under a big tree. He slowly moved his hand surrounded by the bee swarm closer to the tree trunk, gently and gradually. As they watched, the bees crawled onto the trunk in lines and rows.

"It's amazing!" said Huang Xiaoqiu, filled with wonder.

Bowa said, "It looks very magical but in fact it isn't. It is how bees work and live. You let the queen bee climb up the tree and the bee swarm will naturally follow her up."

Once out of danger of being besieged by bees, Huang Xiaoqiu was filled with joy as if she had been reborn into this world. She said proudly, "If one suffers no harm when disaster strikes then the road ahead is unobstructed. Bowa, let's continue up the ridge."

"We can't take this road any more," said Bowa as he looked ahead, "Didn't you see it? At the end of the ridge is a cliff. We have to climb down to the Savage Valley from the side first, and then climb up the mountain after we cross the valley."

"Savage Valley? What if we should meet some savages? That's horrible!"

"Meet some savages? We couldn't be that lucky, could we?" Looking at the Savage Valley down there, Bowa replied as he walked on, "We can't hesitate after we make up our minds. To get to Huiqian Ridge, we must pass through the Savage Valley, even if it is a chasm where dragons hide or a cave where tigers have their lair!"

They walked on the small path beside the Savage Valley without a single halt.

In the woods after the rain, birds were chirping, insects singing, leaves were turning greener, the flowers were more colourful and the air fresher. They were both very tired, but they had something in mind and wanted to hurry up. They walked very fast through the woods beside the river.

Huang Xiaoqiu was too vigilant, worrying about this and that, keeping her eyes busy all the way. Now, she suddenly cried out in amazement, "Bowa, look at the rock wall on the right!"

Tian Shi Bowa glanced at it and said carelessly, "A wall! What about it?"

"There are some characters on it." Huang Xiaoqiu had already walked over to the wall, "Hey, it's a poem."

"A poem?" Bowa became interested and walked closer to take a look at it. Yes, a few lines of characters were written vertically on the wall. Some of the characters were covered by moss, probably due to age. The good thing was these characters had been carved with a chisel and when they wiped off the moss, the characters were clearly visible again. Huang Xiaoqiu was very happy because it was she who had found them first. She read the characters in high spirits:

There seems to be no road leading to the gorge, stopping the boat beside the mountain. White reeds nod and smile; an immortal lives in the Jinyu Cave.

"How funny these ancient people are! The Savage Valley we arrived at via the Guandu Gorge is more like a stream. How would one sail a boat in it?" Huang Xiaoqiu giggled.

"It is a literary work after all. It feels very beautiful to write imaginatively. What's more, it might be possible to sail a boat when the water rises."

"What about the Jinyu Cave? And also the immortal in the cave. What does it mean? Imagination again?"

"Well, let me think." Tian Shi Bowa pursed his lips and said, "Surely, the immortal is definitely imaginary. As for Jinyu Cave, I think they had reasons to say so. Perhaps there is some cave inside the mountain. Who knows?"

They chatted without slowing their pace. It took them more than an hour to cross the Savage Valley, then they began to climb the mountain.

Trees and prickly vines grew densely on the mountain, which made it particularly difficult for them to find the road. They had to make great efforts to maintain their walking speed. When they entered a luxuriant Chinese oak forest, they faintly heard some sibilant sounds made by a kind of animal. Out of curiosity, they tiptoed into the woods to take a look. My! They were both excited and shocked by what they saw. A litter of black-and-brown-striped boar piglets were snuggling with their mum, suckling contentedly while making a harmonious chorus.

Huang Xiaoqiu wanted to come a bit closer to have a better view, but

Bowa pulled her back and whispered, "The mother boar is overprotective at this time and it's better to leave them alone. Let's get out of here quickly!"

Never did they imagine in these silent woods that a tiny voice could be carried over such a great distance. The mother boar, keenly feeling something or perhaps overhearing their talk, indeed sat up all of a sudden, two strong front legs supporting her huge head, her big ears pricking up and drooping down from time to time, listening attentively.

Suddenly, her pair of round eyes fixed on them, which looked timid at first, then watched tentatively and gradually stared straight at them, as if burning with fire.

"Oh, no! Run, quick!"

They turned and ran at once. While they ran, they felt the rustling sound of tree branches following in the near distance. They looked back with fear and, sure enough, it was that huge mother boar baring its white, shining tusks and chasing after them with loud howls.

An old saying that one boar is equivalent to two bears and three tigers shows the ferocity of wild boars. When they were young, adults said never ever try to bother a female boar which not only bites people, but also is able to catch a tiger with a flick of its tusks and throw it into the air. How terrible it would be if it caught them.

"Hurry up! We are no match for her if we just run straight. Let's climb up the mountain."

Tired and frightened, Huang Xiaoqiu was out of breath, panting all the way. They went uphill while the mother boar that was close on their heels was going to overtake them in a second. Bowa thought of the time when he herded pigs in the wild. Those pigs, large or small, were all afraid of being whipped with a stick. He hurriedly asked Huang Xiaoqiu to run ahead of him while he himself broke off a branch and said, "Xiaoqiu, you run up the hill and I will deal with her."

"Be careful! Mother boars are very aggressive," warned Huang Xiaoqiu.

"I'm not afraid of her. You hurry up!" Tian Shi Bowa trimmed leaves and small forks off the branch, leaving a few thick ones. He then stood with his legs apart, staring down and waiting for the female boar.

The mother boar suddenly saw Bowa blocking her way. She stopped to look up at him, as if she had lost her mind and didn't know what to do for the time being. But she was a beast, after all, so big and how could she admit defeat so easily?

Howling scarily, the female boar launched her attack. She charged at Bowa with her mouth wide open while Bowa, without a tremor, held the stick tightly with both hands and beat the boar hard in the eyes. The mother boar shook her head and took a few steps back but her ferocity showed no intention of giving in and in a second she howled and launched another charge. Bowa fought back, waving the stick and continuously hitting the boar hard on the head and eyes. The mother boar could not stand it this time and stopped her attack. Bowa checked the stick in his hand, broken more than in half with less than a foot left. Bowa wanted to find a new one but was worried the mother boar might take the chance to attack again. As he hesitated, he heard Huang Xiaoqiu shouting from above, "Bowa, come up. Hurry up! There is a big cave here with a crack at its opening, good enough for us to enter and hide inside the cave."

Wonderful! Bowa said to himself. He turned back, shouted at the boar and then turned and ran uphill. The female boar was shocked by the sudden scream and retreated a few steps, standing still there for quite a while. She came to her senses when she saw her quarry run away; she raised her four feet to chase after him again.

Tian Shi Bowa ran breathlessly to Huang Xiaoqiu and saw a narrow crack near the wide opening of a cave. Young, slender and thin, they were able to get in while the huge mother boar of course couldn't.

"Great! It will work," said Bowa as he looked back and saw the charging mother boar getting closer and closer. He urged Xiaoqiu to squeeze in first.

Huang Xiaoqiu slowly squeezed her body into the crack but unfortunately she got stuck in the narrow crack when she was only a foot inside.

29

TRAPPED IN JINYU CAVE

"No! The crack is so narrow and my body hurts. Bowa, tell me what I should do!" Huang Xiaoqiu shouted in horror.

Bowa took a careful look and knew immediately that Huang Xiaoqiu was not very good at handling pain and dared not push hard. When she was not looking, Bowa went over and pushed her inside hard on the shoulder. Along with a gentle ripping sound, Huang Xiaoqiu slid into the cave at once. She was in but the left shoulder of her short shirt had been torn open by a stone.

"Are you OK?" Bowa asked, the moment he heard the sound.

"It's nothing. My shirt is torn. Bowa, come inside. It's very spacious in here." Huang Xiaoqiu paid no attention to her torn shirt and shouted at Bowa from inside the cave. Bowa threw the broken stick at the mother boar and when the beast was blocked and slowed its charge, he moved his body quickly trying to squeeze in through the narrow crack. To his surprise, he was stuck there too. Huang Xiaoqiu grabbed Bowa's arm and tried her best to pull him into the cave regardless of whether or not it would work or hurt him. With this force, Bowa pushed himself hard and his whole body went in at last.

She could not get in but was unwilling to admit defeat; she just turned around in front of the cave, refusing to leave.

"Ha..." Huang Xiaoqiu laughed when she saw the female boar turn around helplessly. She teased the beast, saying, "Come and get in, if you can. Wild boar, wild boar, why don't you come in since you are so fierce? Silly beast!"

"We can't stay in the cave waiting like this. Can we walk inside a bit further?" Bowa asked.

"I don't know. It looks so dark and I dare not."

"Relax. Let me try." Bowa felt the ground with his feet. It was hard! He took one more step and at the same time reached out his hand to check, and his head too. There was some space beside the wall in the cave. In this way, Bowa felt his way forward, going up along the winding wall. Very soon, they had walked more than 20 metres.

"Bowa, you won't find any snakes ahead that might bite me, will you?" Xiaoqiu's voice trembled with fear.

"No, it can't happen," answered Bowa briefly.

"Why? A lot of people encounter snakes when they explore caves."

"Xiaoqiu, you haven't thought this through, have you? What you just mentioned usually happens in caves that are descending, humid or full of water," Bowa explained carefully. "This cave is slanting upward, with dry walls. Therefore there would be no snakes and few other animals either."

"This Bowa! He does have a photographic memory! As he said so, I also remembered having read it in a book," Huang Xiaoqiu said to herself without answering back. "With him, such a smart boy, leading the way, is there anything else I should be afraid of?" She therefore followed Bowa closely and groped forward in the darkness.

All of a sudden, Bowa stopped feeling the way, but silently stood still. "What's wrong?" In the pitch darkness, Huang Xiaoqiu could not see him but she didn't let go of Bowa's T-shirt.

"I thought I saw a flash of light somewhere here," said Bowa.

"Hey, Bowa, stop making things up, will you?" Huang Xiaoqiu sounded as though she was making fun of him, "Never think you are indeed a wonder child even if teachers and classmates all believe you are as smart as a wonder child. How could there be a flash of light in such pitch darkness? Show me then. Where is the light? Are you worried about me being afraid? Are you worried that I will become a burden to you and therefore you're trying to comfort me? Ha… I'm not afraid any more. The worst thing would be if we can't find our way out."

"You're good! It's not easy for a girl to hold her nerve in a situation like this!"

"Hey, Bowa. Stop making fun of me. I am good? Forget it. My academic performance is getting worse and worse and I just cannot hold my head high at school! I'm so ashamed."

"It's not your fault. Something happened to your family and you've been affected by it. You will make progress once you adjust to the situation." That was very comforting to hear from Tian Shi Bowa. Xiaoqiu didn't say anything and Bowa continued, "As for the flash of light, I did feel it in front of me, and I am not enigmatic, you know."

"If it did flash, the light should be there. Could the light have got into the stone and disappeared?"

Huang Xiaoqiu replied, "You are taking it for granted. You can't justify it anyway."

"I remember the Science Education Channel once had a programme about it. A few scientists went to explore a very deep cave and eventually they descended to such a depth that there was no light at all. As they continued forward by groping their way in the dark, they felt a glimmer of light flash for an instant and then vanish. Later, before they had gone very far, they did find an exit where light passed through. They did some research and found it had something to do with reflections of sunlight on tree leaves dancing in the wind. When the tree leaves shook, the light was transmitted into the cave, flashing and disappearing immediately."

"You mean we might find an exit soon?" asked Huang Xiaoqiu hopefully.

"Very possible!"

With hope in their hearts, they kept up their motivation to achieve their goal. The two felt the power in their legs and they groped in the darkness and moved forward much more quickly. They climbed up 88 slopes and navigated 99 bends and when they looked up, a sudden light blinded their eyes.

"Wow!" Huang Xiaoqiu called out first. At a place about 20 metres above them appeared an elliptical opening, room-like and irregular in shape. "Bowa, you are so amazing! There really is an exit!"

Great, they could get out of the cave now. Full of hope, they stumbled and climbed up to the open exit. Streams of dazzling colourful rays of sun instantly dazzled their eyes. What a beautiful opening it was! Crystals, fluorites, granite and other beautiful stones, mixed together all sparkled with multiple colours under the gorgeous glow on top of the distant mountain. They saw a vertical line of characters faintly written on a relatively flat rock wall, Jinyu Cave, a blurred signature which could be roughly recognised as Huang…

"Nancheng, yes, the following characters are Nancheng." Huang Xiaoqiu recognised these characters and shouted happily, "Bowa, the person who wrote it shares the same family name as me. How interesting! Look at these handsome strokes! They might have been written by a descendant of Huang Tingjian (a famous calligrapher in Song Dynasty China). What do you think?"

"Maybe," said Bowa as he looked at the characters carefully. "They are not carved on the rock, rather they are written in vermillion. It couldn't have been written a long time ago because the writing is still quite clear. I guess the calligrapher should be a modern person and probably it was the one who found this cave."

Huang Xiaoqiu said, "Anyway, we can leave here safely!"

"Don't count your chickens before they hatch!" Bowa glanced around and said, "Let's go and check around the opening. It is still questionable whether we can leave here or not."

When they went to the edge of the opening, they were both taken aback and gasped.

Outside the cave mouth was a bottomless cliff; there was no way for them to get out!

"Oh heck! That's too bad! What should we do?" Huang Xiaoqiu sat down on the ground, anxious tears streaming down.

"Look at you! What's the use of crying?" Bowa said calmly, "Don't you remember someone wrote something here? There's no need to worry about how to get out of here."

"You're right!" Huang Xiaoqiu broke into laughter. She stood up, wiped her eyes and said, "Let's look for it at once."

The open mouth of Jinyu Cave was located high up the mountain. They walked a few metres straight along the mouth and found a narrow passage. Inside the winding passage, a natural 'skylight' or crack formed on the edge of the rock that appeared every dozen or every hundred metres or so, from which scattered light penetrated, dim inside still but quite convenient for them to walk on. After they had walked about four or five kilometres and turned a sharp bend, the view before them suddenly opened up: a huge cave hall was displayed in front of them. The hall was particularly high and large, as high as a six-storey building and so large that it could accommodate two or three thousand people dancing at the same time. Beside the hall, a lot of cracks in the rock from which lights shone through, gave people a sense of soft serenity when they looked at it.

Around the hall, rows and rows of grotesque golden stalactites had been formed over time, mixed with each other, both large and small. Huang Xiaoqiu ran to the centre of the hall, happily waved her hands and merrily danced the Tujia hand-waving dance. Bowa however searched everywhere for a passage to get out of the cave. When he retraced his steps, he saw four characters engraved on a large milky-yellow Earth-God-like stalactite: *Jinse Dating* (Golden Hall).

Tian Shi Bowa sighed with emotion, "Who was imaginitive enough to name the place like this? Very ceremonial!"

"I couldn't care less. Bowa, I'm starving!" Huang Xiaoqiu suddenly plonked herself down on the ground in the Golden Hall and said to Bowa, "I'm suddenly feeling disconcerted and dizzy too."

"As you say, my stomach feels empty too." It quickly became dark. Bowa looked at the sky and said with some anxiety, "It's getting dark. What should we do? Well, nothing we can do. You take some water first to stave off hunger from the puddle beside the stalactites."

Huang Xiaoqiu drank some water and felt a little better. She said, "It is dark now. Are we going to stay here for the night? No! I have to find an exit."

"I tried that already and I went quite a long way inside but couldn't find one anywhere," said Bowa.

"Have you checked that large opening nearby?" asked Huang Xiaoqiu, pointing at a hole on the right side of the rock wall.

"Did you see clouds and fog floating outside the opening? So bright! There must be a cliff over there. No need to check it," said Bowa.

"Bowa, you always say we should be careful with everything but this time you are not." Huang Xiaoqiu seemed to have grasped the key point and said, "Don't let any hope slip by. Take me there to have a look."

On hearing this, Bowa felt a bit embarrassed. Yes, he should be careful with everything and how could he get muddled up with his work? Bowa said, "Xiaoqiu, you are right. We should go and have a look."

They walked to the opening and stretched their necks to look into the distance. It was really dazzling outside, cliffs standing steep like vertical walls which even the most agile apes would find it difficult to climb down. Huang Xiaoqiu however was eager to find a way. She removed the scales from her big eyes and searched around carefully until she found a poem written on the cliff! It had four lines in total and although it was difficult to read, it could be seen that the poem was written in vermillion:

> The Jade Emperor painted a Jinyu Cave,
> Dreamy and dramatic as if in the Lake of Immortals.
> Where is the winding road leading to the outside?
> An 800-step long vine ladder connects to the ancient pine tree.

"Hey, isn't it leading the way for us?" said Huang Xiaoqiu as if she had found a treasure after reading the poem. She continued, "Hurry up! Let's look for it and I am sure the road must be at the opening."

"How do you know the road is at the opening?" asked Bowa vehemently.

"Isn't it as plain as the nose on your face? *Where is the winding road leading to the outside? An 800-step long vine ladder connects to the ancient pine tree.*" Xiaoqiu said, "In my judgement, a vine ladder is sure to be around or at least very nearby. And the ladder is very, very long; 800? I guess it might refer to 800 steps. Suppose one step is 40 centimetres long, the height of the cliff is at least 320 metres and it connects to the ancient pine tree below the mouth of the cave too. What a long vine ladder it is!"

"Hey, Xiaoqiu, you are really good now, your thinking is more and more resolute. OK, let's find that vine ladder."

They looked around the opening to check if anything was visible but there was no sign of any vine ladder. A slightly protruding keel stone from the left side of the opening caught Xiaoqiu's attention. She looked at it carefully and it was quite a large stone, weighing about a ton. Xiaoqiu said, "Perhaps the vine ladder is under the rock. Come on, Bowa, grasp my hand tight and I'll stick my head out to take a look."

"No. What if I should lose my grip on your hand or you should miss your step? You are done for if you fall over the cliff."

Huang Xiaoqiu mulled it over, agreed and said, "But I am a girl and it is more difficult for me to hold your hand tight."

"You don't need to," said Bowa after examining the rock. "I'll lay flat on the ground and grab the flinty point of the rock while you press my calf down and hold it, and I'll try my best to stretch my neck to check, which I think is quite safe."

"OK." Xiaoqiu nodded in agreement.

Bowa crawled forward, his chest already leaning out of the opening and his head stretching out with great efforts to look at the rock below. He suddenly shouted, "Yes! Yes! Xiaoqiu, I can see it. There is a vine ladder pressed under the rock."

"Really? You've seen it?" Huang Xiaoqiu was excited too and said, "Hurry up, get it up and show me."

"I know the vine, millettia, very thick and strong, but this one looks too dry and crisp. Vines grow from the foot of rocks and probably there was a draught one year and the upper part of the vines withered and died for lack of water," said Bowa as he looked at it carefully. "Hey, I've found something good. New vines have long grown from the old ones but when they clung to the old ones to climb high, some of the old vines broke and the new vines fell down and hung on the cliff wall."

"Shall we try the old vines? What if they are still very strong?" Xiaoqiu was very eager to have a look but she dared not loosen her grip on Bowa's calf but just urged anxiously, "Get it up quickly. Let's try and see whether we can climb down the vine to the foot of the cliff."

"OK!" Bowa reached out his hand to grab the vine ladder, lifted it up slowly and said, "Xiaoqiu, did you see it? I felt it and it's a bit dry, it has probably been exposed to wind and rain for at least 20 or 30 years."

"Grab it tight and crawl back slowly then."

Bowa pulled his body back into the cave. Huang Xiaoqiu grabbed the vine ladder from his hand and pulled it hard. With a clear crack, the vine ladder in her hand broke, falling all the way down the cliff to the ground.

"My! That was close!" They both turned deadly pale, "Luckily we didn't try to climb down the vine!"

"Hey, we are at a dead end. We're really done for!" said Huang Xiaoqiu, looking out of the cave. As she looked, the discouraged look on her face suddenly changed into a happy surprise. "Bowa, look, look opposite."

"What is it?"

"We never noticed it before," said Huang Xiaoqiu as if she had made a great discovery. "Bowa, look at the small hill obliquely below opposite, covered with grass, only a few metres away from us. If we try our best to jump onto it, we won't get hurt when falling on the grass, will we?"

"Ha…" Tian Shi Bowa chuckled, "Xiaoqiu, you are too anxious to underestimate the real distance. It's at least 60 or 70 metres between us and that small hill."

"My goodness. It looks so close anyway. But how do you know?" asked Huang Xiaoqiu a little doubtfully.

"Look carefully! How tall are those pine trees over there?" said Bowa, pointing at the pine trees on the small hill opposite. "Each of them I guess is no less than 30 metres high, isn't that right? Think about it, the diameter of the tree tops would be at least 10 metres. Suppose we fill the distance between us and that small hill with pine trees, a row of six of them side by side might not be enough for us to do so."

"Well, based on your calculation, it is impossible for us to jump onto it."

"Not just us, even a world long-jump champion couldn't do it either."

"Does that mean we can do nothing but wait for death? I don't want to and I need to find a way out of here." Huang Xiaoqiu stared at the valley veiled in the deepening darkness, so worried that she looked like a cat on hot bricks.

"No complaint! Face reality! Keep cool in an emergency! Deal with things calmly!" Bowa murmured these things in his heart. He chose a corner to sit in with a flat, smooth wall behind, found two clean slates to sit on and called Xiaoqiu to come over. He then took a plastic bag out of Xiaoqiu's backpack, and filled it with water for Xiaoqiu after he himself had drunk enough from the puddle beside the stalactites.

Darkness fell in the blink of an eye. Neither of them needed to say anything, both knowing they had to sit there for the night. After a while, Huang Xiaoqiu started to feel the cold little by little. She could not help saying to herself, "How could I have ripped my shirt? How can I face people with this on when I get out of here?"

"A big rip?" Bowa at this time remembered Huang Xiaoqiu's torn shirt.

"You are indeed careless! Didn't you see me holding one side of my shirt all the time?" Huang Xiaoqiu looked quite upset, "One side of my shirt is torn."

"Hey, I remember you prepared for the trip. Why didn't you bring a change of clothes?"

"I folded my dress up for the trip, and some toiletries too. But I was in a bit of a hurry and I forgot to put them into my backpack due to some unforeseen interruptions."

"Well, you have to sew it up," said Bowa.

"Sew it up? Bowa, you must be joking!" Huang Xiaoqiu grumbled as if she was pouting. "Do we have any needle and thread? Or do we use our teeth?"

"OK, I have an idea." Bowa didn't mind a bit about the irony in Huang Xiaoqiu's words and continued, "My T-shirt is good. Let's do a swap. I can tie some knots in the torn parts. You know, it is not a problem for a boy to dress like that. No shame at all."

Huang Xiaoqiu didn't say anything.

"Is that OK?"

"It's OK, but I don't want to trouble you," whispered Huang Xiaoqiu.

"Hey, no need to stand on ceremony!" Bowa took off his T-shirt, handed it to her and said, "Here you are! Put it on!"

Huang Xiaoqiu took it in the darkness and said, "I will take off mine. Don't look at me."

"What are you talking about? Look at what? It's pitch dark here."

"No. Turn round, then I'll take off my clothes."

"OK, OK, it's up to you." Bowa did turn round, and though in fact he could not see anything, he covered his eyes with his hands. "I'm OK now. Take it off and give it to me."

Huang Xiaoqiu put on the T-shirt and then stuffed her shirt into Bowa's hands, "You can turn round and put the shirt on."

Tian Shi Bowa groped for the place where it was torn and tied a knot there. He then tried to button up the shirt, only to find that he couldn't. It was a bit small for him. He just left it open.

Tired and hungry, they both fell asleep leaning against the wall before finding a topic to talk with each other about.

It was summer, but the temperature in the Jinyu Cave was very low because it was located on Huiqian Ridge at an altitude of more than 2,000 metres. At night, after a few breezes swept through the cave, stones heated by the sun during the day became icy cold very quickly. In the middle of the night, chills from the stone wall pierced Huang Xiaoqiu's body making her shudder a few times, and she woke up trembling. She touched her face, which was cold, and her arms, which were cold too with goose bumps all over. She wanted to move her body but it was too stiff to move at all. Before she had figured out what to do, she was shiverering with cold.

"Bowa! Bowa!" She barely had the strength to open her mouth, "Bowa, wake up!"

Tian Shi Bowa was sleeping with his body bent over his knees. He felt the sound, opened his eyes drowsily and glanced at where Huang Xiaoqiu sat, "Are you calling me?"

"Yes, yes, it's me." Huang Xiaoqiu answered in a trembling voice because she was so cold. "I'm so cold…"

"Cold?" asked Bowa, "How can you feel cold?"

"I'm cold and I can't stand it any more," said Huang Xiaoqiu with difficulty. "Don't you feel cold?"

Bowa moved his body and felt his chest and arms; they were cold but not too uncomfortable. He said, "It is a bit cold but bearable."

Why could he stand it? Bowa felt somewhat inferior and lonely when he was very young because of his articulation disorder. Therefore, no matter whether it was spring or winter, he often went to catch fish and crabs in White Crane Stream, which helped him build a strong body to fortify himself against the cold. Also, he fell asleep over his knees and the chills from the stone had not invaded his body and hadn't hurt his vitality. That's why the cold didn't harm him much. He asked Huang Xiaoqiu, "Are you feeling very cold?"

"Awfully cold!" Huang Xiaoqiu's teeth were chattering with the cold, "Bo…wa…, my body is icy cold."

Bowa reached out his hand to touch her arm. "Ah, yes, it's really cold. Xiaoqiu, what's wrong with you?"

"I am afraid of the cold," said Huang Xiaoqiu falteringly. "Perhaps the chills from the stones have pierced my body and now I cannot move. Help… me!"

Bowa touched Xiaoqiu's other arm, legs and feet; they were all freezing. He was in a panic. Without thinking too much, he stood up, bent his body a little and walked to her side. He held Xiaoqiu's shoulders tight and dragged her to him. Finally, Xiaoqiu moved from the wall and sat straight. After a while, she exhaled a long breath and said, "I am... feeling a little... better."

Bowa dared not let go of of her shoulders in case she fell back on the stone wall again. He asked, "Xiaoqiu, what should I do now?"

"I am cold... and I can't sit up."

"What do you want me to do? How about this? Let me hold you for a while, will you?"

"OK!" Huang Xiaoqiu nodded.

Tian Shi Bowa put his arms around her shoulders, rotated her body 90 degrees, pushed his slate close to Huang Xiaoqiu and sat on it himself, pressing his chest tight against Xiaoqiu's back. However, he could not loosen his hands for the time being for fear that Xiaoqiu would fall down. Bowa wrapped his arms round her breast but the moment he made a little effort, he touched two springy lumps. He was startled and quickly moved his hands elsewhere. "Well, Xiaoqiu," Bowa said to himself, "no wonder she is so afraid of the cold. She is physically sick." Bowa moved his hands to Xiaoqiu's belt, his left fingers locking in the right ones.

"Bowa, if... I... die... like this, what should I do? I have an unfulfilled wish."

"What wish?" asked Bowa.

"I owe... a backpack to one of my classmates... He... he didn't accept it."

"He already knows your sincerity and he will accept it." Tian Shi Bowa knew instantly what she meant and comforted her, "You won't die. It is not that serious and you will be well very soon."

Gradually, Bowa's body warmed Xiaoqiu and a few moments later Xiaoqiu's body became warm and soft and she didn't stutter either when she talked. "Bowa, I am so grateful to you."

"Don't mention it! It's good you are not feeling cold," said Bowa. Then he thought for a while and said, "Xiaoqiu, when we go back, I suggest you go to hospital for an examination."

"Bowa, what do you mean? I am not sick; why are you saying this to me?"

"Not sick? Why are you so afraid of the cold then?" Bowa felt Huang Xiaoqiu was somewhat careless. "Don't you know you have two lumps on your breast? That is very unusual! Perhaps that is the reason why you are so afraid of the cold."

"Bowa, you…" Huang Xiaoqiu felt herself reddening. She calmed herself down and said, "Well, Bowa, how should I explain it to you? It is not a disease, rather it's normal growth."

"You are hiding your sickness to avoid treatment, aren't you? Xiaoqiu, in what sense is it normal? Why don't I have it?"

"Ah! Let's drop it. You don't understand anyway." Huang Xiaoqiu pouted.

"It is because we don't know that we need to talk about science. It is scientific to advise you to go to hospital," said Bowa very seriously.

"Science! Science! You only know about science through textbooks," retorted Huang Xiaoqiu impatiently, "Bowa, I have to tell you being too smart is stupid."

Chatting with each other, they drifted off to sleep again.

30

THE WHITE CRANE SPREADS ITS WINGS

Were they roused by the flashing glare of the morning sunlight? Or were they woken up by the rumbling of their stomachs? Maybe both. They woke up anyway.

Their stomachs felt empty, growling so loudly it was as if a few ox carts were running over their bellies one by one. They touched their bellies, which were empty! Their stomachs were protesting with hunger!

"I'm hungry!" said Huang Xiaoqiu, narrowing her eyes. Her lips pouted as she stood up and said to Bowa, "I am starving! My head is dizzy too."

Bowa, who was still sitting there, stretched and said, "Go and drink some water."

"Drink water! Just water! I have no strength at all. How to find a way out?" Huang Xiaoqiu went over to the big opening and saw a group of white cranes flying elegantly in the morning sunshine. She suddenly hit upon a strange idea, "Hey, Bowa, you can call your little white crane to bring food for us, can't you?"

"Xiaoqiu, that's empty talk. How could my little white crane hear my call since he lives in Xiaonanhai dozens of kilometres away?"

"Didn't you say white cranes are intelligent birds that can use sound or whatever to transmit information? A group of white cranes are flying outside the cave now. You could give it a try."

"White cranes? There are white cranes flying outside right now?" Bowa suddenly stood up, walked across to the opening in a few steps and saw a flock of white cranes flying in the sky. "OK. I'll give it a try."

Bowa took out the handkerchief he kept in his pocket all the time, the one Teacher Liu gave him, waved it high in his hand and shouted, "Little white crane, little white crane…"

His shout flew out of the cave and echoed high in the sky.

The flock of cranes that had already flown past the cave came back! They flew over the opening, hovering and circling overhead, cried out and flew away again.

"Xiaoqiu, I tried. Now you're satisfied, aren't you?" With these words, Bowa filled the plastic bag with some water for Xiaoqiu to drink and he himself drank some too. Then he said, "You find a place to relieve yourself, then we will set about finding a way out."

"No. You know, I do want to go, but I really have no strength left at all. How can I do that?" said Huang Xiaoqiu, helplessly. "Can't we wait for the little white crane for a while?"

"It's OK to take a break and conserve some strength, but don't put all your hopes on my little fellow. He is too far away from us, after all." Bowa finished his words and walked away to find a quiet place to relieve himself while leaving some privacy for Huang Xiaoqiu. A few minutes later, he went back to the Golden Hall.

It seemed Huang Xiaoqiu was really hungry and extremely tired. Although the sunshine shone on her face, she looked dull, pale, fatigued and weary. Bowa moved his lips, wanting to say something but at last he gave up. Spiritually relaxing a bit, Bowa felt very hungry and very tired too. All he could do was to lean on the stone wall beside the opening, staring into the distance.

At this time, a miracle happened.

A tiny white spot, approaching from the distance, was getting bigger and bigger and clearer and clearer. It fluttered its wings, black and white, charming and graceful.

"Little white crane! Little white crane!"

Huang Xiaoqiu jumped up when she heard Bowa's shout. When she was about to take a close look, the little white crane, with a loud cry, had already glided into the cave with his wings spreading flat.

They both rushed to his side, "Little white crane, how could you get here so fast?"

"Little white crane, have you been following us closely all the time?"

The little white crane standing erect was head and shoulders taller than Tian Shi Bowa. He brushed against Bowa's body with his long beak and wings, crying at the same time in response.

Since the little white crane had come, Bowa got straight to the point. He said as he made gestures showing fish and feeding fish into his mouth, "Fish, do you understand? Little white crane, go and catch some fish for us."

They didn't know whether the little white crane had understood them or not. This young fellow made a few circles around Bowa first, then clattered toward the opening, spread his wings suddenly and flew away.

As his tiny back became smaller and smaller, the hope in Xiaoqiu's and Bowa's hearts became bigger and bigger.

It paid to wait patiently. Their hopes at last came true. It didn't take long for the little fellow to fly back into the Golden Hall with seven or eight small white carangids (jack fish). Bowa cleaned the fish in a puddle, took one and gave it to Xiaoqiu, who however said, "Are you making fun of me? It's raw fish. How can I eat that?"

"Hey, Xiaoqiu," Bowa wanted to say a few harsh words to her but what came out of his mouth was, "OK, I'll come up with something."

Tian Shi Bowa searched around and found there were some dry branches beside the opening. He went over to break some off and found some fluffy dry grass too. He piled them all beside a stone, then went to look for something in the rubble of the Golden Hall.

"Bowa, what are you looking for?" asked Huang Xiaoqiu.

"Fire."

"Fire?" Huang Xiaoqiu flashed her big eyes and suddenly remembered something. "Bowa, you're looking for some black stones, aren't you? Those shining black stones you once showed me in the White Crane Stream?"

"You have a good memory this time," answered Bowa.

Black stones aroused Xiaoqiu's interest. She hurriedly ran to help Bowa. Maybe her girls' eyes were sharper and Xiaoqiu found a small black stone first and then Bowa found another one.

Over the fluffy dry grass nest, Bowa gripped one black stone in each hand

and struck them together. After striking them together dozens of times in succession, a spark flashed inside the dry grass and then a faint plume of smoke appeared, thickening little by little and turning blue at last. Bowa blew gently on the grass nest and with a slight sound, flames instantly burst out, then took hold of the dry wood. Xiaoqiu hurriedly placed the small fish on the rock around the fire pit to roast.

How delicious the fish smelt! Needless to say, enjoying the delicious small roasted fish, their spirits were soaring, brisk and joyous like the sky where the white cranes spread their wings, soaring high.

Huang Xiaoqiu picked one up from the rock to feed the little white crane who however rolled his eyes at her and moved his head aside, ignoring her.

"Xiaoqiu, the little white crane, unlike you, doesn't eat cooked fish." When Bowa had almost finished his food, he went to his little pal, put his arms around his neck and said, "Little white crane, help us completely or not at all. You have better eyes than us and often fly in the sky, so perhaps you know where the exit of this cave is. Can you lead us out of here? Please!"

The little fellow ran around in a few circles first, then quickly strode toward the opening which he had just flown through.

"What did he mean?" Xiaoqiu didn't understand the little white crane's behaviour and asked Bowa as she stared at him. "I guess he wants to tell us there is no other exit or the only exit is where he just flew in," replied Bowa.

Bowa went up to his pal, stroked his neck and wings, and said, "We want to get out of here. Do you have any idea how?"

The little white crane raised his head high, facing the open mouth of the cave, opened his beak and uttered a long cry. Then he turned back, plunged his head between Bowa's legs, crouching down for Bowa to put his bottom close enough to his body between his neck and wings. He then flapped his wings on the spot.

"Bowa, is the little white crane telling you he wants to carry you out of the cave?" Huang Xiaoqiu guessed with surprise.

Eyes wide, Bowa knew that was the case. But how could it be possible? He moved his legs and slipped off the little crane's body.

"Is it possible?" Huang Xiaoqiu voiced Bowa's doubts out loud.

Bowa knew the little white crane had now grown bigger, taller and stronger. Two years ago, when he went back home from Chongqing after the operation, this little fellow had helped him carry his luggage home along the White Crane Stream. But carrying him was not a joke. There wasn't even anywhere safe for him to put his hands and feet, and if he should fall off its back in the sky, he would surely die. The situation left a lot to be desired. Could the little white crane pick up the millettia hanging halfway down the cliff? Or could he grab it with his claws and bring it to the cave? As Bowa thought about this, he patted the little fellow's wings, brought him to the big rock, and picked up a few vines for him to see and smell. Next, he pointed toward the cliff wall outside the cave, lifted one of his legs up and stuffed a dry vine into his claws. The little white crane clenched his claws and seized the vines tightly as if he could read Bowa's mind.

"Yes! That's it! Good boy!" Tian Shi Bowa praised his little white crane and at the same time patted the stone wall at the opening, saying seriously, "But I don't want you to catch these dry vines; I want you to get the living ones hanging halfway down the cliff and bring them back here."

The little white crane watched Bowa's demonstration attentively until he was finished. He then walked around him, uttered a cry, flapped his wings, dashed forward toward the opening and stepped firmly on the ground near the mouth of the opening with his legs. Instantly he was soaring up into the sky.

Bowa and Huang Xiaoqiu rushed to the edge of the opening to watch.

Hovering in the sky as he circled twice, the little white crane slowed down and glided close to the flourishing millettia cluster clinging to the cliff. He targeted a thick one, flew over and picked it up with his beak. He tried his best to flap his wings to fly up, but it was quite a long one, fresh and heavy containing a lot of water. The little fellow couldn't bear such a weight any more and opened his beak involuntarily. The vine slipped out of the little white crane's beak and rustled noisily back against the cliff from the sky. How could the little fellow be willing to accept defeat? He flapped his wings again, trying his best to chase after the vine. As the vine was approaching the wall, the little white crane opened his strong claws, clutched the vine tight and flew up quickly toward the open mouth of the cave.

"Yeah! Little white crane, you are so good!" Huang Xiaoqiu shouted as she could not help clapping her hands. Tian Shi Bowa was of course very proud of his pal in his heart but he didn't blindly cheer up on account of this. What for anyway? He bent over and stared outside, preparing nervously to welcome the little white crane back.

The little fellow struggled to fly toward the cave, even the sound of his wings flapping rapidly in the sky could be heard.

Clouds rise before dragons rise out of the sea; winds arrive before cranes fly down. The wind stirred by the little white crane's wings blew in Bowa's face first followed by the little fellow as he flew into the cave. Bowa stared at the vine inside his claws. The moment the fellow landed on the ground, Bowa quickly rushed toward it, grabbed the vine tightly with both hands and pressed it hard under his chest.

The little white crane released his claws and jumped aside, panting.

Huang Xiaoqiu came to grasp the vine too and helped Bowa stand up.

"Wow, it is indeed a long vine!" said Huang Xiaoqiu as she looked at the vine with many leaves on.

Bowa still held the vine tightly for fear that it would slip down the cliff. He shook the vine, smiled and said, "The longer, the better. We can coil it around the rock a few more times so that it will be safer."

"Yes, yes, you are right," responded Huang Xiaoqiu.

"The millettia is strong but this one alone is not enough. What if it should get worn by the jagged edges of the rocks and break suddenly?" Bowa said to Xiaoqiu as if speaking to the little white crane as well, "We need at least one more for safety's sake."

Looking at Bowa, the little white crane in fact didn't know what he was talking about. Bowa therefore walked over to him, patted his wings, and pointed to the cliff, telling him to clutch vines one more time.

The little white fellow immediately understood. He spread his wings and flew out of the cave. Familiar with the route already, the little fellow spotted a thick and strong millettia after hovering in the sky for just one circle. He flew straight to the cliff, grabbed the vine with his strong claws, flapped his wings to fly up and quickly returned to the open mouth of the cave.

Tian Shi Bowa handed the first vine to Xiaoqiu while he himself grasped the one the little white crane had just brought back. "Great! This one is thicker and stronger. Xiaoqiu, we are saved."

"It's all thanks to the little white crane and we should be grateful to him," said Huang Xiaoqiu vehemently.

They twisted the two vines together and pulled against the vine to test its tension; it was very strong. They wound the vine around the end of the big rock near the open mouth of the cave three times, with the end of the vine coiled around a flat slate and tucked under the big rock tight, safe and secure for sure.

Bowa said, "Xiaoqiu, you go first. How about your arm strength? Will it be OK?"

"How could it not be?" replied Huang Xiaoqiu defiantly. "Don't you know people in the village have all called me a tomboy since I was very young. I am very strong! What's more, there are many potholes in the cliff and you can conserve strength in your hands if you step on the footholds with your feet and climb down. I am lighter than you and it won't damage the vine if I go first."

"You are underestimating your enemy! Never slacken your grip on the vine!"

"I know I know! You nag like an old woman!" replied Huang Xiaoqiu as she carried the luggage across her body and grabbed the vine.

"No chance for me to nag if something happens!" Watching Huang Xiaoqiu grab the vines and slowly step down on the footholds, Tian Shi Bowa warned, "Every time you shift your grip on the vines, hold on tight! When you reach the foot of the cliff, shout back and wait for me there."

"I know I know!" answered Huang Xiaoqiu from the stone wall outside the cave.

About 11 minutes later, Huang Xiaoqiu's voice came from under the cliff at last. "I did it. Bowa, come down quickly!"

Bowa was half relieved. He patted the little white crane and said, "Good boy, fly! Watch me in the sky as I climb down the cliff."

Very calmly, Tian Shi Bowa grasped the vines, located the footholds, climbed down the vines hand over hand, and looked for potholes below step by step.

When Bowa was halfway down the cliff, the little white crane circled around him, hovering gracefully beside him. The breeze from the little fellow's wings refreshed Bowa, which enhanced his performance like the whistling pine waves, the fragrance of wild flowers, the playful noises of deer, squirrels and hares, the whispering of damselflies, mole crickets, tiny mantis and katydids (like grasshoppers or crickets), the crisp singing of chickadees, rubythroats, thrushes and larks. He stared into the distance with a firm, pure and penetrating look in his eyes. His eyes spied auspicious colourful clouds under his feet, rows of aged green pines and fluffy masses of flowers, all filling him with particular happiness.

Tian Shi Bowa arrived at the foot of the cliff very quickly, where Huang Xiaoqiu was waiting for him.

They found the hill covered with green pine trees and grass opposite the cliff connected to a higher mountain, the very highest one they were going to climb. By bravely embracing danger while climbing a mountain, human beings are sure to conquer the highest summit. They were able to do it because they knew Huiqian Ridge was on the top of this highest mountain.

They ascended the hill and walked toward the mountain top. After quite a few hours' climbing, they finally reached the top and embarked on a relatively wide mountain ridge stretching with twists and turns.

Along the way, the little white crane hopped forward in front to guide them for a while and then flew up to hover above their heads detecting and searching for a way ahead. Bowa loved his little pal. He patted him on the wing and said, "Little white crane, we are very grateful to you for saving us from danger. Are you thirsty? Do you feel lonely? Good boy, go and find a lake to drink some water, go and find your friends to play with. I will call you again when I miss you. Is that OK?"

The little white crane fluttered his wings and responded with a cry. He then spread his wings, ran very fast along the mountain road with his tall, strong legs and suddenly soared up into the sky.

Bowa and Xiaoqiu continued their trip before they could tear themselves away from watching the little fellow fly up into the air. Very soon, they saw a household in a small mountain hollow. They entered the house and saw an old man, so they asked him how to get to Huiqian Ridge. The old man laughed and said, "It is right under your nose. You are in Huiqian Ridge now."

"Really?" Huang Xiaoqiu was overjoyed when she heard this and asked hurriedly, "Grandpa, do you know Huang Cuicui?"

"Huang Cuicui?" asked the old man. "We have two Huang Cuicuis here. Are you asking about the Huang Cuicui who married here from White Crane Village in Xiaonanhai?"

"Yes, Exactly! She is my aunt."

"Little girl, you are asking the right person. She is in our village. Go straight ahead and you will see the big house of her family after climbing over the hillside. You can't miss it."

Xiaoqiu and Bowa found Huang Cuicui very quickly and they also knew that Xiaoqiu's sister Huang Xiaochun had already left Huiqian Ridge to work in Shenzhen.

31
PREFERENCE FOR LOW-ALTITUDE FLIGHT

Tian Shi Bowa was a grateful boy. On the afternoon when they went back to the village, he didn't go home first but went directly to look for Teacher Liu, reporting back and also telling her about their trip.

"Hey! You are back. Perfect timing. Tian Shi Bowa, come on in." The moment Tian Shi Bowa entered the playground, Liu Wanyi in the room saw him and welcomed him into the office, saying, "Bowa, you are beginning middle school life very soon. You know, English is very important in middle school but we don't have English classes in our school, so it is totally new to you. We received a notice from the higher education committee informing us that a national English summer camp is to be held in Beidaihe. It is free! The county education committee has decided to give you this opportunity because of your excellent performance in the national composition contest. You will go there when the summer holiday begins. Make full use of this opportunity and study hard to bone up on your English."

"Wow! It really is a good opportunity! I have been worrying about whether I could keep up with my English in middle school," said Tian Shi Bowa happily. But he suddenly frowned and said after thinking for a while, "Will Huang Xiaoqiu have this opportunity?"

Liu Wanyi hesitated for a moment and said as she looked at Bowa, "Good opportunities don't come to all. You're starting from a low base and you need to seize every opportunity to learn. If you pass it up, you will lag behind. Have you thought about it?"

Teacher Liu Wanyi didn't put it directly. There was so much knowledge waiting for Bowa to learn and what's more, it was she who had discovered and nurtured him, a young sapling with a promising future. In order to help him climb the mountain of knowledge, she had applied to prolong her teaching assignment in the village and to be transferred to the middle school which Tian Shi Bowa was going to attend. She also bought a set of six volumes of the *Modern Chinese Dictionary* and she was also preparing to buy him a complete collection of *Olympic Maths* materials. As for English, of course, it was also important. He had to have a solid foundation in English for his future college education and for studying abroad. But today he proposed to give this precious opportunity to someone else!

"Teacher Liu, I know this chance is very important for me but even if I lose this particular opportunity, it will only delay my starting to learn a foreign language while this opportunity for Huang Xiaoqiu really matters. If it could be given to her as she is still in low spirits, it will perhaps help restore and improve her enterprising spirit and influence her entire life."

What else could she say? Teacher Liu was lost in thought. Even though Tian Shi Bowa was just a child, he was broad-minded. Opportunities are like seeds. Giving one's own opportunity to others means one opportunity becomes two seeds which will definitely sprout with the right soil conditions. Buds grow up and two trees of course are better than one. At last Liu Wanyi said, "OK, I respect your decision." Tian Shi Bowa happily waved goodbye to her.

Huang Xiaoqiu was too excited and couldn't believe it when she received the news that she would be going to the summer camp in Beidaihe. When she was told it was Tian Shi Bowa who had given her this opportunity, she froze for a moment and then cried her eyes out. As she cried things became clearer and clearer to her. She said, "Bowa, I really don't know… how… well, I am so grateful and I will learn from you and reward your kindness with good performance."

In a happy mood, Tian Shi Bowa skipped all the way home. He didn't know a guest was waiting for him at home.

Before he entered the courtyard, Bowa had already smelt the aroma drifting from the kitchen. His mum was preparing dinner! Usually it was not yet time for dinner and Bowa knew they must have guests coming.

He was right! Uncle Qu sat in the wooden chair under the roof, eagerly staring at the intersection leading to the courtyard, hoping he would see Bowa the moment he entered. Of course, he was rewarded. As soon as Bowa went into the courtyard, he stood up and greeted him, "Bowa, hurry up, come and sit down for a while."

"Uncle Qu, you are coming to visit again," greeted Bowa politely.

Coming to visit again? For those who didn't know the story, they would surely feel it was a kind of complaint about frequent visits from others. Uncle Qu however had long understood why Bowa was concerned about him, and that it was difficult for him to walk along the mountain road. But the fact was that Uncle Qu had come to visit again. He was willing and able to and he loved to do it. Since he had become attached to Bowa's family, he had been full of concern about them, often coming to visit them and caring about them. Today was no exception. After he had drunk the tea Bowa poured into his cup, he said, "Bowa, you are going to be a middle school student, aren't you? I want to pick you up to study in the city and at the same time your father could go to my place to recuperate for a while. If so, you could visit your father every week while nothing would distract you from your studies. What do you think about it?"

"Go to study in a city middle school? Great! Middle schools in the city have good facilities and teaching quality. Uncle Qu, you are so kind!" Bowa however smiled and continued firmly, "But I can't go with you. According to the rules, I should attend middle school in the town. The other teenagers in the village and I are equal and when they can't go to study in the city while I can because of some privileges, I am sure to feel guilty. Now some people say studying in big cities is high-altitude flight while studying in the village is low-altitude flight, which I know is meant to make fun of us. But my teacher says that for a pilot, low-altitude flight is the very knowledge that one needs most, depends on the most technique and is the most challenging. I like low-altitude flight! As for my father, let him stay at home. My grandma would worry about being unable to see him at once if anything happened to him. As for me, I also want to take care of him every day when I'm not studying."

"Well, Bowa, I am so happy for you although I do have some regrets," exclaimed Uncle Qu. "How many young people nowadays are there who don't try and chisel their way into the city for further education? But you are different. You have a lofty ambition and you deal with big issues as an ordinary person with a placid disposition. I am very proud of you, Bowa."

"Uncle Qu, I am embarrassed to hear what you said just now." Bowa sat down on the stool beside Uncle Qu and said, "Uncle, your entrepreneurial spirit is truly worth learning. Please don't praise me for stuff like lofty ambition. I just try my best to study well, do things well and be the best I can be. Nothing special."

"Shall we make an appointment?" Uncle Qu made every attempt to try and help Bowa. He said, "Promise me to study in the city when you are a high school student. What about sending your father to my place to recuperate at that time?"

"Well, we can discuss it nearer the time," said Tian Shi Bowa as he thought about it. "Perhaps my father will have recovered by then."

"Right! It's what we all hope." Uncle Qu continued very seriously and solemnly, "Now, you need to promise me one thing, otherwise I will be really upset."

"Uncle, What is it? You look so serious. OK, I promise."

"You have refused to accept any money from me in the past. Now you are going to live on campus in middle school and you need to save money for your family. I want to give you 10,000 yuan a year for your study."

"No, Uncle, You don't have to do that. It's free to go and study in middle school now."

"You think I don't know that? Your tuition is free but you still need to pay for the dorm, transportation, food, textbooks and so on!" Uncle Qu laughed, "You promised me just now and you must accept no matter whether you agree or not."

"Uncle, it's OK for me to accept. Anyway, we should use this amount of money, shouldn't we?" Bowa stopped to think for a while and then continued, "There are more than 20 students in our school who will go to middle school like me but none of us have had the chance to learn English before. We want to find a tutor to teach us English but we have no money. Uncle Qu, I am wondering whether our school could open an English summer school in Xiaonanhai Town and if they can use the money to cover teaching fees and student study expenses. What do you think about this?"

"Good. Bowa, you are such a warm-hearted boy, wise and farsighted and

I support you. We will do this, not only during this summer holiday; it will be held yearly in your name and I will be the sponsor."

Bowa didn't get it right away. Good heavens! In his name? In a boy's name? To make sure he had heard correctly, he thought about it and asked cautiously, "Uncle Qu, you mean you will fund the English summer school for our village every year?"

"Yes, one session a year," confirmed Uncle Qu.

"How much will it cost? It must be quite a lot."

"It doesn't matter. In your name and I will pay for it." Uncle Qu added, "But you should agree to accept my extra support for your study expenses."

"Uncle Qu, you are so kind. It is the most honourable kindness! White Crane Village elementary school will remember your gratitude forever. But please do it in your own name." Bowa stood up and rubbed his cheek against Uncle Qu's, saying, "As for the extra funds for me, we'll see."

The news spread quickly. In a few days, a female reporter, along with a photographer from Qianjiang TV station came to White Crane Village to interview Tian Shi Bowa. She said, "You are Bowa, aren't you? I am Teng Xuefang, a reporter from Qianjiang TV station. We heard you are going to fund an English summer school. Please tell us why you want to do this and how you intend to do it"

Teng Xuefang held the microphone to his lips.

Bowa gasped for a moment, wondering who had been such a gossip as to spread false news. He had already agreed with Uncle Qu that it would be done in his uncle's name but why had it come to this? Perhaps Uncle Qu wanted to encourage him and hoped to give him a good reputation, but how could he accept it? He gently pushed the microphone from his lips and answered, "Aunt Xuefang, you must have made a mistake. Think about it. My father had an accident and has been seriously ill for a long time. He is now still lying in bed and needs a lot of money for his treatment. My family at present cannot even afford to make both ends meet. How could I, a poor country boy, have the money to sponsor an English summer school?"

"Oh, what you said might be true, but leaders from the education committee office in Xiaonanhai Town told me in person that it was you who donated money for the summer school. I personally checked the donation record and found your information. Could you explain what is going on here?"

That was quite a long story. If he recalled the whole story, plus all the ins and outs, it would be all hype, too boastful and too shallow. Tian Shi Bowa, would you do that? Of course, he wouldn't, but how to explain this to the reporter? Aunt Xuefang was holding the microphone waiting for him. Oh, yes, didn't Aunt Xuefang call him 'Bowa' just now? He could tell her Tian Shi and Bowa were in fact two different people and the the donation was probably done by the guy called Tian Shi, and had nothing to do with Bowa. When she went to look for the so-called Tian Shi, he could find somewhere to hide and not come out until the reporter had left. The trouble would be over then. As Bowa turned this over in his mind, he blushed suddenly. "Tian Shi Bowa, what are you thinking about? Isn't it an obvious lie? It is still a lie even if you do have a good reason for it, namely that you're not doing it for yourself."

"Did you forget what Grandma told you and what Teacher Liu taught you? 'Study hard, work whole-heartedly and be sincere.' Did you forget about that?" No, Bowa didn't and never dared to forget.

But how on earth should he answer the question? Tian Shi Bowa blinked, took a look at Aunt Xuefang and then looked up at the flowing clouds in the sky, not knowing what to do.

ABOUT THE AUTHOR

Ku Jin is the pen name of Su Guanghua, an author of central China's Tujia ethnic minority and a member of both the China and Chongqing Writers Associations.

He studied at the Lu Xun College of Literature, and has been published in various journals such as *Youth Literature*, *Spring Breeze* and *Guizhou Writers*. His writing has also appeared in a number of anthologies, including the Chinese Writers Association's *Selection of Chinese Minority Literature in the New Century*, and the *Selection of Literary Works for the 60th Anniversary of New China*.

His novel *Yuanzhai* was supported as a key work by the China Writers Association, and he has received six provincial and ministerial-level awards for his work.